D0560620

RENEWING AND REVITALIZING the genre of Hawai'i noir fiction, Chris McKinney tells his tales of Honoluu's lower depths with an insider's authority and the **zeal of a real writer.** Beyond all that rings true in McKinney's fiction, what elevates it most is the author's **unexpected compassion** for those at the bottom or in emotional jeopardy.

—Tom Farber, author of *A Lover's Question*

This novel begins with a **MEMORABLE STORY** of a Korean girl's achievement of self salvation in a **journey on foot into a new world,** which, she discovers as an adult, is confused by a series of failures in the family of her own making. *The Queen of Tears* has a fascinating lineup of characters, all presented with a brutal honesty, in a story that is rich in description and in the complexity of its plot. Great storytelling from cover to cover.

—Ian MacMillan, author of *Village of a Million Spirits* (winner of the PEN USA-WEST Fiction Award) and *The Red Wind*

What amazes me about Chris McKinney's new novel *The Queen of Tears* are the intricate psychological profiles the author paints of each of his characters; McKinney knows these people, their histories, yearnings, failures, machinations and ultimately their acts of heroism both of the small and of the essential. What amazes me is **MCKINNEY'S GIFT: his deep understanding of our cultures and subcultures,** the nuances of relationships that coexist therein, his excellent prose that tells an intensely felt story with a **stunning fictive music,** his unflinching look at ourselves in a way that is recognizably disconcerting. What amazes me is McKinney's generosity as a writer; he allows his readers to know the characters who people *The Queen of Tears* as the real. He allows us to see our families and friends both the estranged and the beloved. McKinney focuses his writer's lens on the consistencies, allegiances, pretenses, and the betrayals of the most intimate relationships in our lives, showing us how to understand and know them often in spite of themselves. Fans of *The Tattoo* will surely revel in Chris McKinney's new novel, *The Queen of Tears.*

—Lois Ann Yamanaka, author of *Father of Four Passages*

PRAISE for
CHRIS McKINNEY'S FIRST
BESTSELLING NOVEL
THE TATTOO

"...**THIS IS A** book about 'the sins of the fathers,' how anger and pain and patterns of destructive behavior get passed from one generation to another...**McKinney has written a gritty, troubling book and he's done it well.** The issues he raises are key to Hawaii today, and for future generations."

—*The Honolulu Advertiser*

"**MCKINNEY'S VERY FIRST** novel is **thought provoking and revealing** to say the least. The way this first-time novelist keeps the story moving is a credit to his skill as a writer...We highly recommend this book to those who enjoy contemporary fiction, readers who can't get enough of Hawai'i and those who just plain want stories with **good character development**."

—*The Dispatch*

CHARACTERS

Soong Nan Lee—Born to a Korean "comfort woman" and a Japanese soldier during the Japanese occupation of North Korea, Soong reaches superstar status as a young actress in Seoul known as "the Queen of Tears." Banished from her native country in shame, Soong flees to the U.S. with her family. As she watches her three children grow into adults, she wonders if her motherly responsibilities will ever end.

Won Ju Akana—Soong's first daughter, born in Korea before the family fled to America. Won Ju struggles to keep her Waikiki boutique afloat in a severely depressed tourist economy. Haunted by her own dark past, Won Ju is determined not to let her womanizing husband influence her young son, Brandon.

Kenny Akana—Won Ju's husband, and a successful businessman, Kenny grew up on the right side of the tracks. A surfer and member of O'ahu's most elite canoe club, Kenny is the kind of Hawaiian called a "coconut"— brown on the outside, white on the inside.

Brandon Akana—Son of Won Ju and Kenny Akana, and beloved grandson of Soong Nan Lee. A shy, reclusive teenager obsessed with fantasy computer games, Brandon is swept away in the midst of family chaos and struggles to keep himself afloat.

"Donny" Chung Yun Park—Donny's hatred and resentment of his mother, Soong, is constantly at odds with his need for her financial support. After a number of his moneymaking schemes go belly-up, Donny decides to make one more try for success.

"Crystal" Monica Mahealani Sellers—A beautiful, sharp-tongued young woman of mixed Hawaiian heritage, born and raised by an abusive father and battered mother in the tough Waianae neighborhood. Crystal is a stripper at Club Mirage in Honolulu when she meets her husband-to-be, Donny.

Kaipo Sellers—Crystal's massive ex-convict brother lives in Waianae, stealing for a living. While intimidating in appearance and attitude, Kaipo has much to teach his Korean in-laws about kindness and generosity.

Darian Lee—Soong's youngest daughter is the only child in the family born and raised in America. Because her pampered upbringing and education set her apart from her Korean mother and half-siblings, she often struggles to find her place in the family.

THE QUEEN OF TEARS

chris mckinney

MUTUAL PUBLISHING

Library of Congress Catalog Card
Number: 2001118362

First Printing, September 2001
1 2 3 4 5 6 7 8 9

Design by Jane Hopkins
Cover design by Sistenda Yim

Softcover
ISBN 1-56647-515-5

Casebound
ISBN 1-56647-516-3

Mutual Publishing
1215 Center Street, Suite 210
Honolulu, Hawai'i 96816
Ph: (808) 732-1709
Fax: (808) 734-4094
e-mail: mutual@lava.net
www.mutualpublishing.com

Printed in Taiwan

In Bruegel's Icarus, *for instance: how everything turns away*
Quite leisurely from the disaster; the plowman may
Have heard the splash, the forsaken cry,
But for him it was not an important failure; the sun shone
As it had to on the white legs disappearing into the green
Water; and the expensive delicate ship that must have seen
Something amazing, a boy falling out of the sky,
Had somewhere to get to and sailed calmly on.

-W.H. Auden

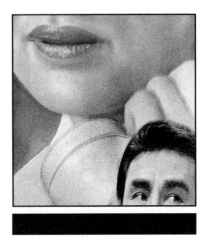

TABLE OF CONTENTS

FEAR OF LANDING BADLY

chapter one

THE PLANE MADE that momentary drop—the one where the passengers know they'll survive, but some doubt they will anyway. Why can't turbulence be seen? Soong Nan Lee asked herself as she squeezed the armrest and looked out of the twenty-year-old plexiglass. Sunlight penetrated it, accentuating the arbitrary scratches on the glowing surface. Soong squinted. Something so big should be tangible. Hot air from the surface grating against the cold, mile-high air should at least create a mixture of red and blue, a deep purple that illuminates the vast emptiness—north, south, east, west. But there was no purple; there was only nothingness shaking her, just to remind her that it was there.

She could not help but look out; she never could. The nausea began to roll in her stomach and scratch at her throat as the Continental 747 sailed way above the clouds. She always got motion sickness, but she'd never needed the sickness bag tucked away in the back of the seat in front of her. She looked out again, willing the nausea away. It appeared as if the plane were not moving forward. The only logical direction was down. The seatbelt strapped firmly across her lap seemed ridiculous to her. The plane made another sudden drop, and Soong closed her eyes. The sudden descent lasted only a second. If you get me through this, God, Buddha, Allah, Shiva, Amaterasu, Ra, or Whomever, I promise I won't fight with the children, she thought. She opened her eyes. The Caucasian businessman sitting next to her put his large hand on her shoulder. "You alright, missy?"

Soong glanced at his hand, and he put it back in his lap. There was a wedding band on his finger, one about as old as the airplane window. Twenty years had a way of aging the most important objects the same way—durability remained, but beauty seemed gone. Soong knew it took more than two decades of aging to restore the facade of beauty, whether talking about jewelry, cars, or marriages. It took much longer than two decades for something to become a quaint antique.

Sandy strands of hair grew above and below the gold ring. His hand moved up to scratch the top of his big stomach. He scratched in between the thin, blue vertical lines of his dress shirt. The hand moved further up to adjust the red tie that hung loosely around the man's thick neck. As he tightened the tie, a fold of white skin and flesh resisted the pressure and spilt over his starched collar. Soong looked at the man's fiftyish face. He may have been handsome once. Maybe he drove an American hot rod as a teenager and dated plump, white cheerleaders. Maybe he picked them off a tree, like pears. But now layers of fat hung loosely off his body. As it was with many who aged, the flesh was shrinking, but the skin was not shrinking with it. He was like a water skin; life was drinking from him, and what was drunk was permanently gone.

After tightening his tie, both of his arms dropped down to both armrests. It would have bothered her that he took the liberty to take the armrest next to her, if she wasn't one of the only adults on the plane who thought of her economy seat as roomy, and even more so, if she didn't feel a twinge of pity for him at that moment. It would be a while until he was an antique, like her. He smiled. "Just a little turbulence, ma'am. Nothin' to fuss over."

He'd almost cried during the in-flight movie. She heard the determined clearing of the throat and the sniffling during the end of the film. It was a piece of typical melodrama, and Soong did not have to keep up with the dialogue to know it. She just watched the faces of the actors twist grotesquely at the end. It had been the same in her country. Didn't moviemakers know that life is full of erosions, not explosions? She'd watched her second husband erode bravely. It may have been braver than anything he did in World War II or

Korea. It's far easier to muster courage to leap into darkness than it is for one to walk slowly into a sloping pool of gradulating dusk every day for nine months while the doctors disassemble you, never replacing any parts. Cut this out, tie this together. Let's make this into this. Intestines were like a second-rate clown's balloon animals to doctors. Soong politely smiled back at the white man sitting next to her, then turned her head toward the window. "So what's takin' you to paradise, ma'am?" he asked.

Paradise? He must have meant Hawaii. Soong turned to the man and said, "Famry."

"Why, you from the Orient, ma'am? It's funny I just assumed you was American. You know, you Orientals, you guys made it all over the U.S. Hell, back in Dallas, Texas, we got you folks runnin' for city council and stuff. I think it's great." He winked. "You know we was all immigrants once."

Soong smiled politely. She only understood about two-thirds of what the man had said. He extended his big, hairy hand. "Well ma'am, I'm Bobby McVie of Texas. I'm going to Hawaii on business. Hawaii may be the great fiber-optics hub of the Pacific Rim, you know. Where you from? China? Japan?"

Soong shook his hand. Yes, to Americans, it was always only either China or Japan. "Korea, but I live Long Island."

"I'll be. Long Island, New York? See I told you. You guys are coast to coast. Hell, I've been to Hawaii twice. Lots of Asians. You'll like it."

Soong nodded. She'd lived in Hawaii years ago for eleven years. Her second husband, the beautiful one that the doctors made a stomach out of intestines for, had been born and raised in Hawaii. She didn't love it. "So who you visiting in paradise?" the man asked.

She was going for her only son's wedding, but instead she said, "My grandson."

Bobby laughed loudly. The sudden boom made Soong jump. "Grandson? Hell, you're too young to have grandkids. What are ya? Forty-five?"

Soong smiled. She was almost sixty. Suddenly the plane made another quick, rapid descent. Soong grabbed the armrest again and closed her eyes. She swore her body separated from the seat for just a moment. Her throat convulsed. "Grandson. You gotta be kiddin' me. Look at you. Five-one, maybe five-two. Hell, you can't be no more than a hundred pounds. Ghost white, too. No one in Texas would believe a child could come out of that bird-body of yours."

Soong kept her eyes closed. Nope, she wasn't more than a hundred pounds. Maybe Newton was wrong, and she'd be the last to hit the ocean when the plane went down. Soong looked at the big white man. Yes, she knew who Newton was.

■ ■ ■

When Soong stepped out of the plane at Honolulu International Airport, the suffocation of humidity filled her lungs. She didn't like the open air. After only a minute, she was glistening and wondered whether the light layer of powder on her face would cake, then crack. Before walking further, she pulled her compact out of her purse and checked her make-up. She immediately missed the coolness and the dryness in the air of an early Long Island spring.

A crowd of faces waited at the gate. She remembered these people. There were more than a dozen tanned faces, some Asian, some Caucasian, some Hawaiian, and some of mixed race. The melting pot of races watched the gate exit and waited for their loved ones to appear. Most of them wore either shorts or jeans. Some wore T-shirts, while others wore tank tops. Soong smoothed out her gray Versace skirt and lightly touched the perfect quarter-karat diamond earring on her right lobe.

From this group of smiling faces emerged a broad, Korean face. It was a thirty-five-year-old face, with squinted eyes covered by a pair of wire-rimmed sunglasses. The face also had a broad, flat nose. The man was wearing a gold hoop earring in his left lobe. The face wasn't smiling. His mustache was thick, except in the middle where hair grew sparsely. The man, who was wearing a yellow Polo shirt neatly tucked into black jeans, was leaning on the last seat of the last row of black chairs in front of the gate. Though his face and nose were broad, the rest of him seemed rather flimsy, and it seemed that was the reason why he leaned on things constantly, because it took all of the body's frail might to hold up that broad face. She walked toward the unsmiling face and greeted it with the same non-smile.

"Hi Mother," Donny said in Korean, already avoiding eye contact.

"Hello Chung Yun," she said, using the name she'd given him. She and her three children always spoke to each other in Korean.

"How was the flight?" Donny asked, as he sighed and pushed himself off the chair, acting as if he were lifting a hundred pounds over his head.

"Ten hours of excruciating horror."

"They almost never crash, Mother."

"But they do crash, Son. And mine seemed as good or as bad as any."

They exited the gate, passing flower lei and concession stands on their way to the enclosed, air-conditioned baggage claim. Tourists, both Caucasian and Japanese, with brightly colored shirts that she imagined were bought at various overpriced tourist traps, walked to and from the gates talking to each other loudly. Others, locals, who wore both darker clothing and skin, also walked the airport grounds. A female voice that sounded like it was struggling to find a tone of politeness was on the intercom announcing departures. The still, humid air painted a thin layer of oil on these white, Asian, and local faces even in air conditioning. Soong wanted to find a bathroom to check her foundation thoroughly, but decided to wait until she got to the car. Then, she instinctively stopped walking and looked back. Donny was loafing about fifteen feet behind her. The children had always complained that she walked too fast, but to her the problem was that they didn't walk fast enough. As soon as Donny reached her, she began to walk quickly again.

After they descended down the escalator and reached the baggage claim carousel, Donny asked, "How many bags do you have?"

Just as Soong was about to answer, a voice boomed far behind her. "Hey beautiful, now don't tell me that's your grandson."

Soong turned around and waved emphatically, like a little girl. She caught herself, and immediately stopped. "He my son," she said, struggling to find her best English.

Bobby, the man from the plane, laughed. Soong waved once, like a matriarch this time, and walked to the other side of the stainless steel carousel. "Made a new friend?" Donny asked, not looking at his mother.

"He was sitting by me in the plane."

"Oh."

"I have four bags."

"O.K."

They grabbed the luggage and walked through the sliding glass doors. Again, the heavy hand of humidity hit Soong, but it was not as bad as it had been the moment she'd walked off the plane. She was acclimating, she hoped. They waited at the curb for the light to change. A huge cement overpass crossed above them. For a moment, Soong imagined it crumbling and falling on them. But then her concentration shifted to the amount of time she was wasting waiting for a light that was way too slow for her tastes to change. As soon as the lighted red hand switched to the white figure in mid-stride, Soong took two steps before the next person even put a foot off the sidewalk. Donny, along with another half-dozen people, crossed the street and entered the multilevel parking garage two steps behind her. The ones who, like Donny, were carrying multiple pieces of luggage, kept a good pace. Suddenly, she remembered that she had no idea where her son parked the car, so she again waited. After he finally caught up, she steadied herself for the effort she knew it would take to walk slowly behind him to the car.

Donny led Soong to a white BMW 328i and smiled. He put the bags down and pulled his key chain from his pocket. Attached to one of the rings was a small, plastic contraption with a series of buttons on it. Donny pressed one, and the trunk popped open. Soong could tell that he was making a concerted effort not to look at her. He was acting as if he were accepting a Nobel Prize with the utmost humility. She shook her head. "How can you afford a car like this?"

Donny struggled, putting the three bags of Louis Vuitton luggage he'd been carrying into the trunk. Then he pressed another button, and she heard the door locks make a dull pop. He opened the door for her. "Don't start, Mother."

She put the last Louis Vuitton bag in the back seat, then waited for Donny to sit on the beige leather. "You're absolutely crazy. You're not even working. When did you buy this car?"

He turned the key. "Actually, I didn't buy it. Crystal leased it."

She knew that she was pulling apart the pride he felt about driving a fifty-thousand-dollar automobile that he was trying not to reveal moments before. But she could not help herself. To leave it alone would have been like not pulling a loose thread off of a piece of clothing. And who can resist that?

They drove through the busy underpass of the airport, following a long line of cars, taxis, and Greyhound-sized tour buses. Exhaust billowed from the back of the bus, choking Soong. She rolled up her window and pulled down the vanity mirror. She checked her foundation, her pink lipstick and the light blush on her cheeks. "So Mom," Donny said, "are you finally going to move here for good?"

She pushed the mirror back in its place. "It depends."

"Mom, Dad died a year ago. You already sold the liquor store. It's time you moved close to family. We're all here."

Exactly, Soong thought. Family. Family gave her a funny feeling in her stomach. It was kind of like being in that plane, feeling it drop, and seeing no escape through a glowing, scratched-up window. She didn't want to look, but she could never stop herself from squinting from the light and looking out. She was searching for beauty in her family, like she was searching for purple in turbulence.

She'd found signs of the color in both of her daughters at one time or another, but she only saw the richness of blue and red mixed together in just one currently living member of her family, and it wasn't her son. "I don't know," she said.

The car slowed in the afternoon traffic. The BMW rolled slowly behind a rusting Toyota truck with absurdly big tires. "How is my grandson?"

"I was wondering when you'd finally get to that."

"What? He's my only grandchild."

"Well, I don't know why you're asking me. He's not my son."

It seemed Donny was always self-conscious about the fact that he never had any children, while his older sister produced the loveliest child in the world. Soong looked at her son, still waiting for an answer. His eyes remained focused on the windshield.

Donny sighed. "The last time I saw him, he looked fine. Turning into a real local boy, though. I wouldn't be surprised to see him driving a truck like the one in front of us in a few years."

Soong shook her head. It was the truck of an uneducated, blue-collar man who blew all of his money on yellow, accordion-looking things to put under his truck, and big tires. Soong had heard of Freud. A penis substitute. Her grandson would never come to that, and she knew that Donny was just trying to scare her in what she considered feeble retaliation. "And how is your sister doing?"

"She's good."

Soong nodded. They entered the H-1 Freeway, which led to Waikiki. Donny lit a Winston cigarette and rolled down the window. He had an effeminate way of smoking a cigarette that bothered her. "You should quit," she said.

The car whizzed by the industrial buildings surrounding the airport. "Don't start, Mom. And besides, why do you demand to stay in a hotel? You should save money and stay with me."

"I can't stand your smoking and drinking. Just drop me off at the hotel. If I stay any longer, I will stay with your sister."

"When is Darian coming in?"

Soong thought about her youngest child with a mixture of fear, lack of comprehension, and pride. Darian was her American child. Why she, like her older daughter, gave her child a name she could not pronounce correctly, she would never understand. Darian was flying in from U.C. Berkeley the following week. "Next Tuesday."

"She can stay with me and save money."

"She'll stay in the hotel like me."

"Figures," Donny said in English.

Soong sighed. Donny seemed always wanting to take any action by her as a slight against him. And some of this, she knew, was warranted. They didn't talk for the next fifteen minutes. Soong peppered the time with light coughs until Donny finally threw his cigarette out. Right before they got off of the freeway, she saw a tiny thread hanging from the sleeve of her blouse, and refused, with all of her will power, to pull it.

When they reached Waikiki, Soong was excited to see how it had changed since her last visit. Waikiki was a lot bigger than she remembered, but also more quiet. She had heard business was bad, and as they passed the lightly populated sidewalks, she believed it. Despite the white beaches, luxurious hotels, and palm trees growing out of the sidewalks, the allure of Hawaii was fading. The fact that the Asian economy was crashing hurt Hawaii even more. There were a few tourists walking the streets, though. Most wore bathing suits and absurdly red tans that screamed "skin cancer" to Soong as they passed vendors selling T-shirts. Others sipped on sodas or licked ice cream cones as they pointed at, but did not enter the surrounding shops. Some were white, most were Asians, and all did not look like they were buying merchandise. She hoped her older daughter's shop wasn't losing too much money. She knew she'd have to be the one to bail her out. "Is business in Waikiki as bad as I'd heard?" she asked.

Donny sighed. "Worse."

The streets of Waikiki were indeed emptier than she'd remembered them. But it looked more modern. The sight that struck her most was the traffic lights. The rectangular boxes with the three lights were no longer simply stuck on the tops of poles, but now most of the traffic lights were attached to shiny brown metal structures suspended over Kalakaua Avenue. The state was obviously sinking money into renovation. Soong laughed to herself. Hawaii was finally caught in the paradox it relied on for survival. Its main industry, tourism, depended on the natural beauty of the state. The fact that it was a state of the U.S., a capitalistic nation, demanded that it spend the money it'd made from tourism on destroying its natural beauty with big buildings, golf courses, and modernization. Hawaii was beginning to devour itself. Soong quickly calculated her assets in her head and wondered if she had enough to keep her children away from the feeding frenzy.

"Which hotel was it again, Mother?"

Soong sighed. She'd told him the name at least a half a dozen times over the phone. She looked down at her sleeve and yanked the loose thread off.

-2-

WON JU AKANA looked up at the movie poster hanging in the very middle of the largest white wall in her living room. A black lacquer frame bordered the colorful print. In the middle of the old poster, a beautiful, bird-like young Korean woman embraced a chubby, round-faced Korean soldier. The soldier looked, in an overly dramatic manner, like he was determined to leave. The woman, dressed in the traditional green Korean wedding dress, held two fistfuls of beige warmonger material, not letting the man walk away. Won Ju examined the angular, flawless face. The eyes were closed hard. But there was just enough in the face to suggest that the woman would eventually let the soldier go. It was funny because her hands suggested quite the opposite. It was a beautiful piece of melodrama captured for eternity. It was like poetry.

This woman had been one of the most celebrated actresses in Korea during the late fifties and early sixties. She had married a famous movie producer when she was seventeen, then after he died, she married a former Korean-American GI. The GI brought her to America with her two children. The second marriage had its ups and downs, and after the birth of their child, the actress found herself back in Korea, allegedly having an affair with a then-local politician and party leader, now one of the most powerful men in South Korea. The well-publicized affair had lasted only several months, then the actress returned to her American husband. In Korea they called this actress: "Noon Mul Ui Yau Wang." The Queen of Tears. Won Ju called her: "amah." Mother.

Someone tapped Won Ju's back. It was her fourteen-year-old son, Brandon. "Hey, Ma, I'm gonna go to the mall."

"Did you ask your father?" she asked, with her accented English.

Her son's dark face looked tired. "He's sleeping."

"Well, I don't know. You know your grandma just came in today. We were going to have dinner with her tonight."

"Don't worry, I'll be back home by six. There's this computer game I wanna check out."

Another computer game. Her son spent so much time in front of his computer. "Maybe you should wait for your father to wake up."

"Ma!"

"O.K., O.K. Do you need money?"

Her son shrugged. She walked to her purse and gave Brandon forty dollars. Before his tall, spindly body left the living room, she asked, "Wasn't your grandmother pretty?"

Without looking back, he said, "Yeah, I guess."

She looked back up at the poster. She wondered why she looked so different from her mother. Won Ju was a little taller, darker, and more voluptuous. Her face seemed to lack the ability to communicate profound conflict or deep feeling. She had a natural poker face, which many mistook as dullness or stupidity. In fact, during most of her waking moments, her head was like a can of soda that she couldn't keep herself from shaking.

Though her darker looks and natural curves had made many men salivate in the past, she still felt fat and ugly compared to her mother. Looking back up at the poster, she saw the porcelain skin, the petite body, and the face that could reflect three different emotions at the same time. Compared to this woman, and to the soap-opera life she'd lived, Won Ju did not feel very dynamic. She felt like a ten-dollar amusement-park teddy bear compared to a thousand-dollar porcelain doll. The Queen of Hugs, not The Queen of Tears.

Won Ju turned around and walked to the kitchen. She had scrubbed the tiled floor and counters twice earlier in the day, but she felt like she needed to go over it again. She laughed. A forty-one-year-old woman still trying to please her mother. She shrugged, opened the cupboard under the kitchen sink, and took out the tile cleaner and rags. She got down on her hands and knees and scrubbed the white tile, square by square. There were a couple of faint, beige stains on one tile square that, no matter how hard she scrubbed, would not come out.

When she was done, Won Ju put the tile cleaner and rags away, and decided to vacuum the carpet in the living room again. But before she started, she remembered that she needed to feed the fish. The rectangular thirty-gallon fish tank, which was her son's birthday present from his father two years ago, had only three fish in it. There were two tiger oscars, one about ten inches long, the other about a half a foot long, and one clown loach, a striped bottom-feeder that kept the tank clean. Won Ju unscrewed the cap of the fish food and sprinkled the pellets into the water. The oscars immediately went for the small, floating spheres, especially the big one. The big, black lips of the big one broke the surface of the water.

Won Ju didn't like these fish. They were such pigs. The oscars, dull, black fish with orange blotches on their sides, had voracious appetites. She'd never seen fat fish before, but these fish were definitely fat, aggressive, and slow. When they'd been a bit smaller and—it was now hard to imagine—cuter, they used to constantly chase the poor clown loach around. Of course they'd never catch it; the loach was always a sleeker, faster fish, but at least back then, they got exercise. Now they simply floated around the plastic plants, waiting to get fed. The tank was too small. The growth of all three fish was probably stunted because of the lack of space. While she screwed the cap of the fish food back on, Won Ju watched the clown loach scramble for leftovers that sunk to the bottom of the tank. It hovered above the gravel, sucking up the scraps. Won Ju got back to vacuuming.

While she was busy pushing the Eureka Enviro Vac with the True Hepa Filter over the plush white carpets of the apartment for the second time, Won Ju's husband stepped into the living room. Dressed in only black Calvin Klein boxer shorts, his usual home attire, his dark, athletic frame looked attractive, but manufactured, in a way. His body was a three-dimensional map of hard mountains and squiggly rivers. It was as if a cartographer drew out what his or her ideal map would look like. Kenny plopped down on the black leather sofa. She turned off the vacuum. "Sorry, did I wake you?" she asked.

Kenny rubbed his stomach. "Yeah."

He stood up, walked into the kitchen and opened the fridge. "What time is dinner?" he asked.

■ ■ ■

Won Ju followed him. "How does eight o' clock sound?"

"What time is it now?" Kenny asked, squinting at the clock on the microwave oven.

"You need glasses."

"Why don't we just take her to the Club?"

The Club. "You know my mother, she only eats Asian food. I made reservations at the sushi bar by the hotel she's staying at."

He took out a bottle of Mauna Loa Hawaiian Natural Spring Water and in one swig gulped half the bottle down. He looked around the kitchen and smiled. "You sure it's clean enough?"

She walked back to the living room and sat at the dining room table. "You know how she is."

Kenny walked in and sat across from her. "Unfortunately. Where's the kid?"

"Oh, out with his friends."

"You didn't give him money, did you?"

"No."

"Good. You know, instead of hanging out at malls and staring at that computer all day, I'd rather see that kid at the beach or something. It's cheaper and healthier."

Won Ju got up and turned the vacuum cleaner back on before he finished.

-3-

"CRYSTAL," WHO HAD borrowed the name from thousands of strippers before her and many who were sure to follow, had been born Monica Mahealani Sellers. As "Monica," she had been a damn hottie in Waianae High School, a bit flat-chested, though. When she transformed herself into "Crystal," or the doctors did anyway for the price of a high school diploma and a year of toil at McDonalds, she began to shed her clothes for money. She remembered this as she looked at Crystal's body in the full-length mirror. Unsatisfied, she walked to her closet and grabbed a pair of four-inch white platform shoes. She put them on and walked back to the mirror. Much better. It wasn't that her legs were short; she was five-eight and had pretty long legs. But she'd always wanted to be taller. Crystal always wanted to be taller than most men.

She cupped her breasts. Worth every cent. She turned around and looked at her buttocks. Still as high as a kite. When she faced the mirror again, she ran her metallic-lavender fingernails through her thin stripe of black pubic hair. She tingled. She stepped back and tried to soak it all in. No tan lines, no wrinkles. A beautiful body, a real moneymaker. Just one problem: a scar. A surgical scar on the lower, right side of her abdomen. It was because something was ruptured, or something was bleeding, that's what she remembered the doctors saying. She'd been in pain and fourteen—naïve little Monica. She ran a lavender fingernail on the scar and felt a different kind of tingling. Then she grabbed her black thong panty from the bed and put it on.

She sat at her dresser and picked up the much smaller hand mirror that lay face-down. She sighed and looked at her face.

She knew she was pretty. Yet for some reason, she was sometimes unsure of it. She'd often been called "the kind of girl who actually looks even better without makeup," but sometimes she just didn't feel attractive. Sometimes she felt her face was too dark. Sometimes her eyes were too green. Her father's eyes. At times, she wanted to pluck them out. It would be like shucking oysters.

Sometimes her chin was too big. Sometimes her eyebrows were too bushy. Sometimes she looked too Hawaiian. Sometimes too white, too haole. Nobody told her, but she suspected that everybody saw either the too-dark or too-light version. Everybody, except for Donny Park, her little yobo boy. Donny was perfect. He was shorter, uglier, and more irresponsible than her. And the best was that he couldn't get it up. He'd make the perfect husband.

They'd met two years ago at Club Mirage, the most well-known all-nude strip bar in the state of Hawaii. She was dancing her third set to the standard, long-haired, hard-partying, now-defunct eighties rock music, when Donny, wearing khakis, a black Polo shirt, and wire-rimmed shades, sat at the stage in front of her. He was thin, a little shorter than she was, and his wide Asian face had the cutest little adolescent mustache. His hair was Asian standard issue; short on the sides, no sideburns, gelled, side-combed. Straight and a little bit spiky. He put his thin forearms on the edge of the stage and let his long, thin fingers stretch across the surface. When she squatted in front of him, he smiled and looked away. This surprised her. She thought the sunglasses were enough for him not to see.

The last song, "Poison," ended. She loved Alice Cooper. Despite the fact that she was completely naked, Donny's eyes never focused on her for more than a couple of seconds. She stood up from her stirruped position, smiled, then put on her florescent green thong bikini and walked off the stage. The green glowed especially bright because of the black lights. Before she made it back to the dressing room, the bartender handed her a margarita. "From that Korean guy over there."

He pointed to Donny, who was now sitting in a booth. He was quick. Crystal thought maybe he was a high-roller. He dressed well and seemed to have no problem ordering her a twenty-dollar drink. He'd sat at the stage, seemingly willing to tip her. At this job, you never knew, though. Even blue-collar guys and college kids seemed to come in here and spend incredible amounts of money. But if you went shopping with them the next day, you'd see them break out into a cold sweat with every item you charged on their credit card. But this Korean guy looked harmless enough, and it was a slow night, the tourist industry crumbling and all, so Crystal sipped her margarita and walked to the booth.

When she sat down across from him, her ass squeaked against the cheap red plastic of the seat. She was still sweating. Bon Jovi's "You Give Love A Bad Name" blared. More inspirational music. The booth shook slightly because of the level of the bass. Donny's black shirt had lint on it. Crystal smiled. "Didn't anyone tell you never to wear a dark cotton shirt to a club or a strip bar? You become conspicuous because of the black lights."

Donny looked down at the glowing lint on his shirt and smiled. His teeth did not glow very much. Hard-core smoker or coffee drinker or hygiene neglecter. "Sorry, I'm not a regular."

His voice held a faint accent. She could tell he was Korean, but now she knew he was first-generation Korean, F.O.B—Fresh Off the Boat. Even though his accent was very light, she still felt uncomfortable. The owner of Club Mirage, Mama-san, was an F.O.B., and she should've been used to having F.O.B.'s around, but she still felt kind of weird around them. She didn't know what it was, but male F.O.B.'s made her feel especially uncomfortable. Their politeness seemed sinister to her. "So where do you normally go then?"

"Korean bars."

Go figure, she thought. Most of the bars in the area were Korean-owned, and a few of them catered especially to Korean customers. Young F.O.B. Korean girls worked at these places as hostesses. They spoke the language, rubbed legs, and sometimes rubbed more for the right amount. Crystal was no hostess, and she was definitely no whore. The "new" Crystal, of which there had been several manifestations (the one who fucked for love, the one who fucked rich guys, the one who fucked girls, the one who fucked for free, or for herself, and now, the one who decided not to fuck anymore), would not rub anything but herself from now on. Two months of celibacy would not be wasted.

Crystal gently took off Donny's shades, looked into his eyes and smiled. He quickly looked away, and went straight for his cigarettes. She saw enough to know that he was wasted on more than alcohol. Maybe acid, maybe coke. She knew; she was an addict trying to kick the habit. Now she really didn't want anything to do with this guy. When she'd been into sex, she had been into white guys anyway. Less hangups, bigger dicks. Besides, she remembered when this Japanese guy was bouncing at Mirage a few years back. He went ape-shit one night and held Mama-san and a couple of cops at gunpoint. Asians. Sometimes violently unpredictable. She stood up. He smoked like a fag—another minus. "Well, thanks for the drink, hon. I gotta get back to the dressing room. Maybe some other time?"

As she stood up, he stood up, too. Like in the movies. She loved movies. What kind of freak was this? Didn't he know he was at a strip bar? She'd smiled and quickly walked away.

But he'd persisted and persevered, Crystal remembered, as she applied her metallic-lavender lipstick. He spent hundreds on her. After a while, the weird F.O.B. vibe faded. Now they were engaged and living together. They both quit drugs, and while she still stripped, he was out scheming on how he could open his own Korean restaurant.

She felt calm for the first time in her life, like her life was going somewhere. After living the lifestyle of a stripper for ten years, she was finally about to escape the Lotus-guys she faintly remembered reading about during one of her many failed attempts to attend a full semester of community college. Since she'd been eighteen, she'd been dancing. But the dance was about to end. Donny assured her that his mother would dig them out of any hole. "The guilt," he'd told her.

Crystal heard the apartment door open. She held the mirror up so that she could see Donny walk into the bedroom. He stepped in and sighed. "I can't believe that lady."

Crystal stood up. She smiled. He had that foreign accent well-covered, but there was still a twang. She could tell his tongue desperately wanted to replaces his "L's" with rolling "R's." But he was better at covering it up than his sister. Crystal picked up a tiny white slip-on dress from the bed and put in on. The brown of her areolas showed through the thin white material, and her nipples protruded. She ran her long metallic-lavender fingernails through her hair, smiled, and asked Donny, "So what do you think?"

"I hope you're not fuckin' serious. My mother would have a stroke," he said without looking directly at her.

Crystal walked up to him and rubbed her breasts against his shoulder. She found his accent kind of cute. To her it revealed a certain vulnerability. "Oh, c'mon honey. She'll love it."

As she nibbled on his ear, then tugged on his gold hoop earring with her teeth, Donny pulled away. "Get serious. Dinner's in a couple of hours. We gotta get there early so I can get good and drunk. I had enough sober-time with that woman."

Crystal walked to her closet. There he went again. The hardships of being raised by an actress mother. He didn't even know hardship. But she knew it; she knew it well. It took focus for her to turn around and smile at Donny. She pulled off her dress and said, "Well maybe I should just go like this?"

Donny laughed. "I'd love to see that," he said without really looking.

-4-

SO I HAD *to go to dinner with the folks, my loser uncle, Grandma, and Crystal (I don't know how she ended up with the loser). We were going to some sushi bar because Grandma likes rich people food. I think that's all old people eat. Even the folks like rich people food sometimes, but they usually stay home. All Dad eats is broiled chicken or tuna, and Mom can't live without her kimchee, or anything else that smells bad. I'd hate to have a friend over and have them see the inside of our icebox. There's jars and jars of something pickled or fishy, always Korean and always hot, sitting next to at least a dozen bottles of Dad's Mauna Loa Hawaiian Natural Spring Water. It's like Mom should go live in Korea again. But I guess the folks are cool. Mom gives me money for Playstation and computer games, and Dad is thick. He paddles canoe for the Hawaiian Canoe Club, and he always wins. I hope I get muscles like him when I get older, but I doubt it. I'm not really into sports and surfing and stuff. I like my computer. I guess I'm kind of a nerd, and Dad gets on me sometimes about it. But he surfs the web with me sometimes. Mom would freak if she saw the porn stuff he has bookmarked. Good thing Mom doesn't use the computer. She also doesn't drive. It's weird.*

So we get to the restaurant with Grandma to meet the loser and Crystal. It's called, "Yoshi-something" or "Samurai-something," you know some Japanese name. Well, we get there, and it's so obvious that the loser is drunk. I think Crystal was drinking, too, because as soon as I walk in, she runs and kisses me. On the cheek. But it was awesome. You should've seen what she was wearing. She had this tiny white dress that was so tight, I don't even know how she got her boobs into it. You could see her bra. Bras are cool. And she was wearing those huge Spice Girl shoes. Some girls in school wear those, but they look nothing like Crystal. They wish. It's like Crystal should be on Baywatch or something.

Well, after she kissed me, Grandma didn't look too happy. You know, old school. I don't know why she's worried; like Crystal would go out with me, a kid. I wish. But she wasn't happy about it, and what made things worse was that Crystal looked at her, smiled, and gave her a giant hug. I never saw anybody hug Grandma before, not even grandpa, when he was alive. Right after Crystal let her go, Grandma started smoothing out her rich, old-person skirt and twisted the big diamond on her right ear. I don't think I ever saw Grandma wear anything wrinkled before. She's like so old, and even her face doesn't have wrinkles, just make-up. Well, after she stroked her skirt a few times and gave the earring a twirl, she walked up to me, pulled out a little plastic bag filled with white tissues from her purse, licked one of the tissues, and wiped my cheek. Some metallic lavender lipstick was smeared on the tissue. I can't believe Grandma did that. What am I, two? I don't want her spit on my face.

Well, everybody said "hi" to each other, and we all took our usual places at the bar on the smallest chairs in the world. Of course, I had to sit between Grandma and Mom, which never made sense to me considering they always spent the whole night talking to each other in Korean. Dad sat next to Mom. Crystal sat in between loser and Dad. Dad and Crystal talked in pidgin, while the loser pigged out on like the most expensive and gross sushi, even that slimy orange stuff, while drinking sake like crazy. Dad liked to speak in pidgin to Crystal, even though he's from Kahala, and she's from Waianae. I went to Waianae a couple of times with Dad to surf, and there weren't even sidewalks. I doubt anybody has computers over there. The Hawaiians there didn't look like Dad either. They were like fat and poor and spoke in nothing but pidgin. Except for certain guys who looked mean, wore thick gold chains, and obviously lifted a lot of weights. I'm surprised Crystal came from there, too.

So I was sitting at some sushi bar not knowing what to do with myself. It's like I don't have anything to say to these people, but everybody kept looking at me, except for the loser. Mom and Grandma would look at me every time they'd stop jabbering in Korean. Dad would look at me once in a while and roll his eyes. I guess he was bored too. He was down. And even Crystal looked at me a couple of times. But I'm such a fag because every time she'd look at me, I'd look away. I remember learning in speech class that eye contact is key, but it's funny, in the ninth grade, you take speech and they try to teach you everything except how not to be nervous. I mean, isn't that important? Well, everybody kept looking at me like I was supposed to start juggling or something, so I started to stare at the clock.

Well, the clock was moving pretty slow. It was like I was in a time warp or something, so I started to watch the sushi chef. He was pretty cool. It was trippy seeing how fast he was. Slice the fish, roll the rice, spread wasabi on it, deliver. Five seconds, tops. He was really going at it, taking orders from the waitresses, taking orders from the loser. He was in the zone. It's like when I play a computer game sometimes, like a real-time game. Everything is happening so fast, and then it's like three hours later. I wanted to try. Every time I'd disappear, though, thinking about making sushi, Grandma would shove the picture of all of the sushis in front of me, trying to get me to eat something. "You pick," she'd say over and over again. Ever since I was a kid, it's like she gets off on making me eat. It used to be cool, but now it makes me lose my appetite. "You pick, you pick, you pick." Jeez, I don't know, maybe there was like no food in Korea in the old days. That's probably why the loser is such a pig.

So I'm sitting there trying to convince Grandma that I'm not hungry, and then suddenly everyone but me starts playing musical chairs because some old Japanese couple needed some seats. So instead of everyone moving over one, it's like chaos. I guess being in a room full of chairs all day during the week does have its benefits. I was about to say something and complain, but suddenly I was sitting by Crystal, with Mom on my other side, and Grandma two seats away from me. Even from two seats away, she was tapping my arm and shoving the picture menu in front of my face. I was about to tell her that I wasn't hungry when Mom leaned over me to talk to Crystal. "So Crystal, how's work?"

Immediately I start ordering sushis. Maguro, hamachi, ebi. Mom is so naïve. Like I don't know what Crystal does.

"Oh you know, the same. It's getting slower and slower. Jeez, five, ten years ago, I was makin' money. But now, people at McDonalds probably make more than me. Too bad I blew all that cash. I was too young to have that kind of money."

God, her perfume killed me as she leaned across me. Her right boob was like on my chest. Dad told me once that he'd take me to a strip bar when I turned eighteen, but that's like years away.

"So are you going to start something else?"

Keep talkin' Mom. I rudely raised my hand. "Two tako," I said, probably too loudly.

Crystal sighed. "Yeah, I'm trying. I think I'll go back to school. You know, I got my G.E.D., so I was thinking about trying business college again. Maybe get a degree in legal aid or something. But in order for me to do that, someone has to get a job."

Go back to school? She's crazy. No wonder why she's with the jobless loser. She's nuts. I was about to say something cool; I was about to tell Crystal in a really suave way that if she wanted to go to school, she could do my homework, but Grandma nudged me and pointed to all of the sushis I ordered, but didn't eat. It was like she was Mr. Fantastic. She's like three-two, and that's when she just gets out of bed, and here she was, reaching me across Mom. Right when I was about to tell her to eat it, Mom gets up, Dad takes her seat, and Crystal turns around to talk to the loser. Dad was going to try to talk to Grandma. I hated when he did that. It was always so obvious that she didn't understand him. "So Mom, tell me if you're looking to stay here permanently. It's a buyer's market right now because of the bad economy. I could get a great deal on a nice one-bedroom condo, for about a thousand a month, five percent down."

Dad's a real estate agent, whatever that is. It has something to do with houses and kissing people's asses. He also day trades on the Internet. He's up at four every morning. Anyway, sure enough, Grandma didn't understand him too well. She just nodded, smiled, and said, "Thank you." Lucky for her, she was interrupted when the old uncle turned pale, jumped out of his seat, and started walking really fast to the bathroom. What a loser. Even Dad laughed. "That son of yours has to learn to hold his food and liquor."

Grandma still smiled, but it was one of those smiles that look like walls. After a pause, Mom came back and told Grandma and Dad that she saw the loser rush past her, and that maybe it was time to go. She said it first to Grandma in Korean, or at least I'm pretty sure that's what she said, because that's what she told Dad right after. I turned to Crystal. She was gulping beer from a big bottle of Asahi. I was in awe.

So two bad things came several minutes later, the loser and the check. It was funny though, one didn't even touch or look at the other. Instead Mom, without even hesitating, grabbed the check. I caught a glimpse of it. Three hundred and fourteen. Old people are crazy. Well, Mom took out a credit card, but before she could put it on the little black plastic tray, Grandma, with her Mr. Fantastic arm, grabbed the check. Then Dad, with his super-ripped, Incredible Hulk arm grabbed it. Crystal was reapplying her metallic lavender lipstick, and the loser was laying his head, face down, on his crossed arms. Well anyway, Dad looked at the check and handed it back to Mom. Mom gave the credit card, tray, and check to the waitress and said something in Korean to Grandma. She then told Dad, "I asked Mom to come and look at our place. She hasn't seen this one yet."

Dad nodded. And for the first time, Grandma, who was reapplying her dark pink lipstick, looked tired. I never saw her look tired before. I understand though, I get that tired too sometimes. Mom gets worried when I stay in my room all day long on weekends sometimes. Luckily, Dad is paddling a lot on weekends, or he'd drag me out of my room. He hates when I get tired.

Well, the check came, the loser and Crystal left, with no kiss this time, it was like they were in a hurry, and I watched Crystal bounce away while Mom gave the waitress three twenties. Dad frowned and said, "That's like nineteen percent."

Mom ignored him, which she always did when he mentioned money. As we got up to walk out, Dad told Grandma, "You should talk to your daughter. She's too careless with money."

"You listen, Kenny," Grandma said. "You listen husband."

"When you pay, you can tip whatever you want, husband."

They were going to start again. It's like when you get old, it's all about making and spending money and complaining about it twenty-four seven. Money's cool and all, but jeez. I mean, when Dad gave me an Ameritrade account on the Internet last year, with three thousand dollars of buying power, I was stoked. I mean, I made a killing on Cisco and Harcourt, but to tell you the truth, I'd rather be playing Everquest or Final Fantasy VIII. But I guess Ameritrade is like Dad's computer game.

I feel bad for Mom, though, when he gets on her about money. Sometimes he gets mean. He'll say stuff like, "That's what I get for marrying a Korean barmaid," or "Why did I marry a Waikiki novelty peddler?" I mean, she'll remind him that she was a bartender when they met, or that she sells designer stuff in her shop, but it has no effect on him. Once the big guy gets rolling, get out of the way. It got especially bad when I made the mistake of printing out an IQ test from the Internet, and we all took it. Mom kicked our asses. I didn't care too much, to be honest, I tanked it a little, I mean, if I score well, the next thing you know, the folks will expect you to bring home straight A's, but Dad didn't take it too well. I think it especially bothered him because the test was in English, or as Mom sometimes calls it when she slips, "Engrish," her second language, and it made him feel even dumber. Poor guy.

So anyway, I blanked out their money conversation in Dad's S.U.V., or tried to, and thought about Crystal bouncing. But from what I did hear, it was pretty tame, Grandma being in the car and all. Grandma was checking her make-up and keeping quiet. I wondered if Mom and Dad would get a divorce. Whatever. As long as they don't blame me for staying together. That's so lame.

THE DEATH OF KWANG JA

chapter two

IN 1952 CHO Kwang Ja walked from a village in North Korea to Seoul. She walked over a hundred miles. That summer, in the sometimes one-hundred-plus-degree heat, her skin baked to a nice, golden brown. Her tiny and bare fourteen-year-old feet developed calluses so thick that they were tougher than the bottom of most people's sandals. She stepped on sharp, jagged rocks and hardly noticed. She stepped on leftover pieces of shrapnel and didn't even feel it. Once she stopped to sit down, and she looked at the bottoms of her feet. She smiled and pulled out the tiny shards of metal. She didn't care. She just wanted to get out of dry, mountainous country. She wanted to see tall buildings, green mountains, and people with shoes. She wanted to get out of Communist Korea.

She wasn't a political person. If it were the Communists who were running Seoul, she would have embraced Communism without a second thought. She wasn't a religious person either. Despite her poor education which left her barely literate, she sensed early in her childhood that religion was used by bigger people to get what they wanted from smaller ones. Confucianism was an example. As was Christianity. Before the white missionaries in the north were finally burnt out by the Communists, she'd seen some of these foreign holy men get what they wanted from young girls using their religion. When Confucianism and Buddhism were outlawed by the Communists, she saw how their religions did not help the priests. Her atheism may have pushed her towards Communism if Communism did not prove as useless to her as God did.

So Cho Kwang Ja was neither political nor religious. But she was ambitious. Ambition drove her over hundreds of miles of dirt roads and rocky, bald, mountainous terrain. Ambition forced her to live on nothing but dirty water and the leaves of plants she could not even identify. And not only that, ambition made her smart. too. She hid whenever she came close to any human contact. Villagers, soldiers, both North and South Korean, were stealthily avoided. She did a lot of her traveling by night to better her chances of not being detected by anyone. Sometimes, during days, she would sleep in the burnt-out skeletons of American or Russian tanks or shot-down planes. But most of the time, she didn't sleep. Ambition kept her awake, too.

Kwang Ja didn't even know where Seoul was, except that it was south. A missionary had once told her that the sun rose in the east and set in the west, and ambition forced her to hold on to that piece of information like it was a piece of perfect jade. So every morning she looked up at the sun and smiled when she knew which direction south was. Then she'd tell herself she'd know Seoul when she saw it. It would be big with a lot of people. It would be a place where American GIs drove around in their beautiful green jeeps, a place with riches oozing out of great buildings. A place that big and magical, as long as she kept walking south, she could never miss. How naive she was.

It wasn't until years later that she knew that she'd owed luck more than ambition for the successful trip. Crossing the thirty-eighth parallel without even knowing it, and accidentally locating and following the Han River, which turned more and more brown further into her journey, she walked right into Seoul. Besides, her ambition wasn't really ambition. She had no real goals. She didn't know what she wanted to be. She didn't even really know what money or success were. Instead, what drove her through the long walk was part hunger and part fear. She was hungry for something different, and she was running from something too sadly familiar.

Cho Kwang Ja was a half-breed. Before her adopted mother had died of lung disease, she'd told Kwang Ja that her real mother was with her in the recreation camps of the Japanese army during the occupation. She told Kwang Ja that her father was a cruel Japanese soldier. When Kwang Ja had asked for a specific name and description, her adopted mother only scowled. "Foolish child. They all wore the same cruel mask to us." Then she'd coughed herself unconscious.

Kwang Ja's mother had been a comfort woman, a Korean peasant forced into sex slavery. But Kwang Ja was six when she was told this, and she did not see the significance. She simply stored it in the soft, spongy part of her mind and watched her adopted mother die.

But on her fourteenth birthday, she'd remembered. She'd finally known, just by looking in the mirror on her fourteenth birthday, that there was a touch of Japanese that contaminated her blood. The narrowness of her face, the subtle difference in the shape of her eyes. To her, her eyes were a darker brown—almost black and all pupil— than anyone else she had seen (though this was not a Japanese trait, she thought its rareness would draw attention to her, followed by questions). She couldn't believe it. Maybe it was because before turning fourteen, she could never see things objectively; maybe it was because her birthday was the first time she'd seen a mirror in two years, but whatever it was, she now knew. Though others did not seem to notice, like she didn't during all of her childhood, she wasn't going to wait around until they did. It was a bad thing to be part Japanese or part anything but Korean in North Korea. The memories of the people, even in her small village, were long. Communism in the North represented for many the cure for the disease of Western imperialism and the monstrosities of Japanese occupation. That night, she walked out of the village with nothing, except for her fear and the knowledge that she should never stay in one place for too long because sooner or later she would be discovered. It would be a year before she would realize that her brown eyes were just as brown as anyone else's, and her sudden awareness of her uniqueness had nothing to do with blood, but had everything to do with adolescence and beauty.

So she made it to Seoul and found that it was neither kind, beautiful, nor magical. It was a broken city, like a shattered piece of china. The great stone wall that surrounded the city was knocked down in many places. Once-beautiful temples with their majestic, sloping roofs were partially burnt or simply piles of bricks. Poor people crowded the streets, and they all seemed in a rush with indifference towards each other. The air was filled with the harmonization of screaming Koreans and honking horns. Female vendors were desperately trying to sell pickled eggs and *pinbae duk*, a Korean pancake with vegetables cooked in it, to all passersby. Occasionally, sputtering cars, with chassises made completely out of American beer cans, would make their ways through the thick crowds.

Two-story buildings were surrounded by beggars, young hustlers, and prostitutes with clothes a lot nicer than hers. Sometimes these buildings pushed the people so close together that it seemed as if there was a river of black hair separating the two structures. The smell of *kimchee* mixed with exhaust fumes made Kwang Ja feel sick. But worst of all, the mountains surrounding the city were not green. In fact, they looked very much the same as the mountains she'd passed during her great walk. As for the city itself, when the North Korean army had attacked Seoul over a year before, it had definitely left its mark.

So Kwang Ja was alone in this great city and all she had with her were hard-callused feet, a golden tan, the knowledge that the sun rose in the east and set in the west, and a promise to herself that she'd commit suicide before she'd go back north. But despite all of this, she felt lucky that no one seemed to suspect or care that her blood had been tainted.

-2-

LUCK STRUCK AGAIN. After two days in Seoul, half-starving in the streets and running out of hiding places to wait out American-imposed curfews, Cho Kwang Ja was hit by a car. She'd been running away from an old woman accusing her of stealing some rotten grapes from her fruit stand, which Kwang Ja was guilty of, when the fancy black car hit her. It didn't hit her hard; it glanced her just enough to knock her off her feet. Still scared of the woman, she slowed her breath and relaxed all her muscles. She let her mouth gape slightly. She closed her eyes, but made sure her lids were not closed too tight. She knew it would be better to look limp rather than stiff. She'd seen people dying before, and she knew that the stiffness came later. She would have looked completely lifeless, except her hand was still gently clenched around the six grapes she had stolen. She was so hungry; she unconsciously refused to let them go. The woman stood above her and shrieked, telling her she'd gotten what she deserved.

The doors of the car opened then slammed shut. A man's deep voice chastised the angry lady. When she felt a pair of arms lift her up, she tried as hard as she could to feel like dead weight. She let her arms dangle and her neck stretch back as far as it could. Nothing alive likes to expose its neck, so she fearlessly exposed it. Someone slapped her in the face. She didn't move. She was slapped again. The few who stopped and were actually interested were murmuring, "She's dead; she's dead."

She wanted to smile. She was proud of herself. She was really good at this. This pride suddenly melted when she felt a hand on her breast. She wasn't good enough to make her heart stop, but if she were, she would have done it right there. She would have died. Her attempts at motionless suicide were interrupted by the laughter of a man. Knowing the ruse was over, but still refusing to open her eyes, Kwang Ja heard the laughing man say, "What we have here is an actress."

She didn't open her eyes. But she felt herself being put into the fancy black car. At first, the leather seat cooled her arms and hands. But then the seat and her skin grew hot, and she felt drops of sweat roll down her forehead. As the car drove on, she listened to the treads of the tires pick up tiny pebbles and hurl them against the metal of the car. She wondered if she should try to sneak a rotten grape or two into her mouth. "Look at all the refugees," the man said. "From the north, from Seoul to Pusan, now back to Seoul.

Even I almost had to run to Pusan. I must go there today. Where are you from?"

Kwang Ja didn't move.

About an hour later, the car stopped. She was pulled out by what she guessed were small female hands. She still did not open her eyes. She realized that they knew she was not dead, but decided to feign injury just in case. The man who had picked her up spoke to the woman who held her up. He instructed the woman to take care of her, and said he would call later to give further instructions. The car door slammed shut, and Kwang Ja heard the car drive away.

She opened her eyes. It was the most beautiful thing she'd ever seen. The house was tall and made of a dark, almost reddish wood. Its roof was like those she'd seen on the burnt temples in Seoul, sloping downward from the center. Behind the house stood a mountain of pure green. It was so unlike the balding mountains of North Korea and Seoul that Kwang Ja could not believe she had traveled so far in just an hour drive. It was as if she flew from the sun to the moon. Then she looked at the woman holding her up. It was a familiar figure; short, slumped over, hunchbacked. It was the body of a woman who, for years, carried tremendous weight. It was a woman who was so used to bowing to men, carrying their children on her back, and holding the weight of an entire house on her shoulders that her back was permanently bent. Women like this lived in North Korea, too. It was Confucianism at its worst. Kwang Ja no longer felt as far away as she'd have liked.

She walked from the woman's arms and went up to the large wooden door. A brass circle which had elaborate engravings of dragons intertwined hung from the door. She rubbed the brass ring, then brushed her fingers on the dragons. Behind her a voice spoke. "So you're not so sick after all."

Startled, Kwang Ja dropped the grapes. A couple bounced once, then slowly rolled toward the woman, but the rest splattered on the wooden porch. The woman stooped over to pick up the grapes. Embarrassed, Soong tried to beat her to them. The woman slapped

Kwang Ja's reaching hand lightly. "I got it, I got it. You ridiculous child, you move as if it were diamonds you dropped."

Kwang Ja stood back up and wondered what diamonds were and what they tasted like.

■ ■ ■

The woman made Kwang Ja wash her bare feet before she went inside. This woman, who was dressed in simple white clothes and wore white rubber sandals, sighed when she saw the bottoms of Kwang Ja's callused feet. Then the servant's old face smiled. She led Kwang Ja into the house.

Kwang Ja saw things in this house that she had never seen before. Things like faucets, toilets, and beds were foreign to her. As were embroidered rugs, framed paintings, glass cases filled with fine china, and wooden tables that shined so much that she could see her reflection in them. But none of these things were as beautiful as the garden beyond the patio in the back. A huge glass door (another thing she'd never seen before) separated the patio from the house, but the glass was so clean that it was like the door wasn't there. Kwang Ja almost walked through it, but the old woman pulled her back and opened the door for her.

The garden, which was about twenty yards long and ten yards wide, was separated from the mountain by a huge stone wall. It was the same kind of stone she saw as temple rubble in the city. While the vegetation of the mountain grew beautifully green, but wild, the garden was meticulously cared for. Each blade of grass seemed of exact equal length. A tiny river ran through the center of the garden where koi, fish wearing beautifully bright and diverse colors, swam above a bed of fine black gravel. Kwang Ja stepped off the patio and walked to the bridge, which was of the same wood as the house. She watched the fish, some bright orange, some white, and some mixed with both colors, swim in the clear water. Their fins fluttered, but they didn't move forward.

Then she crossed the bridge and inspected the flower garden. Sunflowers, daisies, and roses grew out of the darkest soil she'd ever seen, while several bees buzzed around them. To the right of the garden stood an enormous ginko tree, its yellow blossoms covering every branch. A black and white magpie flew from one of the branches. To the left of the flower garden, several bamboo poles were staked into the ground. Vines of ripe, purple grapes wrapped themselves around the poles. Kwang Ja walked to one of these vines and pulled off a grape. She bit into it and tasted the sweet-sour juice spread on her tongue. This was what the woman meant by diamonds, she thought. Suddenly she felt like crying. This garden, this house was what Seoul was supposed to be to Kwang Ja. To her it was the heart of Seoul. Though the body, the city may be contaminated, the heart was pure. She held in her tears, swallowed the grape, turned around to the old servant woman and asked, "What is expected of me?"

The woman hissed. "Only that you become a lady."

Kwang Ja wasn't sure what that meant, but she did not care. She had been tempted effectively, and was willing to pay any price.

■ ■ ■

It was difficult at first. Kwang Ja had to learn how to read better, not only *hangul*, women's writing, but also *hanmun*, men's writing. She had to learn all of the graces of a South Korean aristocratic woman, which meant she had to learn how to ingratiate herself to men, which was difficult considering there were no men at the house. She was forbidden to take one step outdoors so her dark skin would lighten. This meant she did not spend any time in the garden. She had to lose her northern country accent, and cover it with a more gentile one. What they wanted her to do was forget who she was and where she came from. As far as they were concerned, she was reborn during the hot summer of 1952. The Year of the Dragon. And except for not being able to eat the grapes or watch the fish outside, this was all fine with her.

One of the first things Park Dong Jin had done to her was have her calluses removed. Her feet were soaked in water for days, while two women scrubbed the skin off. Every day the soles of her feet were worn down to a bright red, and like a shedding snake, she left a trail of skin wherever she moved.

She also shed her peasant clothes. She was given clothes she didn't even know how to put on. Layers of thin material of white, green, blue, and pink had to be put on a layer at a time, in a particular order. Covering these layers was the *chogori* and *ch'ima*, the loose, long-sleeved blouse and high, wrap-around skirt which hovered less than an inch from the ground. The material was unusually soft, unlike anything she'd ever touched before. Silk, canoe-shaped shoes finished the ensemble. Then there was her hair. The matted texture was combed out by the same two women who scrubbed her feet. For the first week, every day, she left tufts of hair in the teeth of combs. But she did not cry. She acted as if it didn't even hurt, and the two women who combed it believed her. Finally, after her hair was straight and silky, the servants showed her how to make the simple, long braid worn by unmarried women.

For that first year, she didn't even see Dong Jin, the man who had put her in the fancy black car. But she heard his name constantly. Whenever she did something good, like recite the story of "The Old Man Who Became A Fish," or "The Old Woman Who Became A Goblin" flawlessly, or commit to memory Newton's laws of gravity, her *sabu*, her teacher, a middle-aged man with an unusually long graying mustache, would say, "Master Park will be so proud."

Whenever she did something bad, like forget to brush her hair, her nurse, the old woman who had led her into the house, would say, "You stupid girl. If you are not careful Master Park will throw you back out on the streets."

This Master Park for that first year was an entity she'd neither seen nor heard. To her, he became this faceless figure who held her fate in the palm of his hand. He became like that God she had learned about in the book of the white missionaries. He was a deity who could reward or punish in one stroke without even showing himself. At first, because of her atheism, Kwang Ja did not fear or believe it. But as the months rolled by while her skin lightened, her feet and hair softened, and her mind was filled, she knew she was being transformed, and she knew Master Park was the force behind it. At first she felt like a silkworm cocooning herself and changing. But then she realized she wasn't the power behind her metamorphosis. It was Master Park who cocooned her, and with this thought Kwang Ja felt more like a spider's meal than a growing butterfly or moth. She didn't know why, but she was beginning to feel fear. She did not want to be ruled by a god.

On the one-year anniversary of her rebirth, Dong Jin came to her. He quietly entered the house while Kwang Ja was on the patio, playing the *kayagum*. She was a quick study with everything, but she especially had a knack for playing this twelve-stringed zither, and in just a year, she could play some of the most complex compositions. Through the controlled chaos of floating notes, she heard the glass door slide open. The man she had come to know as a demi-god, along with the two servants who'd scrubbed her once callous-ridden feet, walked and stopped in front of her. And in that first instant of seeing him, the very first time she had, her fear and her perception of him as an all-powerful being disappeared. He was definitely a man, and not an impressive-looking one at that. He was middle-aged and tall for a Korean, but this height was offset by a fat belly and bad posture. A thinning head of hair framed his round face. His eyes were small, his eyebrows bushy, and his nose was broad and flat. His mouth was unusually small, and he seemed to lack a chin. The most impressive thing about this man was the dark, Western-style suit he was wearing. Kwang Ja also noticed he was carrying a strange wooden box with him. When Kwang Ja stopped playing and put her head down, she looked at his shiny black shoes, and it reminded her of his car. It seemed that Westerners were obsessed with creating shiny black things and calling them beautiful. It seemed odd to Kwang Ja that they, like their religious men, didn't seem to like bright colors.

He told her to stand up. He put his hand on her chin and turned her face, looking at each profile. She'd found out she was beautiful only the year before when she'd first overheard the servants commenting on it. Without looking at the servants, he said, "Get us tea."

Kwang Ja left her *kayagum*, and they both walked to the other side of the patio. He told her to sit and placed the box on the table. It was a beautiful, lacquered, cherry-colored box. Dragons made of mother-of-pearl shined on the lid. As she stared at it, one of the servants obstructed her view with a kettle and two ceramic cups. They sat cross-legged at the short, wooden table, and he poured her some tea. She carefully put her right hand around the rim and gently held the bottom with her left. She took a brief sip, letting only a few drops in her mouth. Kwang Ja felt Dong Jin staring at her, and refused to look back. "Did you get the chance to taste the grapes in the garden?" he asked.

She nodded, feeling his eyes study her face.

"Who was your father?" he asked.

"I don't know. I am an orphan."

"You call yourself Cho Kwang Ja. Whose surname did you take?"

"Cho was the name of a family in the village that I went to after the missionary orphanage was abandoned."

Dong Jin poured tea in his cup. He picked it up and blew on it. The steam blew in Kwang Ja's direction, but evaporated before it hit her. "You are beautiful," he said in a deadpan manner. It was as if he were pointing at a tree and saying, "That's a tree." He sipped his tea, then continued. "There is an exotic quality to your look. An almost northern Japanese quality. Do you have Japanese blood?"

Kwang Ja jerked her head up and looked into Dong Jin's eyes. She was slipping. "No, I don't."

Dong Jin smiled. "How do you explain the shape of your eyes?"

"My eyes are the same as anyone else's. They're brown," she said, still looking directly at him, even though she knew she shouldn't be.

"So they are. But there's something different," he said. He looked like he wanted to examine her eyes with a magnifying glass. "Maybe to Westerners, Japanese, Chinese, and Koreans look alike. But I know many people of all of these nationalities. I have never seen eyes like yours in any Korean woman."

Kwang Ja thought about this for a moment. Then she shrugged and looked down. "Maybe too much sun."

Dong Jin laughed. "Yes, maybe. You may be scared, but there's nothing to worry about. No one cares if you're not pure Korean. Not here. In fact, I doubt if that's what you're really scared of. You're at the age where you are supposed to be scared. The world is crazy, especially for a young woman. Do you know why I brought you here?"

Kwang Ja thought about this. She had her suspicions that he wanted to make her his concubine, but felt it would be impolite to say so. She glanced at the box. Perhaps it contained a concubine's gift. This man, with his questions and assumptions was angering her. Who was he to tell her what she was really scared of? "You brought me here because you feel guilty about hitting me with your fancy black car."

Don Jin smiled. "Good guess, but no. You see, I make movies. So I brought you here because I am going to make you a star. The way to greatness is found in either creating something new or destroying something old. With you, I plan to do both."

Kwang Ja looked down. She was taught recently that matter could neither be created nor destroyed. "But I'm just a simple country girl who you accuse of being part foreign. How can I be an actress?"

"You're already an actress, child. I just want to show everyone else. From now on you'll take my name. You are a Park. You are from Pusan or Won Ju, who cares, the country is a mess and no one knows who anyone is anymore anyway. You're a distant cousin of mine whose parents have passed. I am your guardian. We will get you another name, one that doesn't suggest a peasant upbringing, like Kwang Ja does, from a fortuneteller tomorrow. Do you accept?"

Kwang Ja sipped on her tea and let silence fill the room. She didn't want to seem too anxious. She put down the cup, sighed, and looked at him again. "I guess."

Dong Jin laughed. "You are going to be a star!"

He opened the box and pulled out a short, simple-looking knife. Its blade was covered by a silver sheath. It was obviously made by a more primitive culture. "Do you know what this is?" he asked.

"It's a knife, an old one at that."

"Has your teacher told you about the tradition of the 'silver knife?'"

Kwang Ja nodded. "Yes. In the old days, it was given to young women as both decoration and protection. A young virgin was always to wear it. But the tradition died, yes?"

Dong Jin nodded. "Yes. In fact, this knife is an artifact. It has been in my family for hundreds of years. But now I give it to you."

Kwang Ja frowned. She couldn't imagine carrying around a knife like some kind of cutthroat. "But who do I need to protect myself from?"

"We all need protection. Sometimes from strangers, mostly from acquaintances, and always from ourselves. But please, think of this as more of a symbol. It is a gift that symbolizes the fact that you are no longer the helpless girl I found in the streets. I have armed you."

Kwang Ja pulled the knife from its sheath. The silver blade drew in the light from the sun and shot it in her eyes. She tightened her grip around its hilt, and tested the blade. It was sharp. She wondered if it had ever been used. Suddenly she felt strong. Her fears disappeared. Yes, she was no longer the scared child starving in the streets of Seoul. She looked up at Dong Jin. "Thank you for the gift."

He smiled. "Keep it in the box. It's an antique. Now, let's talk about your future as an actress. You and I will go to Pusan, where you will be trained in the theater. You will also be taught more Western philosophies there…"

Kwang Ja put the sheath back on its blade and placed the knife back in the box. He was right, it was a symbol, an artifact more than an actual weapon.

"Are you listening?"

She closed the box. "Yes."

It would be years before she would open the box again. And only twice more.

■ ■ ■

The next day, in the streets of Seoul, with envious eyes focused on her, Kwang Ja and Dong Jin asked a whore/fortuneteller about a new name. She was a woman in her forties who spent her days on the streets seeing the future, and spent nights trying to insure that she herself would have one. Kwang Ja thought it strange that a rich man like Dong Jin would choose such a fortuneteller. But he simply said, "The ones who have lived tend to be the ones with the most vision."

The fortuneteller scribbled down what little information Kwang Ja could tell her about her heritage. The woman then threw a handful of beans onto a thin layer of sand in front of her. She carefully studied the arbitrary formation, and Kwang Ja wanted to laugh, but the whore/fortune-teller's manner of seriousness prevented her from doing so. Suddenly, the woman looked up. "Soong Nan. Your name now will be Soong Nan. It will be a very lucky name for you."

The fact that this whore/fortuneteller was living on the street in rags told the newly named Soong Nan that she didn't know the least bit about luck. So she took the name with trepidation. The next day, Park Soong Nan went to Pusan, leaving Cho Kwang Ja buried in the fortuneteller's shallow sand.

THE INSTITUTION
chapter three

IT WAS A small, tourist wedding; the kind of wedding that comes bundled in a package deal with airfare, hotel, rental car, and two anemic steaks and shrimp-sized lobsters. It was held outdoors, in the garden of the Hawaiian Regent Hotel in Waikiki. White wooden lattices, with plastic plants in front of them, served as the backdrop as Donny and Crystal took their vows. Before Donny said, "I do," he looked down at his family behind the security of his two-hundred-dollar, blue-tinted Jean-Paul Gaultier sunglasses. Won Ju, despite the outdoor heat, wore a matching blazer and skirt. Pantyhose, too. She was looking up and smiling. Her husband Kenny, dressed in khaki pants and a dark blue aloha shirt, was looking at Crystal's cleavage. Their son, Brandon, who'd just turned fifteen, was also wearing khaki pants and an aloha shirt. He was also looking at Crystal's cleavage. Soong, who was wearing a white silk blouse and brown skirt, was holding an open umbrella. Donny almost laughed when he saw her look at Crystal's cleavage and shake her head. Donny's half-sister, Darian, who was wearing a short but classy brown dress, winked at him. She had the same bird-face and pale skin as her mother. When she had flown in the day before from Berkeley, she seemed to like Crystal. She didn't regard her with that air of superiority that came so easy to her.

Donny knew that Crystal's family was not going to show. His family members were the only people in attendance. She had long before been disowned because of her career choice, or so she'd told him, and Donny didn't really know how he felt about this, nor had he even met Crystal's parents. It was funny with that Hawaiian family, jail was fine for her brother, but stripping was a huge sin. There was dignity in prison, none in peddling flesh. Sometimes he sympathized with her because he often thought he was a mere step away from being disowned. But sometimes he envied her because she didn't have to deal with family. But on this day he was glad they didn't show. He reveled in the support of his sisters, the envy of his brother-in-law and nephew, and the disapproval of his mother. More people would have ruined the closeness of it all. Crystal had mentioned that her brother might stop by at the reception, but he wasn't worried about that now. Instead he felt good, like he accomplished something. It took a man to do what he was doing. Originally he wanted to do it in Vegas and have an Elvis impersonator marry them. But Won Ju would have none of it. So for her, he'd decided on the Hawaii tourist wedding. He knew he owed his older sister a lot, so he was more than happy to adjust his plans for her. But he couldn't resist. After he politely kissed his bride, Donny looked out at his family, bent down on one knee, and said in his best Southern drawl, "Thank you, thank you very much."

It was a good thing he'd had a couple of martinis at the Hawaiian Regent bar before he got hitched.

■ ■ ■

The reception was at the Hawaiian Canoe Club. Kenny, who'd been a member since childhood, set it up. The private club, which charged thirty thousand dollars for new membership, sat in front of Waikiki Beach. When the super-stretch Lincoln limousine pulled up at dusk, Donny watched as an older, dark-skinned Filipino employee, dressed in dark brown slacks and a beige button-up collared shirt, lit the gas-powered torches at the entrance. The torches, each an iron pole about six feet high with an iron cone at the top, were almost too high for the Filipino to reach. The employee, after he turned the gas on with a wrench, stepped in the bushes of ti leaves and extended his arm with a lit match. Donny rolled down the window and heard the flame appear with a low, soft, popping sound. He smiled, feeling important, like the torches were lit for him on this special day.

The limo stopped, and Donny let everyone out. His mother stepped out first, followed by his sister's family, his half-sister, then finally his bride. Crystal waited for him to exit, then smiled and grabbed his hand. He glanced at the bust of her wedding dress and suddenly wished it were not cut so low. Though he enjoyed the cut at the ceremony, he knew this was an exclusive club populated by a lot of rich and important people. He didn't want people to think, like his mother, that he had married trash. Though he liked his mother thinking it, he didn't want anyone else to. His head began to pound from the afternoon martinis, and he desperately needed another drink.

The family walked to the registration desk where an older Caucasian woman greeted Kenny with a smile. She was wearing a brightly colored muumuu and thick brown-rimmed glasses. "Hi Margie," Kenny said as he signed the registration book. Donny looked around the lobby while he waited. There were wicker chairs surrounding small, wooden coffee tables. There was a magazine rack with issues of *Time, Newsweek, Honolulu Magazine,* and *Women's Health.* The room was lightly decorated with plants. It was like a picture in a magazine. When Kenny finished signing in, Donny walked past with his head down. The woman smiled and said, "Congratulations."

As they made their way from the lobby to the dining room, two Caucasian boys, both blond, tall, shirtless, and skinny, were running out past the no smoking sign. Weird dress code, Donny thought. Then he looked up. The dining room seemed to be the only way to get from the beach to the lobby. Donny took off his sunglasses and looked out to the beach just as the sun was setting. The clouds were lit with splashes of orange and red, while the sky above them was blue and indigo. Red grating against blue. A perfect ending of a day, Donny thought, as the entire family stopped at the hostess podium. Crystal squeezed his arm. It was the first time he'd realized she was even there since they'd gotten out of the car.

The clanging of dishes and the enthusiastic chatter of club members Donny had never met surrounded their table. Every table was filled. Filipino bus boys walked to and fro pouring water and removing dishes. They wore bright purple aloha shirts with black slacks. The waiters, dressed in tuxedo shirts and black vests, were busy taking orders and serving food. Just about every other table was filled with Caucasian club members. Donny was sitting with his wife on one side and his mother on the other when a cocktail waitress came and asked everyone if they wanted anything to drink. Crystal ordered two bottles of champagne. She and Donny were on the same page. There was only one empty seat at the table, just in case Crystal's brother showed.

Amidst the loud voices in the room Brandon turned to his grandmother. "Grandma, why did you hold an umbrella over you at the wedding? There wasn't any rain."

Donny laughed, then spoke with his accent, which even after twenty years, he was painfully aware that he would never shake. "Your grandma is afraid of the sun."

It was the most he'd said to his nephew in the last month. They'd never really talked. Brandon turned to his mother and asked, "What does he mean?"

"She doesn't want her skin to get dark," Won Ju said.

Brandon frowned and looked at his dark-skinned father. Kenny straightened his blue collar, then shrugged at his dark-skinned son and looked at his well-tanned wife. Won Ju, who glanced at her new, well-tanned sister-in-law, said, "In the old days in Korea dark skin was regarded as, well, peasant-like."

Donny looked at his mother. He was enjoying this. Because her English was so bad, she was almost like a nonentity at this table. He knew his mother was smart, maybe smarter than anyone else in the family, but he kind of liked that most of them didn't think so, especially her precious grandson. He smiled just as his mother spoke up. "No, not true. I not think bad because rich, no rich. Look all round. All people here," she pointed to the other tables, "have tan. Rich people. But sun bad for skin. Especially old woman. Wrinkles."

Brandon nodded.

Then she said in Korean, "You do not have to speak for me, children."

Kenny, who sipped on his sweating glass of water, reached over and lightly touched Crystal's arm. He held his fingers there while he talked. "You better get used to this Korean language thing. They could be talking about you, and you wouldn't even know it."

Crystal laughed. Soong spoke in rapid Korean, pretending to say it under her voice. "Learn the language, like we learned yours." She looked at Donny and Won Ju. "Look now, Darian is my only hope. Darian, are you going to make your mother happy and find a nice Korean boy?"

Darian, who was quiet until now, spoke in perfect English. "Please don't suck me into this. Let me just get drunk in peace."

Donny believed he loved Darian, but sometimes she irritated him. To him, Darian always had this pretentiousness about her, like she was the only American out of the children, and that this meant something. Her English was pure, while Won Ju's and Donny's were accented. The fact that she was working on her MA in English at U.C. Berkeley didn't help either. "Besides, Mother," Darian said in Korean, "I'm never getting married. As a great American actress once said, 'Marriage is a great institution, but I'm not ready for an institution yet.'"

It translated badly. Donny expected his mother to come back with a Korean quote qualifying the virtues of marriage, but she didn't. She just shook her head and said in English, "Hard-head girl."

Darian turned to Kenny and Crystal, and said in her weather-girl voice, "I'm sorry. We were just having a discussion on the institution of marriage. It might be a bad choice of topic considering we should be celebrating it, not debating it." Donny hated that voice. She could've said, "It will be sunny tomorrow with a chance of rain," and he would've hated it even more. Not only did its perfect enunciation irritate him, but the voice also suggested that it was saying something important to a lot of people, while most of the time, it was saying something meaningless, either trying to guess at something that couldn't be predicted or stating the obvious.

Just then the cocktail waitress appeared and poured everyone a glass of champagne. Donny caught Kenny looking at her ass as she walked away. He smiled and raised his glass. "Am I going to have to toast myself?"

Kenny laughed. "Sorry. To Donny and Crystal. All the happiness in the world."

Donny quickly emptied his glass, then refilled it. He enjoyed getting drunk. It took the edge off. Everything looked more round. There weren't sharp edges, nothing around that could cut him. The world felt safer when he was drunk. Even his mother's sharp eyes, nose, elbows, and tongue seemed less likely to cut him. He emptied his second glass and poured himself another. He really wanted to smoke a cigarette.

After Donny finished his fifth glass of champagne, the blue and red of dusk blended into a hazy purple, and the clanging dishes and chattering voices faded into a dull hum, a mountain began to slide into the dining room. Donny thought he was seeing things, so he looked around the dining room, but saw that even all of the tanned, white faces were seeing the mountain, too. Maybe it wasn't a mountain; mountains don't move, instead it was a glacier slowly and deliberately moving towards them. Suddenly Donny waited for a male member of the dinner crowd to yell, "To the lifeboats! Women and children first!" The voice never came, but Donny could tell that he wasn't the only one thinking it.

The glacier was a man who was a combination of professional wrestler, prison movie hammer, and geology on the Discovery Channel. He was tanned and had short, curly clown-red hair. His worn aloha shirt, which had faded pictures of Hawaiian hieroglyphs, men with spears, failed to completely cover his stomach. Below his faded black shorts, Donny saw calves the size of his thighs, and slippers the size of canoes. But the most impressive thing about this man was his neck. Donny could easily imagine a guillotine shattering like glass on this man's neck. This was not a Hawaiian Canoe Club member. And despite his roundness, he looked very sharp and dangerous to Donny. Donny put on his sunglasses when the glacier reached the table. The man rubbed his red goatee that turned into a light blond as it crept up his upper lip. Donny thought the contrast of the red hair with the blond looked ridiculous, but he wasn't about to mention it. "Hi Sis," the man said.

Crystal jumped from her chair and hugged her brother Kaipo, whose look pulled more Caucasian than his sister. He lifted her off the ground and she let out a girlish squeal. He put her down and smiled. "So dis mus' be da new family."

Donny shook Kaipo's hand, or it may have been just one of his enormous fingers, like how babies shake an adult hand, then he watched him go around the table and shake everyone else's. Donny noticed his flawless use of the old plantation pidgin English. And when Kaipo got to Kenny, and Kenny stood up, shook his hand, and said, "Eh, wassup bradah," Kenny's pidgin lacked the same fluency. It was like he was forcing the old language. Donny had heard the phrase "coconut" once to describe Hawaiians like Kenny. Brown on the outside, white on the inside.

Kaipo smiled and sat in the empty chair next to Darian. When he put his forearms on the table, it looked like he was about to have make-believe tea with a group of little girls. He looked around. "Ho, dis place is like haole central, ah?"

Won Ju laughed and said sarcastically, "Hey, this is the Hawaiian Canoe Club, we're all Hawaiians here."

Kaipo smiled. "Yeah, whatevas. Jus' because dese white guys paddle Hawaiian canoe, no mean dey Hawaiian. Hawaiian is one race, an I no mean one canoe race, not one club."

Crystal reached over to Kaipo. "Now relax. Besides, look at you. The red head. You're half haole."

"Not my fault."

Everyone was watching Kaipo except for Soong. She was staring at her grandson. Always the actress. Donny turned to Kaipo. "So I guess you're my new brother."

"Yeah, I guess."

Crystal ordered another bottle of champagne. Won Ju looked at Kaipo with an almost smile. She liked him. Donny felt that only he could decipher the emotions that his older sister subtly displayed. His half-sister Darian, who had the bad habit of not leaving anything to decipher, spoke. "You know, I've been reading some stuff up at Berkeley about the effects of Western imperialization on the indigenous people of the Pacific. How even today the disenfranchised, like the Hawaiians, are still like second class citizens. First in heart disease, first in felony convictions. Some are becoming diasporatic and moving to the continent. Kaipo, how does it feel to be sitting in this dining room with these people?"

Donny was amazed that she got through it without saying a single version of the word "problem." With her, things were always "problematic," or "problematized." Kaipo laughed and pulled a pack of Kool Filter Kings from his pocket. He popped one in his mouth and lit a single match with one of his gigantic hands. The cigarette looked like a toothpick hanging out of his mouth. Several club members, as if trained to do so, were about to remind him that there was no smoking allowed at the club. Then they thought better of it, and looked away, pretending it wasn't happening. "I neva even get half of what you said, but I goin' say dis. I jus' got out of prison two months ago. Wuz fo' grand theft auto, possession, and assault on one police offica." He looked at Kenny. "One Hawaiian cop of all tings. Now fo' one yea' I stayed in one jail dat Hawaiians neva build because I stole one car dat Hawaiians neva make, fo' drugs Hawaiians neva bring in, and fo' punching one cop dat stay on one force dat Hawaiians neva create. Seems to me dat I neva look fo' trouble, instead trouble came to me, came to Hawaii. Shit if neva have haoles, I would've probably been paddling one canoe jus' like da kind dey get now. Now I cannot even afford one paddle. But den again, maybe I jus' like revenge. Steal back."

He had a big voice. People on the other tables overheard, and played with their continental cuisine with their silverware. Kenny scratched his face. "It's the evolution of the world, my friend. All of us Hawaiian brothers have to adjust."

Won Ju quickly rolled her eyes. It was a rare, betraying gesture from her. Kaipo smiled. "Yeah, maybe evolution. But dat don't make it right."

Darian was staring at Kaipo. Kenny was looking down, and Won Ju was smiling. It amazed Donny to see his sister make such a spectacle of herself. Soong spoke. "When I was born Korea, Japanese everywhere. Very bad to Korean people. When I was little girl. When teenager, American GI everywhere. Before all them, Chinese, Mongol, white missionary. No, not right."

Donny was surprised. He'd never considered his mother a politically liberal person. In fact, he considered her a racist and elitist who didn't even like most Koreans. Donny glanced at Brandon, who seemed bored by the entire conversation. He seemed to be the only one in the entire dining room not affected by Kaipo's presence. It was like the glacier pushed everybody, except this tall, spindly fifteen-year-old, away to make room. Kenny, on the other hand, looked like he was pushed all the way to the beach. Then Donny got tired of looking. He had a job to do. The waiter came and took their order.

"So Mom," Donny said in Korean, "I have a business proposition for you."

Soong looked at Darian. "Is this proposition going to cost me a great deal of money?"

"Absolutely not, think of it as an investment."

Darian laughed. "An investment is probably what a degenerate gambler calls a bet."

Donny glared at Darian. She was the spoiled one. She'd never had a life like him or Won Ju. "No Mom, not a bet. I want to open a restaurant. Crystal and I wanted to open a restaurant."

Crystal stopped eating when her name was mentioned. She looked at Donny. Donny tried to send her a reassuring side-glance. "Anyway," he said, "it'll be a loan. You can charge me interest and everything."

"You mean," Darian said, "you'll be reconsolidating this with your previous loan."

Donny was getting angry. How could Darian even say anything when their mother had been pumping thousands of dollars a year into Berkeley for her? Not to mention her degree was virtually useless in the real world. An MA in English, what a laugh. Before he could snap at her, Won Ju spoke. "Let him ask," she said.

Kenny laughed. "There they go again, talking behind our backs right in front of us." He looked at Crystal and Kaipo. "Maybe us Hawaiians should leave."

Won Ju looked at her husband. "Please feel free," she said.

Kenny's face, even from far away, looked angry. Kaipo spoke. "Jus' let um talk bradda," he said.

Soong put her fork down, ignoring the non-Korean speakers. "How much?" she asked.

Donny cleared his throat. "I need to borrow about twenty thousand to start."

Soong sighed. She looked at Won Ju. "What do you think?"

"It's not my money, not my decision."

Soong wiped her mouth with a napkin. "Listen, Chung Yun, I really don't have too much. You know your stepfather spent most of the money I made in Korea on the farm. Your sister also borrowed to open her boutique in Waikiki. Your other sister is not finished with school yet. How badly do you want this restaurant?"

"Crystal and I really need it, Mom. And I know it will work."

Darian laughed. "How could you know?"

She is trying to protect her precious fake-world tuition, Donny thought. "I know," he said.

"This is the last time?" Soong asked.

"Absolutely."

"So Mom," Won Ju asked, "are you planning to stay in Hawaii?"

"I think I might have to."

"Why?" Darian asked.

"Because it seems I'm betting on it. Besides, at least I can keep an eye on Brandon."

Brandon didn't even flinch at the mentioning of his name. He never seemed to. Donny supposed the fact that he was the center of his grandmother's universe seemed as uninteresting to him as the fact that the sun is the center of this solar system.

"Well, Mom," Darian said, "I might be staying a while too. You see, school's not really working..."

Won Ju closed her eyes. Soong sipped her glass of chardonnay while Darian talked. Donny felt really good for the first time in months. Bye, bye, tuition. He winked at Crystal. But she didn't see. She was talking to her brother, while Kenny glared at Won Ju. They never suspected that he saw so much behind his blue-lensed, two-hundred-dollar Jean-Paul Gaultier sunglasses and through the champagne buzz that was slowly turning into nausea.

■ ■ ■

After dinner, they all walked out to the limo and said goodbye to Kaipo. Donny, in a mild drunken haze, hugged his brother-in-law. He imagined it was like hugging a stuffed grizzly bear. Imagining it as a live bear would've been too scary. This bold act instantly told him he was properly drunk, and he slouched into the limo. First they dropped Darian and Soong off at the hotel. Then the car took the Akana family to their condo. Before Brandon could make it out unscathed, Crystal smothered his face with drunken kisses. Kenny laughed while Won Ju playfully slapped her hands away. Donny looked at the boy. He was growing tall and handsome. Donny sighed as the family congratulated the couple. The car drove away, heading towards Donny's and Crystal's apartment. Donny lit the cigarette he'd been dying for for the last three hours.

Crystal rolled down the window. "So, what'd you think?"

Donny sighed again. "It was O.K.."

She lit a cigarette and laughed. "We got ourselves a weird extended family."

"Yup."

"You know your mother hates me."

"Yeah, and Kaipo hates Kenny. Kenny hates Kaipo. Brandon hates me. Darian loves Kaipo. Won Ju loves everybody, except for maybe her husband, and I hate..."

Crystal turned to Donny. "And you hate?"

"No one."

She took a long drag from the cigarette. "You hate her, don't you?"

"What the hell are you talking about? She's giving us the money."

"I thought she was loaning it?"

"Don't talk stupid."

"So you don't hate her?"

"I thought I talked to you about this before. I don't hate her. I just hate the way she raised me and Won Ju."

Crystal threw the cigarette out the window. "Won Ju doesn't seem to have a problem."

Donny sighed. "Don't let her fool you. If she wants to she can keep a straight face about anything."

"And what about Darian?"

"She grew up different. Her American father saw to that. Besides, my mother wasn't working when she was growing up. She never lacked the attention."

Crystal laughed and put her arms around Donny. "Poor little Donny. Don't worry, I'll take care of you."

Normally this would have infuriated him. But he was too tired. He felt like puking, but he was even too tired to do that. He simply leaned against Crystal and let her tease his hair. When the limo pulled to the apartment building and Crystal pulled Donny out, he laughed. She'll take care of me. One of these days, I've got to learn to take care of myself.

-2-

IN THE ELEVATOR, Won Ju heard her son ask a wincing question, the kind that everybody asks themselves, and despite much speculation, can never find an answer for, partially because it is a genuine mystery, but mostly because they're afraid of it. "Why did Crystal marry Donny?"

He might as well have asked, "Why can human beings be so cruel?" Kenny laughed, sounding proud that his son asked the question. "They love each other," Won Ju said. "And remember, it's *Aunty* Crystal and *Uncle* Donny." She knew she gave him a Santa Claus or Easter Bunny answer.

The elevator doors opened. "He isn't my uncle," Brandon said as he stepped out first.

Won Ju looked at Kenny. He shrugged then pointed at her. "Don't start. I have my own gripe with you."

Won Ju followed her son into the hallway. "What are you talking about, he's not your uncle?"

Brandon stopped and turned around. She suddenly became aware of how much taller he was than she. He was fifteen and already about five-ten. But it was weird with children. She still felt like she was looking down at him. "Dad told me how he used to steal Grandma's jewelry and pawn it."

She was surprised her husband had told their son this, but she was even more surprised that her son cared. He never seemed to take a genuine interest in his grandmother, despite the obsessed interest Soong had in him. "You don't know how Donny was brought up. You know nothing about him. And remember, he is my brother, he is your uncle."

Brandon turned around, pulled out his keys, and opened the door. He took off his shoes and walked to the kitchen. He opened the refrigerator door. "But he's a loser," Brandon said.

After taking off her shoes, Won Ju looked back at her husband. He smiled. She closed the refrigerator door and put her hands on his shoulders. She was about five-three, so it was a high reach. "I'll say this once," she said. "He's your uncle and that's that."

Brandon pushed her hands away. He walked away, biting into an apple he grabbed from the fridge. "Yeah, yeah," he said as he made it towards his bedroom. The door shut.

Won Ju turned around to look at her husband. He was sitting at their glass dining-room table with the newspaper lying in front of him. "How could you tell him that?" she asked.

"Well it's true, right?"

"That's not the point. Donny is his uncle and he should show him respect."

Kenny picked out the sports page from the *Honolulu Advertiser*. The sports and business sections were the only two portions in the paper he read. Though, a couple of times, she caught him reading the funnies. He opened the sports section up, which he had already read in the morning. Won Ju could only see a large picture of Shaquille O'Neal hanging from a basketball rim. "Listen," he said, "I like Donny. I really do. But I don't want my son showing respect for people who don't deserve it. He's getting older and deserves to know about human nature. I told him the story, and he made his own moral decision."

"His own moral decision? Fourteen-year-old boys who never had to make any real decisions yet are not in any position to judge others who have. It's not right."

Kenny put down the paper. "He's fifteen. And like I said, I like the guy. I like him more than I like your mother. But your mother deserves some damn respect. What was he pitching to her tonight? Another one of his quick-cash money schemes? Your Mom's a pain in the ass, but I respect her. Your brother, Brandon hit it right on the nose, he's a loser."

"Kenny, fuck you."

"No, fuck you. And what was that shit tonight? Feel free to leave? Don't smart-mouth me like that, especially at the Club."

Won Ju walked into the kitchen. The Club. She hated that place. She'd felt the haole members watching the table full of Koreans. She knew they looked down on her and her family. Them with their smug smiles and Filipino servants pouring them water and washing their dishes. She hated that the Filipinos worked their lowest-paying jobs. She felt a kind of kinship with the Filipinos because the Philippines got it just as bad as the Koreans did. There was kinship in pain. The Spanish, the Japanese, the Americans. She'd learned much of her English reading the school books her brother never read in high school. Even though the books downplayed it, she knew what happened. This was why Kenny's love for the haoles went from puzzling her to angering her. He was Hawaiian. The Hawaiians got it so bad from the whites that there were hardly any pure-blooded Hawaiians left. But Kenny wasn't pure Hawaiian. His mother was German-Irish and his father was half-Chinese. However, the rule in Hawaii was if you have any Hawaiian blood, you can call yourself Hawaiian. But Kenny grew up rich. So his liking white people was probably a class thing, not a race thing. Won Ju felt you could not choose pride in both class and race. Kenny was proud to be Hawaiian, but to her it was like he didn't deserve to feel that way because he didn't suffer the poverty that many Hawaiians did. And when he said, "Don't smart-mouth me like that, especially in the Club," she was livid. He couldn't have his little, docile Asian wife disrespecting him among those of his class: the rich whites. So with her mind running like this she walked to the table, picked up the newspaper, and threw it on the floor. She stepped on Shaquille O'Neal on the way to the bedroom, wanting to leave her husband, but feeling like she wouldn't and never could.

"Hey, stop being such a fuckin' brat," Kenny yelled as Won Ju walked through the bedroom door.

Brat. He even spoke to her like she was a child. Right now, he was probably sneaking a peek at Snoopy sitting on his doghouse having another moronic WWI biplane fantasy, and he had the audacity to refer to her as a child. After he'd read the funnies, he'd probably go to bed and take about three seconds to fall asleep. Then he'd wake up at three-thirty, in turn waking her up, if she could even get to sleep by that time, to watch the stock ticker on CNN. Degenerate gambler. Asshole.

He'd looked so good on paper when she'd decided to marry him. Wealthy, good-looking, college-educated. She'd never even thought until recently that the combination of these three things often create something toxic. It was like when she was a bartender. Chivas, Glenvivet, and Patron may be quality stuff on their own, but mixed together? Well, you got the stuff you squeeze out of a bar rag. When did she start hating her husband?

She went to the fish tank to feed the fish. When she opened the lid, the larger oscar rushed the surface, and his fat black lips broke the surface of the water. He waited there. Won Ju closed the lid. Let them starve. She walked into the bedroom with the cylinder of fish food still in her hand. She was going to fight with her husband, and she needed something to throw at him.

-3-

SOONG SAT AT the small circular table with Darian in the hotel room, missing Long Island. The air conditioner hummed as she put a coat on. She hated air conditioning, but in a hotel in Hawaii, you either left the thing on or sweated out a pound of water. Their conversation in Korean started. Though Darian could not write in Korean, her spoken Korean was eloquent. "So what's this about leaving school," Soong asked, "are you getting bad grades?"

Darian stood up and looked into the mirror above the wooden dresser. "No Mom, my grades are good. I don't know, maybe Dad's death is finally getting to me."

It had been over a year since the stroke came that finally killed Soong's second husband. It took four to kill the tough ex-army captain, but the years of cigars and Scotch whiskey had finally caught up to him. Strokes and stomach cancer. Soong missed him too. Despite everything, he had been the love of her life. Darian was the only one who'd flown to New York for the funeral. "He wouldn't want you to use his death as an excuse." She couldn't think of anything else to say. Sometimes a cliché is all that's left.

"I know. But I don't know, lately I've been feeling like what I study there, I don't know, like it's worthless. Like you're spending thousands of dollars on nothing."

Darian walked back to the table and sat down. Soong looked at her daughter's face. She was a very pretty girl. In fact, she looked like Soong when she was young, only more American. Soong did not know what this meant, and couldn't pick out a physical trait which was not Asian but distinctly American, but to her Darian would always be her American child. "I told you to study something more practical."

Darian sighed. "I know. You know what's funny? You know what I'm studying in the English Department at U.C. Berkeley? I'm studying you."

"I don't understand," Soong said.

"I'm studying literature written by first-generation Asian-American immigrants. I'm reading the works of their children. I'm reading about us."

"And it seems worthless?"

Darian stood up again. "It's not that it's worthless; it's…" She paused and said in English, "Problematic." Then she reverted back to Korean. "It's a problem. Sometimes I feel like we're studying ourselves with a kind of detachment that's scary. I don't know what they called it in Korea, but here we call these intellectual learning centers 'ivory towers.' It's sad. A bunch of people who may have grown up Asian, saying their thoughts and experiences are the valid ones. Turning isolated experiences into rules of thumb for entire races. Feeling sorry for themselves because they think they're second-class citizens."

Darian sat back down. "Kids like me, Mom. Second generation. Some can speak their ethnic language but not read or write it, like me. Some can't speak, read or write. Only a few can do all of it. But we all pretend like we know what's going on.

But in truth, we're just twenty-something-year-olds swapping sob stories and using ridiculously big words to rationalize our experiences. Ivory tower, Mom, looking down on the masses, isolated, out-of-it."

Soong frowned. "And what does your father's death have to do with all of this?"

"Dad was second-generation Korean. His parents came and worked the sugar plantations of Hawaii. He grew up dirt poor, he was in World War II and the Korean War because he thought that was his only way out of plantation life. He liked to drink Scotch and tell stories. I loved him. You were a famous actress in Korea who came up from nothing. You lived through national scandals and immigrated to a foreign country not being able to speak any English. It's like what right do I have to dwell on my heritage and call it my own when I never experienced any of the stuff you guys experienced? I feel like a self-righteous fraud."

Soong thought about this. "Maybe your father and I earned your right to dwell for you. Maybe it is a right that's inherited and doesn't need to be earned."

Darian shook her head. "It's like meeting Kaipo tonight. You know, Crystal's brother."

How could she have forgotten that man, his neck, and his absurd red hair? His bravado reminded her of her second husband, but it wasn't a childlike arrogance and will that motivated this huge man; Soong knew it was anger. She'd seen that anger in some of the poor faces in Korea years before. Ex-soldiers missing limbs or women missing innocence. It was horrible. But didn't you have to get over the anger? "He's trash like his sister."

Darian frowned. "No, they're not. You know, back at school there's this girl from Hawaii. She writes papers on being Hawaiian, being local. But she's never done drugs, never stolen a car, never been in a fight. She's never been abused by a parent, never had to buy food with food stamps. How can she write about being Hawaiian or local without these experiences? She has no right to represent people whose lives are much different than hers. It'd be like Kenny writing a book on the contemporary Hawaiian experience. This girl, like Kenny, is local, but only a certain kind of local. I'm Korean, but only a certain kind of Korean."

Soong laughed. "You cannot always pity those who refuse any attempts to better their position. A lot of these Hawaiians don't even try. That's why I sometimes hate this place. They're like the blacks in New York, the Mexicans in Fresno. Complain, complain, but don't do. I walked over a hundred miles for a better life when I was fourteen."

Darian smiled. "That's true, Mom, and I respect you for it. But you know what? Crystal just may be you, if you didn't get hit by that fancy car in Seoul that day. Crystal could be you."

Was it dumb luck that changed Soong's life? She'd asked this before, and sometimes she believed it, and sometimes not. Tonight, she decided not to believe it. "No way. There's a difference. I was starving. People don't starve in America."

Darian shook her head as she walked to the door. "Think about it, Mom, you could have been Crystal."

The door shut. Education. The highly educated always looked at others as if they were waiting for the people around them to discover some archaic punchline so that they could finally pat them on the head. Maybe Darian was right; her education was a waste of time. Soong sighed and made her way to the bathroom, where she began to disassemble herself.

Soong meticulously wiped off her make-up and dressed for bed. She brushed her teeth. Looking in the mirror, she thought, what is it that make-up manages to conceal? When she'd been young, it was used to accentuate features. Redder lips, whiter skin, more luscious eyelashes, sharper, cleaner eyebrows. But now it was for repair. Not as many wrinkles, not those dark bags under the eyes, not as tired-looking. These were two very different types of masks. She missed the first one immensely.

She thought about her children. She thought about the money. She was almost sixty years old, and her children still cost her money.

When did the duty end? The tightness of her second dead husband made it more difficult for her children to get money, but now she was facing them unarmed. She couldn't say no to any of them. She should've stayed in Long Island, but without Henry, it seemed stupid. Long Island was their life together, but now that life was over. She spat out toothpaste and sighed. When did a mother stop being a mother?

She turned off the light. She walked to the bed and carefully slid under the covers. The air conditioning was blasting away. When her eyes finally adjusted to the darkness, she laughed. It never used to take that long for her eyes to adjust. She thought about the money again. If only she had more. Once she gave, not loaned, gave her son the twenty thousand, she would be down to her last twenty. If her older daughter's business failed—and considering the poor state of the tourist industry, it eventually would—her daughter would need help again. If her younger daughter went back to school, a year of tuition would be more than she would be able to afford. And she knew her son's business would fail. He was a failure. Considering that the price of gold was down, her jewelry would not be much help either. Now, if she died, it would be a different story. She had a one-hundred-and-fifty-thousand-dollar life insurance policy that the kids would split in three. Now there's a solution, she thought. If only I were to die. In a split second her life flashed before her eyes. She told her mind to do it. It was a good life, an exciting life. Yes, perhaps it is best to die penniless, she thought. That's maybe how I'll know I'm finished with life. It will be done when I no longer have anything to give my children but my death. She smiled. Then why spend twenty thousand on my thirty-eight-year-old son? Because she knew she would. But that was O.K. She was afraid of many things: heights, flying, the ocean, going over sixty in a car. She was afraid of pain for her children. But she was not afraid of death. In fact, this night, as she closed her eyes, the thought that they might not open again soothed her. Her breathing slowed and her thoughts became misty. That night she dreamt of how nice it would be to live until she saw her grandson happily married, then die. She wanted to see her grandson in an elegant tuxedo eagerly waiting to enter the Institution. That would be when he would begin the most interesting journey this life has to offer. Yes, she thought, I'll wait for my grandson to find his mate, then die.

-4-

LIKE EVERY OTHER morning, including weekends, Won Ju opened her shop in the Pacific Beach Hotel at six o'clock A.M. When she had first signed the lease for the twenty-by-thirty-foot shop ten years ago, she felt as if she had a sure thing. The Pacific Beach Hotel had a large Japanese clientele, who as everyone knew spent the most money in Hawaii. And this particular hotel had an attraction that was hard for the tourist mind to resist. In the middle of the hotel, serving as a backdrop to two of its restaurants, the Oceanarium and the Neptune, stood a two-hundred-and-eighty-thousand-gallon salt-water fish tank. Almost a thousand fish of about one hundred and twenty-five species swam behind this twenty-six-foot wall of glass. Most of these fish were indigenous, like the stingray, the ulua, and the uhu, or parrotfish. Others were imported, like the Florida native, the tiger-striped jack. But all could only be seen swimming together in this florescent lighted tank. It was artificial. Deep-sea fish swam in the same water as reef fish. Sand dwellers, like the stingray, fed with the nocturnal red menpachi. They were all forced together under the white lights that made the fish glow unnaturally. And Won Ju had put her faith in this ecological experiment. She'd believed that the tourists would never stop coming to see it.

And they hadn't. They'd just stopped spending money in the shops like hers. At first it had been great. The Japanese had the money to spend on the expensive goods she sold. The Bally leather belts, the Louis Vuitton purses, the Ray Ban sunglasses. She'd once sold thousands of dollars of goods a day. She'd made more than her husband did when she'd first opened. But much of this money went into expanding her inventory. She bought more and more expensive watches, more and more gold jewelry. She knew, like every other shop-owner, that Asians, especially the Japanese, could get this stuff much cheaper in Hawaii than in Japan.

Then Asia took a financial hit. The tourists kept coming, but slowly stopped buying. Won Ju's shop was overstocked, and just as suddenly over-employed. Her business, which had once employed six girls, was now down to one. She opened her shop at six A.M. and closed it at eleven P.M. At least four days a week, she would stay all seventeen hours. Her last girl was forced to work sixty-hour weeks. She knew if she closed down and dumped her inventory now, she'd have just enough, with her savings, to pay off the rest of the lease and pay her mother back the fifteen thousand she owed her. But after that, she'd have to rely on Kenny. Kenny the Tightwad. Kenny who would give her a bad time with every twenty-dollar bill she would take. She'd also have to stop giving her son money. And she loved giving him money, because even though she knew she might be wrong, she felt it made her a good mother. With every twenty she gave him, she felt like she was giving her son choices. No, he did not have to paddle a canoe at the Hawaiian Canoe Club, he could go to the movies. No, he did not have to surf, he could go to the arcade. No, he did not have to come home and scrounge for food, he could buy a meal anywhere. She wanted to give her son choices. She did not want him to become like his father if he didn't want to.

So when she opened her shop at six A.M. the day after her brother's wedding, she did so with a pounding headache. Her hangover from the champagne the night before combined with the stress of money made her head hurt. She slid open the glass door and turned on the lights. She grabbed a pink feather duster and brushed it against the rack of belts, purses, and the glass cases that held the jewelry and watches. She turned on the cash register and sat on her stool. She thought about the fish tank and cursed it. Then she wondered if, since her mother seemed to be staying in Hawaii, she would want a job, or maybe even a partnership. She chided herself for the thought. Her mother had enough trouble already. She pretended to dust for most of the next eight hours.

■ ■ ■

At one o'clock Donny walked in. He was dressed nicely as usual; black slacks, a tucked in blue Polo shirt. His face wore the look of a healthy-sized hangover. He walked up to the counter and leaned against it. He smiled, took off his sunglasses, and started the conversation in English. "I just talked to Mom. She's going to give me the money."

"You better not blow this one," Won Ju said, thinking about how her brother dared her to continue this conversation in English. "I'm pretty sure she's running out of money."

"Don't worry. The restaurant will be a hit."

Won Ju didn't believe him. That was what he'd said when he decided to open the photo studio, before he'd met Crystal. It went belly-up in a little over a year. He hadn't known anything about photography. Won Ju rearranged some jewelry in the glass case in front of her. "What do you know about restaurants?"

"Hey, I know how to cook," he said. "It'll just be cheap Korean food. Like a plate-lunch place. The property is in Kailua. You know a lot of hungry Hawaiians and surfers will come to my place."

Won Ju was worried. She'd heard that about eighty percent of restaurants go under. She resisted the urge to start in Korean. She thought before she said, "What's going to draw them away from the places that they eat at now?"

"Good food, Sis. Good food."

She couldn't imagine her brother slaving over a grill for ten hours a day. Hard work never took with him. Worse, she couldn't imagine Crystal doing the same. She wasn't the grease-under-the-long-lavender-fingernails type. "So when's the grand opening?"

"I'll get the money this week and sign a lease next week. I'll renovate for a couple of weeks, then open. Crystal put in her two weeks at Club Mirage."

Won Ju smiled. "Does Mom know what she does?"

"I don't know. I'm sure she suspects something. Maybe prostitution, who knows? I don't care."

"Well, at least Crystal will be a draw with all those hungry Hawaiians and surfers. Maybe she should wear a bikini?"

Donny laughed. "You might be on to something. Big boobs and kalbi. Like a combination plate."

"And you could name it 'Silicon Inn.'"

"Hey, that's my blushing bride you're talking about."

"Yeah, the day I see her blush."

Donny laughed. "Stop, stop."

"So what are you doing here?"

Donny sighed. "I came for a business proposition."

"What?"

"Come in with me and Crystal at the restaurant. Dump this place already." He lifted his hands and looked around. Then he said in Korean, "There's nobody here."

He was right. She hadn't sold over a hundred dollars' worth of stuff in two weeks. What if the entire family got into the restaurant? This idea caused her to think about the fish tank again. All those different fish swimming together. In a way, it reminded her of her own family. Darian, the imported tiger-striped jack. Kenny, the indigenous kala, horned, brown, and not great eating. Crystal, the kahala, big and bold. Her son the menpachi, meek, vulnerable, but beautiful. And Donny the stingray. The bottom feeder. She didn't know who her mother was. Then it dawned on her. She was the girl with the scuba tank who fed the fish. It never occurred to her that she didn't think about who she was in the tank. "I don't know, Donny," she said in English. "I'm not like you. I have a child to think about. I can't afford failure."

"You know, you sound like somebody I know," he returned in English.

He was talking about their mother. "In some ways, she was right about how she raised us."

Donny grinned. "She didn't raise us. I'll tell you something. More than financial support, your son needs you there. I mean think of the options. He could work with us on weekends."

Won Ju had resolved her ill feelings towards her mother long ago. Donny hadn't. She thought about her own son. He was beyond the age of needing an affectionate love-giving mother. In fact, as a teenager, this love embarrassed him. Won Ju disagreed with Donny. Brandon needed a mother who could provide him with money. One who could buy him a car when he turned sixteen. One who could help pay for his college tuition. She had given her son affection, in fact made sure of it, because of the lack of affection she and her brother lived through as children. But a new type of parent was now needed. One who wouldn't close down and reopen businesses on a whim. "Donny, I can't. Brandon needs stability backing him."

Donny sighed. "Stability? Is this what you call this shop?" He looked around. "I think the word you are looking for is stagnation. In fact, it's worse. Listen, in the restaurant, Brandon could learn about work. He could make his own money." He smiled. "Look at me. I'm living proof of what happens when a person doesn't learn work ethic early."

Won Ju was surprised. His command of English was still growing. Words like "stagnation" were beyond her spoken vocabulary. He'd always been a better English speaker. She knew what the word meant, but she would've been afraid to try to say it. She felt a current of pride and envy. "You win," she said in Korean. "Do you remember Las Vegas?"

Donny smiled. "I'll never forget how you took me with you."

The memory of Vegas haunted her. Donny didn't know. He didn't see the sacrifice their mother had made. She switched her concentration to the early, good memories of Sin City. "Remember how we refused to speak to each other in Korean so that we would learn English faster?"

"I remember."

"I don't know about this restaurant idea."

"It's my turn, Won Ju. You did it in Vegas. Now it's my turn to take the lead. I will not fail."

"What about Mom and everyone else?"

"I send the open invitation for anyone who wants in."

A new beginning, Won Ju thought. If it worked, she would not have to depend on Kenny. If it worked, Brandon would get the things every American teenager craves. If it didn't work... Life would get hard fast. She thought about her mother. Her mother knew hard. The story of how she had ended up in Seoul at fourteen was awe-inspiring. Courage won over better judgment, and Won Ju said, "O.K., Donny. But if it doesn't work, I'll kill you."

Donny hugged his sister. It was an odd move by her brother. Though she knew he loved her, he almost never showed affection, except when he was drunk. Her son was the same, though not as bad. Instead of thinking about the turmoil that the restaurant's failure could bring, she tried to enjoy the moment. Hugging was such an American gesture. How people hugged strangers, acquaintances, and enemies was beyond her. But it felt good sometimes. She squeezed back hard.

-5-

SO MOM AND *Dad really had it out last night. It was about money again. While I was playing Everquest, and my druid was about to level up to twenty and I was about to go to Lake of Ill Omen, and while I was enjoying my apple, I heard Mom slam the door and start screaming. It was kinda weird. She's usually pretty quiet, even when they argue. But not last night. Then Dad started yelling. Man, talk about ruining the moment. My druid about to level up and all. He kicks ass.*

So here I am at school. IPS. Making NaCl. Sodium Chloride. Why is "Na" the chemical symbol for salt? I don't know, they never seem to tell you the interesting stuff at school. Even this sodium chloride stuff. Is this stuff even used for anything? I guess it's supposed to show us that some things mix and some don't. Or that if you have something mixed, and you heat it, well one of those things will evaporate. Mom and Dad are probably going to get a divorce. Some of the kids in this class have divorced parents.

Brian Kelsey. Thinks he's hot shit because he's a freshman and he plays varsity football. I don't know what the big deal is. I mean, Punahou has a decent team, but everybody knows Saint Louis is going to be state champs yet again. Well, maybe it's not only because he plays varsity. He's also one of the only freshman with a car, a Mercedes to boot. His dad bought it for him. His dad's a member of the Club, too. Brian's parents got a divorce last year. But you should see his dad's new wife. She's pretty killer. I think she was a student at UH right before they got married. I think she dropped out of school when they got engaged. Sometimes I hear some of the old people at the Club talking smack about it.

Mary Keller. Cool girl. Hot. She's lighting the Bunsen burner right now, acting all scared, like the room will blow up when the sparks from the clicking thing hits the gas. I wonder how girls learn to get that scared look and look all cute and all. Do they practice in the mirror? I mean, it's obvious that she's not really scared. It's like, just ask Brian to light your Bunsen burner for you. I think her mom was married three times. Her mother's a Club member, too. It's like you have to have parents who are members of the Hawaiian Canoe Club to go to this school or something. Mom screamed something about her paying my tuition last night, when Dad yelled something about paying the lease and utilities. I don't even know what a lease is. I don't want to know.

My NaCl is starting to boil. I guess the chlorine is supposed to disappear, and leave behind the salt, and I'm supposed to "oo" and "ah" about it. Like I don't know what's going to happen.

It's not like Brian and Mary told me about their parents. I don't even really know them too well. It might be because I only just started going to this school. It might be because it's like all the white kids hang out with each other, just like all the Japanese kids hang out with each other, and the small amount of Hawaiians hang out with each other. There's pictures of some seniors in the glass case at the Wo International Center, if anybody needed proof. White, white; Asian, Asian; Hawaiian, Hawaiian. I guess I can pass as either Asian or Hawaiian. But I usually just keep to myself. I'd much rather play Everquest than hang out with these people at the beach or the mall all weekend long. Sometimes I wish my brain had an on-and-off switch.

I wonder what Dad would say if he knew I wasn't popular at school. He probably was. You can just tell. I bet Kaipo and Crystal were popular, too. But they went to Waianae High, and Dad went here. Kaipo must've played football or something. Crystal, cheerleader? Nah. She was probably one of those hot girls who always got busted for smoking. Kaipo probably threatened her boyfriends and stuff. Now look at them. Just like the other adults. Talk, talk, talk. Do they ever have anything important to say?

Just like I thought. Just salt left. Now I have to weigh it. Not that I couldn't listen to Crystal all day long. I have a feeling she might have just been acting last night. I bet she can talk about real stuff. I mean, if I were alone with her, I wouldn't talk about computer games and stuff. Just about life or something. God, when the limo dropped me, Mom, and Dad off, and she started kissing me? I know I could talk to her. I still can't believe she married the loser. His weak Elvis impersonation after he takes his vows. God, what a loser.

I can tell Grandma doesn't like the loser, too. I guess she has to do stuff for him because he's her son and all, but she doesn't like him. But it's almost like she doesn't like anybody else, either. I mean, really, I don't even think she likes me. I mean, I know she'd do anything for me, and she always talks about me and worries about me, but does she like me? I mean, she doesn't even know me. It's not her fault. I mean, it's not like I know her either. It's not like I sip tea with her and ask her, "So Grandma, tell me about your life?" I mean, I know about some of it, how it was tough and all back in the day, and how she was like famous and all in Korea, but I don't know what she's thinking, and I doubt she knows what I'm thinking. Besides, there's the language thing and all. But it's more than that. I doubt Brian and Mary know anything about their grandparents either. Look at them. They're always lab partners. I like not having a lab partner. I can do this quicker. Their NaCl didn't even boil yet. I'm already weighing my salt. Mr. Cooper lets *me read my gaming magazines when I finish early, but today I feel too tired to read, not sleep tired, just veg tired.*

Grandma. I don't know anything about her. It's like she's the chlorine that evaporated. I can't even see it. But I guess right now it's all around me in the air.

THE QUEEN OF TEARS

chapter four

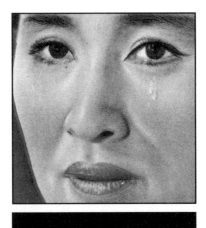

AT NINETEEN, PARK Soong Nan was a star. After doing seven movies that did modestly at the box office, she hit it big with *Chun Hyung Jun*. It was a Korean historical drama based on Shakespeare's *Romeo and Juliet*. Soong Nan was given the lead by her husband Dong Jin, who produced the film. It was a hit in Seoul. A lot of people went to see it more than once.

Suddenly she was one of the most desirable women in all of South Korea. She was their version of an up-and-coming Elizabeth Taylor, a Western actress who Koreans loved, a combination of youth, talent, and beauty. And for her it was easy. Because she was so small and thin, the audience ached with sympathy when she acted vulnerable. And when she acted courageous and unbending, the audience saw a brave little sparrow fly into the eye of a typhoon. They began calling her "The Queen of Tears."

Then Soong Nan got pregnant. Putting her career on hold, she stayed at the house and relaxed in the garden. She read books, worked on learning Japanese, and ate grapes to her heart's content. She did not really have any of those strange cravings that many pregnant women do, except during the summer of her pregnancy, when the purple grapes in the garden grew plump. Every day she ate them by the dozens. After the vines of the gardens grew bare, she ordered them from the markets all over the city. Though they were expensive, Dong Jin did not care; he doted on his pregnant wife so vigilantly that whatever she needed she got without complaint. She knew he would have grapes from France imported for her if she ate all the ones in Seoul.

During those months in the garden, her skin turned a light tan. Though she spent most of the time underneath a big umbrella, the sun managed to touch her every now and then. She did not care. Besides, her skin did not seem to darken as quickly as it did when she was a child. A fall and winter indoors would quickly take care of the tan.

Soong Nan was content. Sitting underneath the umbrella, she thought about the incredible turn her life took, and smiled. She no longer feared the things she used to. Her fears changed from threatening to trivial. Instead of fearing hunger, she now feared riding in her husband's car when the driver accelerated too quickly. Instead of fearing a life of prostitution, she now feared the occasional plane trip to Tokyo. Instead of fearing the exposing of her foreign blood, she now feared the pains of childbirth. Her fears became those that every human being should have the luxury to own. And she owed it to her husband, Dong Jin. Sitting under the umbrella, many times she asked herself if she loved him.

When she asked herself this question, the answer she came up with was always the same. Yes, she loved him. But her relationship with him was completely unlike the relationships she portrayed in her movies. Her marriage lacked the irrationally charged emotions that her characters felt. If her older husband died before she did, which he probably would, she would not lose her mind and commit suicide. Their relationship was not like that. Instead she would honor him by caring for his children and making sure they knew what a great man he was. Because her marriage was unlike those of her movies, she wondered how she could pull off faking love and passion so easily when performing in front of the camera. She thought maybe it was because deep down inside she craved the craziness.

But during the summer in the garden, she would not have traded her situation for anything in the world. All she wanted was the devotion of her husband, a healthy child, and a bucket full of sweet purple grapes. When her daughter was finally born in August, she had all three.

After two months of caring for her child, whom they named Park Won Ju, it was time to go back to work. After the grueling search for a nanny whom Soong Nan felt she could trust, Dong Jin was ready to start filming. After an appropriate caregiver was found, one of the most qualified women of Seoul with the required bent back, they started on the next movie. It was another historical drama. It would be the first of many.

■ ■ ■

Park Dong Jin was losing money, and Park Soong Nan's career was stagnant. For two years, they worked seventeen hours a day, making about a movie a month. Park Soong Nan was still a star, but a star whom the critics and audience felt was wasting her talent on mediocre scripts and subpar directing. Most of these films were historical dramas, and considering that Korean history was five thousand years old, there was not a shortage of stories. Most of the films Dong Jin made depicted aristocratic regimes from the Shilla Kingdom of the eighth century or the Choson Kingdom, which, after five hundred years, fell to the Japanese in 1910. And because this kind of re-creation cost a lot of money, Dong Jin's movies were not making their money back. The sets and costuming were killing him.

Soong's contentedness was disappearing. She never got to see her daughter; instead she watched her husband stoically lose money. Though he did not complain to her, his hair seemed to get grayer every month and his weight was dropping dramatically. Obsessing over history was making him old. She found a real fear again. She suggested that they take a break, but Dong Jin refused. Sitting on the patio in front of the garden one night, having tea at the very same table he had made the fourteen-year-old Kwang Ja the offer, the twenty-one-year-old Soong Nan confronted him. She sat down in front of the brooding Dong Jin and poured him and herself tea. She did not feel afraid in broaching the subject with him. They, unlike many traditional Korean couples, shared an open dialogue. Though it was tradition that she be spoken down to, he never seemed to do it. What she did fear, however, was the possibility that he would not heed her advice. She knew if he went on the way he did, his life would be cut short.

"Perhaps we should slow down," she said, after sipping her tea.

Dong Jin smiled, then sighed. "We can't afford to."

"But it seems that not slowing down will cost us more."

Dong Jin scratched at the short wooden table with a single fingernail. "Do you remember the first time we had tea at this table?"

Soong put her hand on his. "Of course. I'll never forget that."

Dong Jin laughed. "You were a real firecracker. I knew I had to marry you even then."

Soong smiled. "I didn't. I didn't know much of anything back then."

Dong Jin scratched at the table again, then looked into her brown eyes. She felt completely comfortable when he did it. It may have been the training in acting that enabled her to do it; of course she was no longer the skittish girl who feared everyone was looking at her, but then it was just her husband. She'd seen the face so many times, it was as comfortable to look at as her own. "You knew the most important thing any living thing should know," he said. "You knew how to survive. I don't think you'll ever lose that."

"I owe it to luck. I owe it to you. Besides, you gave me the silver knife. After that, the idea of survival became easy." She shook her head. "The Japanese thing. What a child I was. You taught me that I was just an adolescent fearing men, as most adolescent girls should. The knife took care of that fear. You took care of it. I'm on to you. Always the storyteller. Always using symbols."

Dong Jin shook his head. "No, you do not owe me or that knife for your survival. You owe no one but yourself. The money, yeah, maybe you owe me a little."

Soong laughed. "How much do I owe you?"

Dong Jin looked into her eyes again. "You don't owe me anymore, I owe you. You've made me truly happy."

Soong put her hand on his cheek. "Then why can't we just slow down and enjoy our happiness?"

"Do you still have the silver knife?"

"Of course."

Dong Jin smiled. "You never even needed it. But if I were to..."

Soong interrupted him. "I will always have the knife. And when it's time, our daughter will have it."

"I hope she never needs it."

"Do you notice that she doesn't cry?"

Dong Jin's face lit up. "Yes. Sometimes I watch her in the mornings before the sun comes up. She wakes early every day. But she does not cry. She waits. Can you imagine? Having consideration as an infant?"

Soong smiled. "She is pure goodness."

Dong Jin began scratching the table again. "Why do you scratch at the table?" Soong asked.

"Look at this worn mark over here," he said, pointing to a smooth groove which looked like the beginnings of a canoe. "This was my grandfather's table, and this is the exact spot where his fingernail constantly grazed the surface. He was a nervous man but also a great aristocrat. Many big decisions were made at this table. Most importantly, he decided that our family would not resist the Japanese occupation."

Soong thought about the occupation. It was brutal on many Koreans. The Japanese were perhaps the cruelest people in the world at the time of the occupation. But she'd also learned that perhaps those who were the most cruel were the Koreans who acted with the insurgents. She looked at the groove on the table and guessed then that the Park family had collaborated with the Japanese. Only a man lacking a clear conscience could have scratched at a solid surface so hard. "I did not know," she said.

"My father was enraged. He went against my grandfather's wishes. He called him a traitor at this very table. When I was old enough to make my own decision, I opted to side with my grandfather. Because I had made it into the university in Tokyo, and I did not want to forgo my future by chasing some romantic dream my father had of Korean independence."

Dong Jin sipped on his tea. "Back then it was almost impossible for a Korean to get to Tokyo for studies. I worked very hard for it. So my father was killed, my grandfather managed to hold on to some money, and I left Tokyo with a degree in philosophy."

Soong Nan sipped her tea. "And this is why you're concentrating on making as many historical dramas as you can? To somehow make up for it?"

"Now it's my turn to scratch the table."

Soong grabbed his scratching hand and kissed it. "Maybe we should take a break."

Dong Jin pulled his hand away. "I can't."

"I'm pregnant again."

"You can break."

"Not without you. I'll do one more."

Dong Jin stood up. "I just need one good idea."

Soong Nan looked into her cup of tea. Then she looked out in the garden at the green mountain behind the stone wall. It was so unlike the dusty mountains of North Korea. She thought about her husband's guilt about his father. The wind blew in her face. The wind. It was an ancient wind, the same wind the old shamans recognized as the breath of god. The shamans were here before Confucianism and Buddhism were imported from China. It often amazed Soong how old Korea was. Five thousand years. When the wind disappeared, a thought was left in her mind. It was as if the ancient wind brought a seed for her then left. "Maybe you should not look so far back in history," she said.

Dong Jin turned around. "What do you mean?"

"Maybe a movie about the Japanese occupation."

"And?"

"Maybe it should be a movie about a man who defies his family to fight against the Japanese. Maybe this man can have a young wife who begs him not to go. Maybe he dies in her arms."

Dong Jin pulled a cigar from his shirt pocket and lit it. Then he began laughing uncontrollably. He laughed so hard, tears welled in his eyes. They poured down his face in streams, his eyes were like mountains filled with rainwater. "Noon Mul Ui Yau Wang," he said. My Queen of Tears.

-3-

THE MOVIE TOOK two months to make. By the time they were finished, Soong Nan was six months pregnant. They wrote the pregnancy into to script to add even more to the melodrama. She and Dong Jin worried that the work would have a bad effect on the pregnancy, but it seemed fine. Soong craved grapes again, but because it was winter, they were not in season. She did not bother to try and get them imported because she was too busy. She sometimes felt guilty that she was not providing her second child with the nourishment that she had provided for her first. But she knew her husband needed this movie to be great.

When they went to the premiere in Seoul, Soong Nan looked at the poster. It was perhaps her greatest. She was holding onto the beige army shirt of her movie husband. Her hands held the material tightly. Her eyes were closed tightly. But the look on the face was subtly deceiving. At first glance it appeared that Soong was refusing to let go. But if you looked at the poster carefully, at the face and the position of the head, you could tell it was the moment right before she let go. Looking at the poster, Soong smiled. It was perfect. Walking in the theater, she convinced Dong Jin to get her a framed copy of that poster. Maybe she would give it to her daughter when she was older. Like always he agreed without argument.

■ ■ ■

It was a huge blockbuster success. It was nominated for ten awards, including Movie of the Year and Best Actress in the Great Bell Awards. After their second child, a son, Park Chung Yun was born, they left the children with the nanny and went to the awards ceremony. All of the biggest producers, directors, and actors showed up at the theater on Seoul's version of Broadway. Red carpets, flashing cameras, hairdos that took hours to create. Tuxedos, sequined evening gowns. It was all very knock-off American. Very Hollywood.

Soong sat with her husband at the awards. The movie had lost some of its nominations. Best Score was out, as were Best Cinematography, Best Costume Design, and Best Editing. Soong glanced at her husband every once in a while. He kept his stoic face. Only when he was drunk or talking to Soong would his face convey strong emotion.

The next presentation was in the Best Actress category, which she had been nominated for. Dong Jin squeezed Soong's hand. She felt as if she were going to bounce to the ceiling. She wanted to win for him.

When they called her name, she screamed. It was not a bragging scream, but the kind of scream a child voices when their father sneaks up behind them in the dark and yells, "Boo!" It was loud enough so that everyone around her heard. Soong quickly covered her mouth. She stood up to walk onstage. Before she took her first step, she looked back at her husband. He was crying. She quickly turned around to prevent herself from crying, too. She made the awkward walk in front of the sitting people. She said, "Pardon me," to everyone she passed. When she made it to the aisle, her leg buckled. She screamed again. Everyone was laughing. As she walked towards the stage, she heard the applause. When she finally made it to the podium and accepted her award, she forgot the speech she had come up with the night before. When the applause slowly died and she put her mouth in front of the microphone, she felt the heat from the spotlights above her. She didn't know what to say. Silent for a several seconds, she put her hand, salute style, against her forehead. She was looking for her husband. The man working the lights immediately got what she was doing. Suddenly a light hit her husband. She smiled. "I feel like I just got hit by a car," she said.

Mild laughter filled the air. Her husband was smiling and crying. "This is for my husband," she said. "This is for him and his father."

It was one of the shortest speeches in Korean award history. But to Soong and her husband, there was power in brevity. And when Dong Jin won the award for Best Picture of the Year later that night, he said, "Now I know what it feels like to get hit by a car. It's the second best thing that ever happened to me. I dedicate this to my wife. The Queen of Tears."

For Soong it was a moment of clarity when her husband won too. Life was good. Life was actually good. Since she'd been a child, she considered life a struggle to learn how to live. But now she knew why the struggle was worth it. It was about trading months of toil for moments like these. Yes, the Westerners are right about capitalism, she thought. Everything costs. And the most expensive stuff is the stuff most worth having. She thought about her children and wanted to go home.

■ ■ ■

Soong and Dong Jin had to make the social rounds. It would have been bad manners not to do so. But after the second party, Soong kissed her husband on the cheek and said, "I'm going home. I need to see the children."

Dong Jin, who was very drunk, nodded. "Take the car and tell the driver I won't need him. I'll find a ride home."

"Not too late now. You already had too much to drink."

Dong Jin kissed her on the cheek. "Don't worry. Stop being a nag. You're too young and beautiful to be a nag."

Soong playfully slapped his arm. "Soon I'll be an old nag, and you better appreciate it."

"Yeah, yeah, go home. Tell the kids I said goodnight."

He went back into a conversation with the two directors he had been drinking with all night. He was already talking about his next project. Soong Nan left the party and went home to be with her children.

At four in the morning, Soong knew something was wrong. She had been waiting up for her husband and didn't hear a word from him. There had been nights when he'd stayed out even later, but he'd always made sure that she knew when to expect him. By Korean standards, he was generous that way. Soong told herself maybe he forgot because it was such a great night, but she knew he was not a forgetful man. She looked out the window into the garden. Snow had been falling since midnight, and a cottony layer covered the lawn. She wondered about the fish, but it was too dark to see anything but the snow. Looking at the whiteness of the ground, she thought back on her young life. It seemed to her she owed everything to the man she waited up for now. Especially this night. It had been one of those rare nights when, for a brief time, her usual contentedness rose to happiness. And again, she owed her husband. Even though the film had been her idea, it was Dong Jin who'd made it, it was he who'd taken the skeleton which she provided and added the flesh. Good ideas in this world were thought of every day, but to create something great from an idea, she knew this took commitment and sweat. She was so proud of her husband and his tireless efforts of creation.

Just then she heard the baby cry. It was her son Chung Yun. Soong closed the curtain and walked towards the nursery. It was the cry of hunger. Unlike her first child, Chung Yun ate voraciously. She wondered if it was because she did not nourish this child during her pregnancy as well as she had nourished the first. He also seemed to spit up half of what he'd eat. Before she reached her crying son, there was a knock on the door. It scared her so suddenly that the taste of bile briefly entered her mouth. She picked up her screaming baby and walked to the door. The two women servants also woke up and followed her.

When she opened the door, two men in tuxedos carried her limp husband in. Soong handed her crying son to one of the women and led the men to the living-room sofa. They laid the body down. Soong felt Dong Jin's forehead. It was cold. She unbuttoned his tuxedo shirt and put her ear over his chest. She could not hear his heartbeat, but didn't know if it was because of her son's screaming or her husband's death. She felt his face. His closed eyes were motionless. "I closed them," one of the men said.

She looked up at the men. They stood there seemingly almost expecting the touch of this woman to revive their friend. But he did not move.

"What happened?" she asked.

The taller man, one of Dong Jin's fellow producers, shrugged. "He collapsed at the party. We picked him up and told everyone we'd take him home."

It was the days before emergency-room care, of huge hospitals open twenty-four hours a day. Seoul was greatest city in Korea, but it was still a poor city, one scarred by a recent war. It was still tradition to take an ailing person to their home. Soong nodded. "Thank you very much. Thank you."

The men knew it was their cue to leave. Soong and the two men politely bowed to each other. The servant not holding the screaming baby opened the door for them. Soong's husband was still motionless on the sofa.

The little girl Won Ju emerged from her bedroom. She rubbed her eyes and walked across the living room without looking up at anybody. The skirt of her nightgown covered her tiny feet. She had a blanket draped on her shoulders. When she reached her father's body, she touched his hand. Soong watched as her daughter put the blanket over her father. With no emotion on her face, Won Ju put her small hand under her father's nostrils. Then the four-year-old tried to open his eyelids. She sighed. "Mom, tell Chung Yun to keep quiet. Daddy's sleeping. He's only sleeping."

Won Ju walked back to her room. Soong Nan told the servants to put the baby to sleep and go to bed. Over the faint sounds of her hungry and crying baby, Soong Nan cried. It was a soft, gentle cry. Though the tears flowed down her face, sound did not exit her mouth. She took out Dong Jin's handkerchief and blew her nose. The tears kept coming. She was the Queen of Tears. And suddenly she felt like an orphan again.

THE TANK

chapter five

THE RESTAURANT IN the Kailua Shopping Center was called "W & D Korean Take-Out." It was a small eatery with ten feet by twenty feet of pane-glass window, six small yellow tables with six chairs each, and a stainless-steel counter separating the customers from the soda machine, huge rice cooker, and the boxes of straws, cups, plastic utensils, foam food containers, napkins, and wooden chopsticks. Behind this area was the kitchen, which was unseen by customers because of the swinging door. To the passerby there was nothing really different about this property except the name. It had been "Tony's Drive-Inn," but Tony wasn't making money, so he'd left. The W & D of this new operation, Won Ju and Donny, were hoping that the new name and new food would change the luck of this property.

It was decided that it'd be a family operation. Open seven days a week from ten in the morning until ten at night, there were enough shifts for everyone except Kenny, who wanted nothing to do with it anyway. "It'll sink in a year, then I'll have to bail you out," he'd said. Won Ju and Soong, both of whom did not drive, caught the city bus every morning together and opened at ten, Monday through Saturday, staying until five each day. Donny and Crystal came in at five (except on Sundays, when they stayed the entire shift) and closed every night at nine. Brandon and Darian worked part-time on weekends, coming in at eleven and leaving at seven. They served as extra help during the busiest times. Crystal's brother Kaipo sometimes came in during weekday lunches, when business picked up.

It had been Donny's first successful idea. Like he'd hoped, the surfers and local residents came. Crystal, with her baby T-shirts and long, lavender fingernails, with glittery silver shooting stars on each nail, was becoming the stuff of local legend. So W & D was fast becoming one of the most popular eateries in the small town of Kailua. And the shifts worked for everyone. Donny, Crystal, and Soong rarely worked together. The hot air was not grating against the cold.

But after a while Crystal began to tire. She'd never really thought about it before, but this arrangement had her spending all of her time, day and night, with her new husband Donny. And for the first few months, this was fine. Crystal had learned a while back how to tune Donny out, how to simply lower the volume knob and nod her head to the soft repetitive beat of the music. Besides, because his new fatigue was added to his impotence, little physical affection was required of Crystal. So for three months she happily worked clothed for the first time in her life. She was selling man's second most valued commodity, and liking that it cost her very little.

However, after these three months, two things began to change. First, Donny began to change the beat of his music. His success catalyzed a conceitedness which Crystal found overbearing. He began telling her what to do. He began to snap at her when she made mistakes. He also became more aggressive sexually. He wanted to try sex every now and then, and unlike before, became angry with every failure. Sex had never been a part of their deal. Crystal had always thought about their relationship in terms of a constructive symbiosis. She provided him with a wife his mother hated and most men envied. She gave him a sense of ego. In return he gave her stability, an alternative source of income, and a break from self-destruction. He gave her ego because she knew he was in a sadder state than she. But suddenly he seemed to want not just a wife, but what she thought of as a traditional Korean wife. He wanted one who would put up with all of his shit and scratch it up to wifely duties. Crystal was getting scared, especially when Donny leaned closely toward the television when that Bob Dole ad on Viagra would show. And besides that, the other thing started to change.

Crystal, after those first few months, was losing her hatred for the male gender. Away from the slobbering wanna-be gynecologists at Club Mirage, she began to find some men attractive again. At first, she caught herself saying, "nice ass" here, or "nice eyes" there. Then she began fantasizing about having sex with some of these customers. These were not elaborate dreams of men dressed like slaves catering to her queenly needs, not Liz Taylor in *Cleopatra* fantasies: instead they were purely erotic images of her and a customer having feral sex. But she wouldn't act on these impulses. She'd instigate some harmless flirtation and return to work not thinking about it. Or she'd look at her husband and her sexual impulses would evaporate. It was funny, she thought, that at the same time she stopped hating men, she started hating her husband.

■ ■ ■

One Friday night, five months after the opening, a young, shirtless surfer walked to the counter. He was tall, and his dark skin grabbed tightly around his dense muscles. His aloha-print surf shorts were a size too big, and they hung low on his waist, revealing a severe tan line where his muscular stomach and slender hips met. He was also handsome. His dark face was angular and a muscular jaw sat below big, brown puppy-dog eyes that seemed to glow with simplicity and innocence. His eyes were not like the wanna-be gynecologists of Club Mirage, instead they were the eyes of a man who simply loved to surf, and was looking for something as simple as a bite to eat. Crystal felt her hand brush back her bangs and the erotic images chaotically twirled in her head, not like ballerinas, but like figures falling down in fits of seizure. "May I help you?" she asked.

"Yeah, can I get the Special and a jumbo Coke."

Crystal scribbled down "Special," which was a mixed plate of kalbi (marinated Korean short ribs), barbecue beef and chicken, two scoops of white rice, and kimchee, and she dropped the order off to Donny in the kitchen. Not saying anything to him, she quickly went back to the counter where the surfer was waiting. She looked at the brick-colored floor of the restaurant and saw how his large, bare feet tracked sand from the door. "Sorry," he said.

Crystal smiled. "You better get a broom and sweep that up."

The surfer looked stunned. Then he smiled. "You're kidding, right?"

She gave him a deadpan look. A Won Ju look. "Not at all."

"Uh, oh, I'm sorry. I don't have a broom."

Crystal was having a ball. But in a way, his stupidity irked her. "Sorry, I was kidding."

The surfer sighed. "Cool."

"So how were the waves?"

"Shitty. Blown out."

Strong wind did have a bad effect on waves. Perfect, rolling swells were meant to build up and peak into perfect, swirling cylinders, but if a strong wind came, waves seemed to shatter on reefs. The wind should learn humility, she thought. Before she could continue the conversation, the surfer walked to one of the yellow tables and sat down. Crystal was annoyed. She made his soda and walked outside of the counter to give it to him. "So, do you like surfing?"

The surfer grabbed his soda and forced down a large sip through the straw. "I go every chance I get."

"Where do you go?"

"I went to Sandy's today."

"I love Sandy's."

"Do you surf?"

"I used to a lot. But I don't have time anymore."

"You have to make time."

This guy was way too involved with his surfing, Crystal thought. She looked up at the counter and saw Donny approach it. He put the styrofoam container filled with food on the counter and walked back to the kitchen. Crystal smelled the familiar grilled meat and sighed. It was a smell she had a hard time getting out of her hair every night. She bagged the container, put a plastic fork and knife into the bag along with a few napkins and gave it to the customer.

He stood up and took the bag from her. His eyes never met hers. Instead, he looked longingly at the white styrofoam container he was holding. As he exited Crystal called out, "Come back anytime."

She sighed and went back to the counter.

■ ■ ■

After closing that night, Donny and Crystal took the long and familiar drive up the Pali Highway. As the car scaled the green mountains of the Koʻolaus, Donny rolled down the window and lit a cigarette. Crystal rolled down her window and lit her own. "Maybe we should get rid of this car," she said.

"The lease runs for another five months. We can't just get rid of it."

"I'm tired of it."

Donny laughed sarcastically. "You don't even drive. All you do is ride like some kind of princess. How can you be tired of it?"

"Well, I leased it. Isn't it my decision?"

"No. I like the car."

Crystal threw her cigarette out the window. "Lease your own."

The car entered the tunnel. Crystal turned on the radio to 97.5, the alternative rock station. No Doubt's "Spiderweb" blared out of the speakers, mixing with the noise of driving through the tunnel. The wind and acoustics of the tunnel, along with the music, made Donny's response inaudible. His voice was just a part of the strong wind blowing through the open windows. The smell of exhaust entered the car. Crystal found the fumes intoxicating. The smell reminded her of stopping at gas stations as a little girl in her father's truck. She'd loved the smell of pumping gas. It was before everything went wrong. After they passed through the first tunnel, Crystal lit another cigarette.

In the second tunnel Donny turned the radio off. "You know I hate that music," he said loudly.

Crystal shrugged. When they exited the second tunnel, they began their descent down the Koʻolau Mountains. The BMW sped up to seventy, and in fifteen minutes they would be back home in Honolulu. "Why don't you learn how to drive already?" Donny asked.

"Believe me, I'm considering it," Crystal said.

■ ■ ■

At their apartment, Crystal walked into the bathroom and locked the door. She heard Donny turn on the television. She recognized the sound. It was one of those nature documentaries on the Discovery Channel. He loved those animal documentaries. The night before, he'd watched a crocodile one. She remembered seeing his amazed trance as a lizard-sized baby was peeking out of a cell made of its mother's teeth. The teeth were the size of boar tusks, or so the narrator said, and the baby was quite safe in its mother's mouth, but it still looked like it wanted to get out. She also thought it was kind of neat.

Crystal undressed and turned on the shower. Before she stepped in, she smelled her hair. The scent of marinated cooked meat clung to every highlighted strand. She checked the temperature of the water, slid the curtain back, and stepped in. The shower had become a sanctuary for her. It seemed to be the only time during the day that she was not with her husband. Sometimes she would stay in even after the hot water ran out and the water turned cold.

The warm water poured over her body. She shivered and tilted her head up. The water blasted against her closed eyes. Then she thoroughly scrubbed shampoo in her barbecue hair and rinsed. She repeated the process three times before giving up, telling herself that too much shampoo would damage her hair. Next she rubbed a bar of soap into her soft washcloth and began scrubbing her body. Suddenly she remembered the surfer who ordered the "Special." She closed her eyes and listened for Donny. She couldn't hear him or the television. Then the twirling images returned. The naked surfer kissing her body, working his way down to her pelvis. Then his body thrusting into hers. The images emerged like she was watching them on a randomly patched-up strip of porno. There was no sense of chronology with these chaotic images. When Crystal finally opened her eyes, she was sitting in the shower with her legs shaking. Feeling an unfamiliar guilt, she turned off the shower, quickly dried off and dressed.

Donny was watching some documentary about little light-brown monkeys in Sri Lanka. They all had long tails, pink faces, and heads of hair like Moe from the Three Stooges. Crystal sat on the sofa and began drying her hair with a towel. The monkeys were having some kind of civil war. A new faction had arisen and challenged the old leader. Donny was immersed in the program. "Is it that interesting?" Crystal asked.

"It's amazing. It's like they're human beings."

"Or like we're monkeys."

The new faction, led by a big monkey the narrator called "Duce," won. Duce reminded her of her father. Big, cocky, beady-eyed. While the tribe surrounded the body of the fallen leader, "Hegel," Duce looked at his victim with indifference. He perched himself on the low branch of a tree and watched the other monkeys touch the overthrown king. It was strange. It was like they were sad.

"Look at that prick Duce," Crystal said.

Duce was the new leader and with victory came the spoils. The females of the tribe were his, as was the fear of the other male monkeys. Duce almost immediately abused this power. He mounted the female monkeys violently, and he abused the baby monkeys that he did not recognize as his. It was a direct contrast to the previous king, who was stern, yet affectionate, or so the narrator said.

"This is amazing," Crystal said.

"Shh."

What happened next mesmerized Crystal. The rest of the monkeys, even the ones who supported his move for leadership, plotted against him. Evidently, according to the narrator, a revolution, led by the disgruntled females, was brewing. Suddenly the film panned to Duce. He was sitting by himself. There was an enormous gash in his head that parted his Moe-like hair. One of the previous leader's lieutenants was the new leader. Duce, scarred for life by the experience, seemed to be in a state of exile.

"Wow," Crystal said, "it's like Shakespeare or something."

Donny turned off the television. "What do you know about Shakespeare?"

"Not much."

Donny stood up and stretched. "Let's go to bed."

Crystal turned the television back on. "I'm not tired."

Donny grabbed her hand. "C'mon."

Crystal sighed. "O.K."

She turned off the T.V. and threw her damp towel in the hamper. She followed Donny into the bedroom and began to undress. Leaving on a T-shirt and underwear, she turned around to walk towards the bed. Donny was sitting on it, naked. "Let's try," he said.

His body was unappealing to her. It was thin, and there seemed to be a complete lack of chest muscles. In fact, there was a dent in the middle of his chest whose depth was exaggerated by a slight rise in the stomach area. His torso was hairless, except where a few long strands of black hair grew around his nipples. His legs, which were extremely thin, bent off the bed, and between them was a cock (she always liked "cock" more than "penis," "dick," "ding-ding," "prick," or the many other euphemisms that were constantly being created, like "ole one-eye") that seemed to be hiding in a bushy thatch of black pubic hair. Now I'm hot, she thought. She shrugged and took off all her clothes. She plopped on the bed. Just like every other time before she had sex with a man, even if she got completely wasted from booze, coke, or even ecstasy, she thought about her father. The drugs seemed to just limit the duration. But now she was sober.

Kaipo inherited his size and that red hair of his from that father of theirs. He was an Englishman, not a James Bond Englishman, but a green-eyed, hulking, tree-carrying Englishman, whose father arrived in Hawaii from England with his wife and instantly became a "luna," leering at plantation laborers from horseback. Well, their father inherited the leering, and when Crystal had been twelve, and their Hawaiian mother was leered at so much that she became as unnoticeable as a piece of furniture, their father began leering at her. It was an old story, one that stretched even far beyond the stories Crystal had heard in high school of young girls disfiguring themselves during the Middle Ages so that their fathers and brothers would discontinue raping them. But to Crystal it was a new story, one that she was completely unprepared for, as if anyone was ever prepared.

There had been none of that buildup that she'd heard about from some of the other girls at Club Mirage. A long kiss on the cheek turning into an embarrassing kiss on the lips two weeks later. A hand on a skinny thigh, moving gradually further and further up as months pass by and the thigh becomes more plump. A finger inside, turning into two fingers, three, then... There was no "This is our little secret." She'd come home from the beach one day in an unflattering, second-hand, one-piece pink bathing suit, and her father walked into her bedroom and raped her. All the while she was gazing at her poster of Jon Bon Jovi that she pulled out of *Tiger Beat*, trying to imagine his music instead of hearing the creaking of springs under her bed. The leering didn't begin until after that. And he'd never said "This is our little secret." He simply blew out of the room while she lay bleeding. She did remember him mumbling, once, "You're not really my daughter. You're too dark." And at first, she wanted to believe it, but she always knew, just by looking at her eyes in the mirror, that it was not true. This had gone on for two years. And when it all ended very badly, the end cost her the ability to have children. Three years later, her mentor, her older cousin Stacy, who was now married to a haole plumber and had three kids by three different fathers, the plumber being none of them, got her to drop out of Waianae High ("They don't even give you books for all your classes," she'd said. "If they don't take school seriously, why should you?"), and got her into stripping.

Donny was instantly on her. He grabbed her wrists and kissed her hard. Crystal closed her eyes. She felt his hard kisses move down to her breasts, his tongue like a slug, leaving a saliva trail from her neck to her chest. But at the same time, she felt nothing. It was about as arousing as kissing her own arm or something. Donny let go of her wrists. His kisses moved down to her stomach. She wiped the saliva from her neck and breasts and rubbed her wet hand on the sheet. His spit left a smell on her hand. It was the smell of wetness in heat. Almost like a combination of sweat and soapless laundry that had been left sitting in the washer too long. Donny's face was now in her crotch, and again, she felt nothing.

After about five minutes of this Crystal began nodding off. Then her eyes snapped open when she felt him stop. His face shot up to hers. "Suck it," he said.

He turned on his back. His flaccid cock drooped to the left. "What?" Crystal said.

"Suck it. C'mon, I did you, now you do me."

Crystal sat up. "Are you crazy?"

"C'mon. Don't act like you've never heard that before. You're a stripper. C'mon."

"I was a stripper."

"Yeah, whatever. C'mon, I did you."

Crystal stood up and put on her T-shirt. She wanted another shower to get the smell of spit off her body. Donny stood up and looked at her. She stuck out her middle finger and said, "Suck this."

Donny became angry. He leaped out of bed, and it was the first time she saw him do leaping of any kind. As far as angry male faces went, it wasn't very intimidating. Crystal was from Waianae and grew up with Hawaiians who could rip Donny's arms out of their sockets. But he was a man. And Crystal knew, even a weak man's body was built for violence better than most women's. The wind will always bend the wave, even a weak wind. "Don't you fuckin' talk to me like that," Donny said.

Crystal thought about her own toughness. She had been beaten many times in high school for supposedly being one of the school sluts. She couldn't fight. But she knew she could take pain. Her body was poor at offense, but great at defense. She carefully looked at Donny and any previous fear or apprehension she had evaporated. "I'll talk however the fuck I want to talk."

"It's that fuckin' surfer tonight, isn't it?"

She had completely forgotten about the surfer and her shower. Masturbation was so underrated. "What about him?"

"You want to fuck him."

Crystal was thrown. This outburst was not like Donny. It was a possessiveness she'd never seen from him. "So what if I did? I'll tell you, I'd rather fuck that fuckin' monkey Duce than you right now."

Donny's open hand slapped her the side of her face. It stung and shocked her at the same time. She smiled. The fuckin' pussy doesn't even know how to throw a punch. Crystal clenched her fist and let it fly. The lack of balance in her body told her she was doing it wrong, but she didn't care. The punch landed on his nose. Two of her purple nails cracked.

Donny held his face for a couple of seconds. Then he started to laugh. His hands dropped and he said, "Get the fuck out of here."

"Fuck you, you get out."

"You."

"I don't know how to drive."

Donny laughed. "I'm fuckin' naked."

Crystal looked at his naked body. His skinny arms and narrow shoulders. The dent in his otherwise flat chest and his slightly bulging stomach. She turned around and put on underwear, jeans, and shoes. She walked out of the room and grabbed the keys and her mini Prada backpack from the counter. As she left, she heard the door slam behind her.

While in the elevator, Crystal, rubbing one of her cracked nails with her thumb, started to panic. It was an old feeling for her, but it was one of those feelings that, no matter how many times she experienced it, was always just as intense as the last time. She didn't know what to do, which struck her as funny, because she always did the same thing whenever she was in this state. Get drunk. Get high. Go to Club Mirage, lay down her plush white faux fur mat, which was slowly becoming a light beige, on stage, lean back on it, and make money. A garter full of one-dollar bills usually made her feel solid. "Just make the money, honey," her cousin Stacy used to tell her. "The rest is candy. And always bring your mat. There's nothing worse than stage burn on the ass." That and the fact that a boob job could bring in about thirty-four percent more revenue was the sum of the wisdom that came from her cousin.

When Crystal got to the parking lot, she stood frozen outside of the car. She had tried to drive once, but that had been ten years before. And even then she was horrible at it. She felt like a ten-year-old child running away from home. She sighed and walked back towards the elevator. She would apologize and he would forgive her. If she didn't have a place at the restaurant, she would probably start stripping again. She would apologize and he would forgive her. She pressed the circular button by the elevator, and it lit up into a dull orange. She'd often wondered why elevator makers picked such an ugly color to signify the returning or leaving of home. She thought maybe elevator makers were unhappy with their lot in life. They only got to make things that go up and down. Wouldn't horizontal elevators be neat? They're called cars, she thought.

When the doors opened, Crystal turned around and said, "Fuck him."

She found herself standing in front of the car again. She stuck the key in the door and stepped into the driver's side. When she put the key into the ignition, her hand was shaking. She took a deep breath and turned the key. The engine hummed in German. She adjusted the seat, then laughed uncomfortably, because she did have a clue as to what the proper distance from the steering wheel and pedals should be. She nervously pulled her cigarettes out of her purse and lit one. She then peeled one of her cracked nails off and looked at the rearview mirror. "What the fuck am I doing?" she said.

She rolled down the window and threw her cigarette out. She put the car into reverse, then laughed. It amazed her how something as trifling as an automatic transmission just changed her life. If the BMW had a manual transmission, she would probably have been apologizing to Donny right now. She slowly pressed on the gas with her right foot, then quickly pressed the brake with her left. This went on for the few minutes it took her to get out of the parking lot.

When she got on the road, she still had no idea where she was going. She carefully watched the red lights of the cars in front of her glow in the darkness as they slowed down. She looked into the rearview mirror at approaching headlights, thinking that every car behind her was going to ram into her. It was chaos. But she wasn't really thinking about that, she was just trying to focus on the road. Her life had been filled with flashing red lights and on-coming traffic, so the adjustment to driving wasn't as difficult as she thought it would be. And once she figured out that it was easier to work the pedals with one foot, she felt very clever and very sure of herself. She ripped off the last cracked nail on her right hand, doing it while driving.

-2-

WHEN YOU LIVE in an apartment building with your husband, mother, and son, there's next to no privacy. One picks fights with you, another criticizes you, and the last expects you to give him what he wants even though he never tells you what he wants. Actually, they're all kind of like the last. Being a wife, daughter, or mother, they all want something from you, and you never know quite what it is. Won Ju thought about this as she stood in the living room in front of a slightly cracked open window. She tried to make sure all of the smoke was getting out, but most of the time the highrise winds just blew the smoke back in her face.

It was close to midnight. Won Ju was losing the lifelong battle to quit smoking. She had stopped for three years, but a month before, at the restaurant, Donny had left a pack of cigarettes in the kitchen. She didn't know why she pulled one out of the pack and lit it. Being a smoker on the wagon meant that every cigarette tempted you, but she had lasted for three years. She didn't know why on that particular day, in that particular second, she had smoked. The Winston was strong and she coughed. She had only finished half of it, but that night, she found herself buying her own pack. She bought a pack of Camel Lights because she hated menthols and there was a coupon inside the cellophane, a picture of Joe Camel smiling. Kenny's cheapness started to rub off on her.

Brandon was snoring. Since her mother had moved in, her son took the couch. That was two months before. She knew that little late-night access to his computer was making him unhappy.

It would last for two more weeks. A one-bedroom had finally opened in the same building, and it was Soong's for a thousand dollars a month. Won Ju was relieved. She saw her mother every day, and that was fine, but to see her every night, too? It was too much for Won Ju.

Footsteps approached in the darkness. Brandon turned over and stopped snoring. Won Ju threw her cigarette out of the cracked window and closed it. She put her fist up to her mouth and coughed. Kenny pulled a clear plastic bottle of water from the fridge and took a long swig. "Smoking again?" he said.

"Just one."

"It's bad for you, and those around you." He looked at Brandon.

"I heard that somewhere before."

"You should stop before it gets out of hand."

"Yeah, I know."

Kenny screwed the cap back on the bottle and opened the refrigerator. The light from the icebox threw light and shadows on his dark, chiseled body. It was a body that Won Ju was once attracted to, but now she did not know. It used to make her feel safe. Like the muscles were there to defend her. And when she'd met Kenny, she'd thought she needed a defender more than anything else. But now she felt like the body had somehow turned on her. It was hugging her tightly, and she could not breathe in the smothering. It was a feeling she knew and a feeling that brought up old nightmares. "You're up late," he said.

Kenny walked to his son and stood over him. He pulled the blanket over him. Won Ju laughed. "What?" he asked.

"You watch too many movies. It's like eighty degrees and you put the blanket over him."

"Ha, ha. So is your mother going to be able to cover the rent at that other apartment?"

She knew he couldn't believe that the restaurant made enough money to support that many people. It did, but barely. There never seemed to be enough left over to save just in case business became bad. It was a precarious way to live, just as her shop in the Pacific Beach Hotel had been, but for now it was producing. "She should be fine."

"What about Darian?"

Won Ju's younger sister had a knack for making friends. It had taken her two weeks to find roommates and a place to live. Evidently, whenever she was new in any town, she just went to coffeehouses and made friends "like her." Won Ju hated coffeehouses almost as much as she hated the Hawaiian Canoe Club. Coffeehouses represented another closed society where the self-described elite perched themselves, looking down upon the unknowing masses. They acted as if they really knew what life was about, while Won Ju always admitted that she didn't have a clue. These were the same people who would drink imported or microbrewery beers at some trendy yuppie bar after work and use words like "full-bodied" or "citrusy" to describe the taste. She doubted that Darian and those like her knew much about life. In fact, if Darian wasn't her sister, Won Ju would have probably hated her. A bunch of unmarried, childless pseudo-intellectuals talking about their existential angst over modish ales that cost four-fifty a pop. "Darian's fine. She's thinking about transferring to U.H."

"The University of Hawaii? She might as well go to school in someplace like Puerto Rico. I heard Robert Kakaula, a local sportscaster of all people, was the keynote speaker at U.H.'s last graduation ceremony. Prestigious, huh? She should stay in Berkeley."

Kenny had always been proud that he went to school in the mainland, even if it was some half-ass small private school in Northern California that would admit anybody willing to pay the exorbitant tuition. "Well, I'm going back to bed," Kenny said.

Won Ju nodded. When he disappeared back into the darkness, Won Ju pulled another cigarette from her purse and cracked open the window. Maybe he wasn't trying to smother her, but she felt like he was as she inhaled deeply from the cigarette and futilely blew the smoke into the wind. There's something wrong with me, she thought.

■ ■ ■

At about twelve-thirty, while Won Ju was convincing herself about how she was getting old and liking the fact that her looks were fading, and how once her son became a man that it'd be all over, the phone rang. It was Crystal calling from downstairs. She was rambling about driving a car and horizontal elevators, whatever they were, flat escalators at certain airports, Won Ju imagined, when Won Ju finally had to cut her scratchy intercom voice off by telling her she'd be right down. She put on her sandals, put a coat on over her thin nightgown and walked out the door.

While in the elevator, she wondered what brought her sister-in-law there so late. She could guess, but she found herself anxious to hear specifics. She also wondered, if the fight was bad, who could work with Donny during the next day's night shift. Because she had overdosed on her mother's company, she decided it would be nice to work with him, not only because she wouldn't have to take the bus, but also because she'd get to hear his side. However, the thought of Crystal and her mother working alone together during mornings made a new schedule impossible. Soong would never work alone with Crystal. The language barrier was too strong. Not only in terms of speaking, but also in terms of entirely different attitudes on life. No, they would never work together.

When the doors opened, Crystal was standing behind the glass door. She was wearing shorts, a T-shirt, and big black platform shoes. Her hair was piled on top of her head and held together with a chopstick. She was excitedly wringing the straps of her little leather backpack. Won Ju could tell she wasn't wearing make-up or a bra, but then, she often wore neither, so Won Ju couldn't guess whether it was because she was in a rush, or whether it was Crystal just being Crystal. But besides the huge chest, Crystal looked like a little girl wearing a backpack too small for her and shoes way too big for her. Won Ju opened the door and stepped out. "So what's up?" she asked.

Crystal dug in her bag and pulled out a cigarette. She smoked Virginia Slims. Menthols. "It's over between me and your brother."

"What happened?"

Crystal lit the cigarette and took a drag. "He was being a cock. Ever since the place started to make money, he thinks he's some kind of fuckin' Korean warlord. Or some kind of king monkey."

Won Ju didn't get the monkey thing, but she kind of knew what she meant. Money can often turn men into pricks. "Did you guys have an argument or something?"

Crystal blew out smoke. "Yeah, something like that. Can you believe that asshole wanted me to suck his little flaccid dick? Like he was ordering a burger from McDonalds or something."

This was way too personal for Won Ju. But then, she knew about the blowjob thing. Kenny always thought he deserved it after he went down on her, only he could never get enough of it. "Crystal, you have to understand. It's a cultural thing." She was consciously, but also innately, trying to defend her brother with what she knew was bullshit.

"Fuck that. You can't tell me there are drive-thru blowjobs in Korea. You can't tell me that every man in Korea is a cock." Crystal was on to her.

Won Ju laughed. "No, that's not what I'm saying. It's more like they think they can be."

"Well that fucker thought wrong."

"O.K., just calm down. You can sleep over here and we'll straighten everything out tomorrow."

Crystal dropped the cigarette and stepped on it with her enormous black shoe. "O.K. Thanks, Won Ju."

"By the way, how did you get here?"

"I drove."

"I thought you didn't know how to drive?"

"I don't. But I guess I do now."

Won Ju opened the glass door for Crystal. She was impressed with Crystal's recklessness. Won Ju, like her mother, was always afraid to learn how to drive. She thought Crystal was the same way. She looked at Crystal's hand. "What happened to your nails?"

"Fuck my nails. They were a pain in the ass anyway."

When they got in the elevator, Won Ju realized that there was no place for her sister-in-law to sleep. Not only that, but her mother would freak seeing Crystal in the morning. She shook her head. "I'm sorry, Crystal. You don't mind sleeping on the ground, do you? I'll set up a pillow and blanket. My mother's in Brandon's room and Brandon is on the couch."

Crystal shrugged. "I don't mind. As long as no one minds if I sleep naked. It's so hot nowadays, I can't fall asleep with clothes on."

Won Ju hoped to God she was joking. "And tomorrow. What do you think? Maybe I should call Darian and see if she can work for you?"

"Yeah, her or my brother. I'm sorry, Won Ju, just one day. We'll straighten everything out in the morning."

The doors opened. Won Ju led Crystal to the door. "Don't worry about Brandon. He's a heavy sleeper."

"Good," Crystal said. "It means he's probably not doing drugs."

Won Ju was surprised by the remark. This was definitely a different kind of woman.

Won Ju brought out a big comforter and pillow for Crystal. They set everything up at the foot of the sofa. Brandon did not move. Won Ju said, "Good night."

Before she walked out of the room she heard Crystal. "This is bad timing. The business was doing so good, I was about to start thinking about going to school."

Won Ju smiled and went to bed.

-3-

CRYSTAL'S EYES SHOT open. It was still dark and terribly humid. She felt her body and smiled. Sometime during the night, she'd stripped naked while sleeping. She'd stripped half asleep before onstage, so why not during R.E.M.? Not even the blanket was on her. As her eyes adjusted, she remembered she wasn't alone in the room. Her back was facing the sofa. She quietly turned around and saw the whites of Brandon's eyes. He quickly shut them. She had a difficult time holding in her laugh. She quietly looked for her thong panties and slipped them on. She found her T-shirt and put it on, too. She looked at Brandon. Her eyes were good in the dark and she could see his eyelids flutter slightly, trying too hard to feign sleep. He was so cute. He kind of reminded her of a smaller form of the surfer she had seen the night before. He was tall and thin. He would grow up to be a lean, nicely built man. And the innocence was there. Once, she had thought of innocence as the same as naivete, but now it was beautiful to her. Not being able to help herself, she touched Brandon's cheek. Only when he turned over did she see his hands buried by his crotch under the blanket. Not as innocent as she thought. Suddenly the movie *The Outsiders* popped into her head. Wasn't there a line in the movie capturing something about lost innocence by some poet that everybody had to read in high school? She made a note to herself to talk to Darian and ask her about it, that and about a dick monkey in some Shakespearean play who offed the good king, took over, and was offed by a new king. She tried to fall back asleep while the images of Brandon, a brown monkey with a gash on his head, and school caused what she considered her insomnia. But then, isn't insomnia something that prevents you from sleeping like ever? She almost always managed to find sleep before the sun rose. For a second, she considered herself full of it, but before she could mentally comment on her moment of self-awareness, she slipped out of consciousness.

-4-

IT WAS NO picnic working with the Queen of Tears the next morning. After an hour bus ride, hearing her complaints about the sex-crazed Crystal sleeping in the same room with her grandson, Won Ju was tired of listening to her mother. For someone who had been known as the Queen of Tears, her mother did very little crying, in fact the only time she'd seen her mother cry was on-screen, but she did do a lot of complaining. It was never a whining complaining, but it was always stern, like she was a movie director tired of seeing her actors not deliver their lines in the way she wanted them to. Maybe the industry had more of an effect on her mother than she thought. It was like she was working the process of her family's life into a final scene. Once the film ended satisfactorily, she would walk off the set. Won Ju thought that it was too bad that there wasn't editing in life, her family. Their lives could use some editing, but then she realized that there was editing. It's called nostalgia. Won Ju turned her head toward the window, but Soong continued, even after they got to the restaurant. Once she was on a roll, that was it. There would be no film worth salvaging at W&D Drive Inn today. While Won Ju was chopping cabbage in the kitchen, Soong asked the same question she'd asked at least eight times on the bus. It was one of those questions that didn't search for an answer, but searched to accuse instead. "Are you crazy? Allowing that woman sleep by Brandon?"

"Where else could she sleep?" Won Ju answered for the ninth time.

"You should have sent her back to Chung Yun."

"Mom, she was not about to go back to Donny. She was upset."

"That woman knows nothing about marriage."

Who does? Won Ju gave Crystal credit for her courage, even though she was upset that Crystal just did what she felt like doing, despite the repercussions. Who did she think she was? "And you are an expert at marriage? I remember when you left one time."

"That was different."

A marine walked in. The Korean chatter stopped. Won Ju took the man's order while Soong went in the back to cook it. He was a typical customer from the U.S. marine base in Kailua. He sat at one of the tables and drummed his fingers. Won Ju walked into the back where her mother was cooking three pieces of chicken on the black grill. Won Ju sighed. "Let me get it, Mom. Relax."

"No, I have it."

"You have to respect a woman who just gets up and leaves. Sometimes Crystal reminds me of a man."

Soong shook her head. "She's a little girl who left over a stupid fight. No, you cannot respect a woman who just gets up and leaves. Look at Chung Yun. I left, and look at him. Crystal reminds you of a man. There is nothing great about being a man."

"You have more options."

"Options are things valued by those who cannot make decisions and live with them."

Soong pulled the chicken off the grill with her long chopsticks. She put it on a disposable plate. Won Ju took the plate to the front and added two scoops of rice, one scoop of macaroni salad, and a small plastic container filled with kimchee. The marine stood up and picked up his plate. Won Ju made his Coke and handed it to the marine. He paid in exact change, then sat back down to eat. Won Ju returned to the kitchen. "Sometimes I think of leaving."

Soong was putting the stainless-steel container with the raw marinating chicken back into the enormous stainless-steel refrigerator. "Don't think that way," she said as she leaned into the cold metal box. "You have a son to think about."

"Mom."

"Yes?"

"Why are we scared of driving?"

Soong looked at her daughter with a frown. "I'm not scared of driving. I just see no sense in driving if you do not have to. Driving all the time is hard business."

Won Ju didn't understand the response. "Well, I'm scared. All of that thinking, all of that traffic. All of that potential to get into an accident."

"Like I said, why drive if you don't have to? Men like to drive, so let them. You can always navigate."

Won Ju shrugged and started chopping more cabbage. Can't one person do both?

-5-

CRYSTAL ARRIVED AFTER the Saturday afternoon rush, feeling state-of-the-art sleek with short, unpolished fingernails. The first person she saw was Darian, who had been there helping out her sister and mother, and now she was leaning against the counter, reading *Vogue*. Crystal put a hand on Darian's arm. "Hey, what's up?"

Darian, not putting the magazine down, smiled. "I heard."

"I'm sure you did."

"Did he deserve it?"

"Yup."

"Cool. Hey, your nails."

"They were kind of tacky anyway, right?"

"Yeah. But beautiful, Las Vegas-style, nonetheless."

Crystal walked behind the counter. Darian was wearing denim shorts and a black halter top. If she stripped, she would make some good money. She'd make outstanding cash with a boob job. "Is your sister back there?"

Darian turned the page. "Yeah, her and my mom."

Crystal liked the way Darian spoke. Her English was so well-enunciated that she sounded as if she put a great deal of concentration in it. She sounded like one of those women DJ sidekicks she'd hear on morning radio. "Oh, I wanted to ask you something. Is there a play by Shakespeare with a dick king who kills a good king and is killed at the end?"

Darian put down the magazine. "Well, a lot of kings bite it in Shakespearean literature, but the one you're talking about sounds like *Richard III*."

"Does a good king take over?"

"Yeah. Henry VII. He was a Lancastrian. Actually, the first Tudor."

Crystal put down her purse and pulled out a cigarette. "Wow. I saw a monkey documentary just like that."

Darian looked over her shoulder. "Hey, can I have one?"

Crystal pulled another cigarette out of her purse, put both in her mouth and lit them. She handed one to Darian. "O.K. One more. What was that poem in the movie *The Outsiders*?"

Darian smiled. "It was a book before it was a movie. One of my male professors at Berkeley said it was a book obviously written by a young woman. The poem you're thinking about is 'Nothing Gold Can Stay.'"

"Ain't that the truth. Jeez, I gotta go to school."

Crystal stepped into the kitchen. Won Ju was mixing a batch of macaroni salad in a big stainless-steel bowl while Soong was marinating thinly sliced beef. She walked up to Won Ju and hugged her. "Thanks, Sis."

Won Ju nodded. "My mother wants to know if you're working tonight."

Crystal turned to the little Korean woman putting thinly sliced beef into an oily, black soy-sauce-based marinade. "I'm so sorry. But I have to say, your son has been a prick for the last two months."

Soong looked befuddled. Won Ju laughed. "I don't think she knows what a prick is."

Crystal turned to Soong. "You know 'asshole'?"

Won Ju grabbed Crystal's arm. "She knows; she knows."

"Anyway," Crystal said, "I want to switch with one of you for now. Is that cool?"

Won Ju translated it for her mother. In Korean, Soong said, "See all the trouble this causes?"

Won Ju responded in Korean. "What can we do? One of us either works with Donny or Crystal."

"You want me to choose? One hates me, the other is crazy."

"Just work with Donny, Mom."

"O.K.," she said, waving her hand at Won Ju in annoyance.

Won Ju turned to Crystal and reverted back to her in English. "You and I will work mornings."

"Cool," Crystal said. "You guys weren't talking shit about me, were you?"

Won Ju smiled. "No, my mother loves you."

"Yeah, right."

"How did you get here?" Won Ju asked.

"I drove."

"Over the mountain?"

"Yup. It was scary, but scary in a good way. That hairpin turn, I thought for sure I was going to end up in the railing. It was fun, though."

Crystal walked back to the front. Won Ju followed her. Darian was taking an order from a cute marine with blond, spiky hair wearing a tank top. His arms were thin, but well-muscled. The veins on his biceps and forearms were like the ones on that famous statue of that cute guy in Italy. She really needed to go back to school.

His eyes instantly focused on Crystal's chest. Crystal kissed Darian on the cheek. Then she went around the counter and headed to the door. When she passed the marine she squeezed his arm. "Keep dreaming," she said.

He smiled. "Thanks, sister, I will."

"Hey, let's talk," Won Ju said to Crystal.

The marine was the only customer in the restaurant, so Crystal, Won Ju, and Darian walked out to smoke a cigarette in front. Won Ju took her purse, a nice Louis Vuitton number, Crystal noticed, identical with one of Soong's purses. "Listen," Won Ju said as she lit her cigarette, "my mom is going to be moving into her own place really soon, so you can stay as long as you want, if you don't mind sleeping on the floor for the next few weeks. Oh yeah, and stay away from Brandon. My mother has some kind of fear that you are a sex monster waiting to gobble him up."

All three of them laughed. "Thanks, Won Ju," Crystal said. "It must be hard. He's your brother and all."

"Fuck him," Darian said.

"Yeah, if he could get it up." Crystal knew she crossed the line with that statement. She tried to read Won Ju's reaction, but her sister-in-law was calmly taking a drag from her cigarette. She regretted saying it, nonetheless. Darian, on the other hand, reacted with bulging eyes. "I knew it wasn't about sex with you two. How could it be?"

Crystal wanted to change the subject. "So Darian, possibly soon-to-be ex-sister-in-law of mine, how about loaning me a copy of Shakespeare."

"Sure, I have a mother anthology. Riverside. I'll loan it to you. Though I'd recommend *Hamlet* before *Richard III. Hamlet* is the one about male inadequacy."

"Thanks. I'm actually looking more for the meaning of life. I heard Shakespeare had all the answers."

Darian didn't say anything for several seconds. Then she said, "Come to think of it, they're all about male inadequacy. Richard has a hump on his back. Othello's paranoid. Lear, Prospero, Macbeth. It could be said that none of them could get it up. Anthony could, but boy, does it cost him anyway."

Crystal noticed that Darian talked about these people as if they were real, like they were friends or something. She turned to the quiet Won Ju. "So what about it. What's the meaning of life?"

Won Ju dropped her cigarette on the cement and meticulously put her shoe on the cherry. "I've looked and haven't found anything yet."

"Where did you look?" Crystal asked.

"Buddhism."

"Me too," Crystal said.

"In God."

"My God, me too."

"Oh shit, here we go," Darian said, as she tugged on Crystal's arm for another cigarette.

"Astrology."

"Which one, haole or Chinese?" Crystal asked, handing Darian another cigarette.

"Both."

"Now we're getting into the depths of self-delusion," Darian said.

"Amnesty International."

"What?"

"It sprang from the Christian stuff. Help your fellow man."

"What happened?"

"It lasted for about a month. I never thought that to get into human rights means to have to look at so many human wrongs." She looked at Darian. "And I'm not talking about Shakespeare. I'm talking about real life."

Darian ignored her. Won Ju continued. "Get rich quick. Tony, what's his name? Tony Robbins. Also *Chicken Soup For the Soul*."

Crystal laughed. "Me too, on both."

"Amway."

Crystal screamed, jumped up and down, and clapped her hands. "Me too."

Darian shook her head. "I heard they have a church now or something. It's like a cult."

"Being a vegetarian. I felt guilty after turning my back on human rights and running to money. I figured I could at least help poor animals."

"Me too," Crystal said. "What happened?"

"About two months. Poor animals taste too good."

Both Crystal and Darian laughed. "Me too," Darian said, meekly raising her hand.

"Should we go back in?" Crystal asked. "We're finished smoking."

"I'm not done yet."

"You're kidding," Darian said.

"Scientology."

"Well, that's pretty new stuff," Darian said. "When was this?"

"About a year before Crystal's wedding. I went to a meeting downtown and everything. That's when business started to get really bad."

"That explains the desperation," Darian said.

"Wait, what's Scientology?"

"You know," Darian said, "Tom Cruise, John Travolta."

"Oh yeah. I'd love to do Tom Cruise. Even Travolta in his Danny Zucco, Tony Manero days."

Won Ju sifted through her purse and pulled out a crumpled piece of laminated paper. She read from it. "'If it is true for you, it's true. And if it's not true for you, it's just not true, that's all.' L. Ron Hubbard."

Darian grabbed it from Won Ju and shook her head. "You still keep it. Jeez, look at this. He probably thought this one up while sitting on the can. A Descartes he's not. Look at this. There should be a semicolon between 'true,' or should I say the fourth 'true,' and 'that's'."

Crystal grabbed it and looked at the black-and-white photo of a sixtyish white man pensively looking away from the lens, with his hand under his chin. She didn't know about Descartes, but a Tom Cruise he was not. She pointed to the man's neck. "Is that a scarf?"

Darian tugged at the picture and said, "Ascot."

"I took a test with about a hundred multiple-choice questions," Won Ju said. "They recruited me right on Bethel Street in Downtown. Well, guess what? After evaluating the hundred questions, they discovered that I was unhappy."

"Eureka," Darian said.

"Really," said Crystal.

"So now what?" Crystal asked.

"I don't know," Won Ju said.

"Agnosticism," Darian smiled. "Or welcome to existentialism. But then that turns to nihilism, which is a lot like what you said about the human rights thing. Most don't have the stomach for it."

"Do you have a boyfriend?" Crystal asked.

Darian laughed. "I had one in Berkeley. I just broke up with him before I came here. He was a self-proclaimed Marxist working on a PhD in lit. He wore Donna Karan shirts and drove a 1989 Grand Marquis station wagon. I couldn't stand being with someone with that much inner conflict. I guess I'm like Diane Court in *Say Anything*. I'm looking for something basic."

"No one is basic," Won Ju said.

"You're such a humanist. Your husband? I mean I like the guy and all, but he knows exactly what he wants. Christ, we're talking about a guy who probably gets his philosophy from Yoda, or worse yet, L. Ron Hubbard."

Crystal was surprised that the words didn't seem to offend Won Ju. Suddenly an angry Soong Nan was pounding on the window, looking as if she were locked in or something. Won Ju began walking to the glass door. She pushed even though there was a sticker that said "pull." She turned back toward Darian and Crystal. "I always do that. By the way, about my husband, you can have him. I tried that one, too." She pulled the door open and walked through. Won Ju and Soong headed for the kitchen.

"Well, I gotta grab my stuff and take off," Crystal said. "But you should check out my brother. I mean, don't let the pidgin and prison fool you, he's not basic. But he's good. And goodness beats basic any day. I want pure."

"Be careful, pure and good may not be the same thing."

Crystal and Darian walked in as the marine was ordering another plate from Won Ju. "For dinner," he said.

As Crystal walked to the back to grab her keys and backpack, she began singing "Dreamweaver" and was gratified by the marine's laugh. Then she thought about the conversation outside. She had that weird feeling that too much was said. Too much was put out there. She shrugged. She felt that she put very little out. It was Won Ju and Darian, especially Won Ju, airing their dirty laundry. She didn't like publicizing hers. Physically naked, fine. No dirty underwear to see. She picked up her things and walked towards the door.

Right when she pushed the glass door, Donny stepped in front of it. Crystal jumped back. Donny ignored her and walked past the counter without saying anything to Darian. He was wearing a T-shirt. It was the first time she'd seen him wear one in public. It wasn't even tucked in. Crystal closed the door and sat at one of the tables. In about a minute, she heard the muffled sounds of Donny screaming in Korean. Soong screamed back. Donny screamed again. Soong screamed. Won Ju was silent. Donny swung open the door and walked past Darian. He put his hands on Crystal's table. "Give me the keys."

Crystal frowned and looked up at him. "Fuck you."

"I will not have my mother catching the bus."

"Is it you who refuses to catch the bus, or your mother? You didn't mind her catching the bus until today."

"Just give me the fuckin' keys, you slut."

She almost laughed. The word "slut" didn't exactly roll off his tongue. But then she decided to get serious. She didn't want Soong catching the bus either, but she certainly wanted Donny catching the bus. She pulled the keys from her purse and gave them to him. Just as he grabbed them, the marine was standing by him. He put his food on the table. "Is everything O.K., ma'am?"

Crystal smiled. "Fine."

Donny looked at the marine and smiled. "She's my wife."

The marine stared back at him. "Where I come from, you don't call women sluts."

"Where are you from, Disney World?" He turned his head to Crystal. "What are you fucking this guy or something?"

The fist hit him on the bridge of the nose. He fell. Another fist smashed the top of his forehead, leaving a red cut. Now that's how you throw a punch, Crystal thought. She'd try to re-create it in front of the mirror in the bathroom at Won Ju's after she got back. Or maybe she'd start taking Tae Bo.

The marine calmly picked up his plate from the table and said, "Sorry, ma'am," then left.

Donny was holding his nose. Blood oozed between his fingers. Saying nothing, he walked out of the restaurant. Crystal smiled as Darian began to laugh, covering her mouth with her hand. "Sorry," she said in between laughs. Crystal walked to the door and looked out. Donny was sitting in the car holding his nose with one hand and the gash on his forehead with the other.

-6-

CRYSTAL, WON JU, and Soong stayed the entire shift. After they closed, all three rode the bus up the Ko'olau Mountains. "I miss driving already," Crystal said. Won Ju looked at her mother, who was looking nervously out the window. As they approached the Pali

Tunnel, Won Ju could see the Pali Golf Course below. It was so far down that she could barely see the golf carts and the little men trying to get their little white balls close to the hole. Won Ju had a disliking for most sports, but she hated golf the most. It took up so much space.

As she looked down, Won Ju was thinking about the day's events. At first, nothing surprising had really happened. Her mother was unhappy with Crystal's decision to leave. She got tired of hearing her mother's take on what a wife should and should not be, even if she agreed with some of it. But when Donny came in, all puffed up and angry, demanding that Crystal be thrown out of the business, something surprising came out of Soong's mouth. She defended Crystal. She called her son stupid and childish. She told him he was an improper husband without even knowing exactly why Crystal had left. Won Ju had been tempted to tell Soong about the blowjob incident, but shied away from it. When Donny yelled back, Soong yelled louder. And no one could yell louder than the ex-actress, the ex-Park Soong Nan. She could've been an American scream queen instead of Korea's Queen of Tears. It was always amazing hearing that thunderous voice come out of that tiny body.

So Donny had left, and grabbed a knuckle sandwich to go on the way out. After things calmed, Darian left, and Crystal took over as cashier, Soong went right back to repeating in Korean what a spoiled little girl Crystal was. She also insisted that she stay somewhere else, away from Brandon.

But Won Ju couldn't think of any other options as far as where Crystal could stay. She looked at Crystal, who seemed to be staring at Soong's fingernails. She probably didn't have enough to put down first month's rent and a security deposit in any apartment, and Donny was definitely not going to help her out. She was also afraid that Kenny would give her a hard time about Crystal staying too long. She looked at Crystal and Soong. They were quietly sitting on separate seats. Won Ju thought about the huge fish tank at the Pacific Beach Hotel and smiled. All of these different fish forced together behind a wall of glass called "W&D Korean Take Out." Won Ju shook her head.

When the bus arrived at their stop, the three of them waited for the hydraulic hiss of the bus doors opening. They got out and walked towards the apartment. The moon was out. Cars whizzed by. For the first time that night, she thought about her brother with a sudden and depressing amount of pity. She knew it had been his fault, but she wanted to go to him and help him. It was an instinct she'd always had when it came to her brother. No matter what he did, she'd always wanted to protect him. He certainly wasn't going to protect himself.

When they got to the apartment, Kenny and Brandon were watching television. It was the same monkey documentary Crystal had seen the night before. She shot to the sofa and wedged herself in between Brandon and his father. "Did it just start?" she asked.

Kenny looked up at Won Ju with a frown. "Your brother called," he said.

Soong went to Brandon's room, then the bathroom. The shower turned on. "Won Ju, you gotta see this," Crystal said from the sofa. "It's like Shakespeare's *Richard III.*"

Won Ju sighed and picked up the cordless phone. The apartment was way too crowded. She felt like a bartender during happy hour. All these people to serve in this tiny space. She walked to her bedroom and closed the door. She dialed Donny's number. "Hello?"

They spoke in Korean. "It's me. Are you O.K.?"

"I'm better than O.K. I'm glad she's gone."

"Good, good. Wait, just a second." Won Ju stepped out of the room. Kenny was giving Crystal's breasts the side eye. "Hey, Kenny. Why don't you take Donny out?"

Kenny's eyes immediately focused on Won Ju. "Is that him on the phone?"

"Yeah."

"Tell him I'll pick him up in a half an hour."

Won Ju walked into the bedroom and put her mouth back to the phone. "Donny, go out with Kenny tonight. He'll pick you up."

"O.K, Won Ju. Tell him I'll be ready."

Won Ju hung up the phone. It went way too easy. Neither of them gave her a hard time. She walked outside. Kenny got up and walked past her toward the bedroom. Crystal reclined in the empty spot and put her feet slightly under the sofa cushion Brandon was sitting on. Brandon did not move, but Won Ju sensed sudden discomfort flicker in his face. She looked at Crystal and suddenly saw a dangerous animal that had the power to devour her husband and son whole. It's amazing how admiration can turn into fear and loathing so quickly, she thought. She looked at the light brown monkeys on television. "Africa?" she asked.

"Sri Lanka. Wherever that is," Crystal said.

"Good. I don't like animal documentaries in Africa. Lion ones are the worst."

Crystal looked up. "Why?"

"Because they never show the people. There's probably a hundred times more film on the lions of Africa than there are on the people."

"Mom, stop being weird," Brandon said.

"Yeah, Mom. Lighten up," Crystal said.

Won Ju turned around to leave the room, but there was not an empty room in sight. She looked toward the window. For a moment, she recognized it as the only way out, and the thought of spattering on the pavement from twenty stories high seemed very tempting. She'd finally be able to get some sleep.

-7-

KENNY AND DONNY found themselves at Club Mirage. They sat at the stage with a beer in one hand and a wad of dollar bills in the other. They were looking into the crotch of a fake-breasted white girl wearing nothing but make-up, white platform shoes, and bleached hair. "Hey, Donny," Kenny said as the stripper spread her legs and repeatedly thrust her crotch inches from his face, "I wish I was a gynecologist."

Donny smiled and sipped his beer. He put a dollar in the stripper's garter. Some loud eighties hard-rock band was blaring from the CD jukebox, so Donny had to yell. "Do you want a drink?"

The stripper smiled. "Aren't you Crystal's man?"

"Not anymore."

"Liar." The stripper went to the other side of the stage and squatted in front of two local men wearing Honolulu Police Department T-shirts.

Kenny put his hand on Donny's shoulder. "What was her name again?"

"Serenity, I think."

Kenny laughed. "Well, I knew it wasn't Chastity."

It kind of amazed Donny how much fun Kenny was having. He was acting as if he'd never been to a strip club before. "Hey, Kenny, let's sit in a booth."

Kenny responded with a disappointed shrug. "O.K."

Donny ordered two more drinks. "So I suppose you heard about the breakup."

Kenny laughed. "Yeah, I heard. Not much, though."

"You don't sound surprised."

The waitress, who was wearing a red bikini with pictures of white hibiscuses on it, put the bottles of Bud Light on the table. "Ten dollars," she said.

Donny gave her a twenty, and she gave him ten dollars in singles. He gave her one of the singles, and she smiled and walked away. Kenny's predatory eyes followed her. Donny was never a prude, but he didn't really enjoy Kenny's antics. He always felt that Won Ju was the only person in the world who truly loved him, and he felt protective of her.

Kenny took a gulp from the bottle. "Anyway, no, I'm not surprised."

Donny lit a cigarette. Kenny continued. "I had this friend in college in my frat. A real party animal, but really smart too. He told me something I'll never forget. He said, 'Never get seriously involved with beauty contestants, psych majors, or strippers.'"

"Why?"

Kenny smiled. "Because all three are too self-involved and think they're the shit. You can't marry someone like that. That's why I hooked up with your sister. She was pretty enough to be a pageant girl and had the body of a stripper, but at the same time, she was always worried about other people and not herself. Her ego ain't strong."

Donny didn't know whether his sister was being complemented or criticized. "That sounds like good advice."

"It totally is. I'm telling you, you're better off without her. Girls like that, they only live for themselves."

"So which one's the worst?" Donny asked.

"Which one what?"

"Psych majors, beauty contestants, or strippers?"

"Oh, you might have it easy. Psych majors are the worst. They get into it because they want to find out why they're so fucked up. And I'll tell you, there's no worse psychologist than the one who analyzes herself. Talk about digging a deeper hole."

"Sounds like you know from experience."

"Yeah, I'm dating one now. She's probably at home trying right now to analyze why I didn't call her. She's wondering, is it me? Does he have intimacy problems? When the fact of the matter is, I've done my own self-analysis, and come to one conclusion."

Donny was shocked that Kenny trusted him with the knowledge that he was cheating on Won Ju. He was also surprised that Kenny referred to it as dating. "What?"

"I'm a womanizing pig. I'll tell you, Donny," Kenny said as he put down his beer and looked directly at Donny's eyes. Donny turned away. "It's us against them. You think of life as competition, and it simplifies things. It's all a game. Your problem is that you have Los Angeles Clipper mentality. Once you get so used to losing, it gets so you expect it and start looking for a scapegoat. You know how many head coaches the Clippers went through?"

Donny took a gulp of beer and tried to forget what Kenny had just told him. He tried to focus on what was said about Crystal. He agreed Crystal was a selfish bitch who thought she was better than him. But Won Ju? No. "So why do you pursue this psychology person?"

Kenny smiled. "Shit, if you have them wired, they're the easiest to control. Deep down inside they're still fucked-up little girls. In fact, now that I think about it, Won Ju could have majored in psych, but I'm glad she didn't. What happened to her in Vegas, man, it was fucked up. It was so fucked up, it fucked me up for a while, and it happened way before we met. I wanted to kill the son of a bitch. When I told her that, she got really quiet, more than usual. I guess it was a one-conversation deal."

Vegas? Donny thought.

"But getting into psych would've just fucked her up more. So I'm glad she goes through her phases. You know, all that zodiac, scientology bullshit. It keeps her harmlessly distracted. But I'm a little scared that she's running out of stuff. Hell, even I was a phase, marriage and all, I suppose. And I tried. Vegas, I wanted to kill. But a larger part of me wanted to break her fear. But it was bad. She had to get sloshed every time before we'd have sex. In fact, that's how I knew we were going to have sex. She hasn't gotten drunk in a long time."

Vegas? Donny asked himself again. She was mugged, and beaten pretty bad, but he didn't think that it was that scarring for her. His mother had gone ballistic when she had arrived from the airport to the hospital, and seemed to, of course, immediately blame him. He always shamefully thought of the ordeal as more traumatic for him than his sister. "So anyway," Kenny said, "Who cares? I missed WWII; I missed the sixties. If a documentary on Native American genocide is on PBS, one of those docs that Won Ju loves, and it's on at the same time as *Who Wants To Be A Millionaire*, you better believe I'm watching Regis. I'm not the solution to the world's problems, and I don't pretend to be. Does that make me evil?"

"Vegas wasn't that tough on her, was it?" Donny asked Kenny.

Kenny nearly spit a mouthful of beer out. "Are you kidding?"

"She was mugged and beat pretty bad, but…"

"You don't know?"

"Know what?"

"I shouldn't say if the old dragon lady and Won Ju didn't say anything. But I'll say this, I'm glad I'm a man."

Just then the bleached blond walked to the table. Her white thong bikini glowed under the black lights. "So you were going to buy me a drink?" she asked.

Kenny made room for her on his side of the table. "Sit down. I'll buy you one."

Serenity sat by Kenny and asked, "So what's your name, sweetie?"

Kenny smiled. "Whatever you want it to be." Then he looked seriously at Donny. "Remember, I said I'm glad to be a man, not proud to be one."

Rape. But why was it my fault? Donny asked himself.

-8-

KENNY WALKED INTO the dark apartment and closed the door. He took off his shoes and felt the carpet between his toes. Home. He missed his single-man apartment. He remembered the tiny one-bedroom in Salt Lake with nostalgia. One room contained his surfboards, paddles, golf clubs, and other sports equipment, and the living room, the first room a person saw when they stepped in, contained his twenty-seven-inch television and his king-sized futon bed. He'd loved bringing women over. The first thing they saw was the bed. There were no chairs, only the bed. Once he got them upstairs, he batted a good .900. He never referred to it as his Bat

Cave, which many of his friends called their single-guy apartments. He'd called his "The Spiderweb."

But now this two-bedroom was home, and he thought the carpet in this apartment felt more plush than any other carpet he felt. But there were way too many people on his carpet. Here he was, entering like a ninja into his own home. He took a few cautious, drunken steps and stopped when he saw the faint outline of two sleeping heads. One was on the sofa. The other was on the floor. He waited in stillness for his eyes to adjust. The silhouettes became more distinct, and the shape of Crystal's body began to materialize. Kenny looked towards his bedroom and let out a quiet sigh.

There were no two ways about it. Kenny was drunk and horny. He stepped quietly towards the sleeping body on the floor and squatted in front of it. He looked at his sleeping son, then his eyes darted towards his bedroom again. After waiting a few seconds, his hand slowly extended towards the head of long, dark brown hair.

His hand stopped. He looked around. He remembered he'd awakened in the middle of the night the night before, and his wife had been smoking a cigarette by the window. He looked towards the window. She wasn't there. His eyes focused on Crystal again. Still in his squat, he took a step closer to her. He felt his penis harden in his jeans while he stared at the shape of her breasts, covered by a cotton T-shirt. He wanted to dive into the neck of the T-shirt and start sucking away. He looked towards the bedroom again. Again, no movement.

He held his breath then exhaled. He crawled closer to her and lightly touched her breast. He pulled his hand away quickly. He felt like an awkward teenager copping his first feel. He felt

like a bobcat wondering how he was going to eat a porcupine. His hand moved forward again. This time he let his hand stay on the breast longer. He put her nipple between his index and middle finger and squeezed gently. With her eyes still closed, Crystal let out a quiet moan.

The excitement was overwhelming. She moaned! She knew it was him and she moaned! He had to force restraint on his desire to rip her clothes off and smother her with his body. He looked towards the bedroom again. Again silence. He put his other hand on the other breast and began rubbing it, feeling the nipples become erect. Suddenly, it was as if his drunkenness left him, it was like he was aware of every sound and movement around him. She wanted him. He would take her right here with his wife in one room, his mother-in-law in another, and his son not more than two feet away. He looked at his son. Brandon did not move. It was crunch time, and he wasn't about to stay seated on the bench. Coach, put me in, he thought.

He began taking off Crystal's shirt. As the shirt moved up slowly, he saw a smile flicker on her face. She wanted it. When the shirt moved up to her chest, she opened her eyes. The scream that followed shook Kenny so badly that he tasted the bile that leapt to his throat. His erection was lost in a matter of a split second. He stood up and stared at his bedroom door, knowing what was coming next.

Both bedroom lights turned on. Both Won Ju and Soong, dressed in robes, came out and turned on the living room light. Kenny was standing over Crystal. Crystal had her hand over her eyes. Brandon, who was also awakened by the scream, looked up at his father with a questioning face. Kenny, for a few seconds, imagined his life falling apart. His wife would leave him, his son would go with her, he wouldn't be able to find strippers to ease him because Crystal would have him blacklisted, and this little crazy Korean woman who now stared at him would hire someone to have him killed. He felt like Scott Norwood missing that last-second field goal at the end of Super Bowl XXV. Scott "Norwide."

But Kenny was a die-hard optimist. None of these things would happen, he was not the missing-last-second-field-goal type. All he had to do was think and outsmart this bunch—a stripper, a housewife, a foreigner, and a teenage child—and put it through the uprights. He could outsmart them all. He looked down at Crystal and heard himself speak. "Jesus, Crystal. I'm sorry. I didn't even see you. Are you O.K.?"

Crystal looked up at him. Kenny tried to convey a pleading look, but knew he wasn't very good at it. Crystal smiled, "It's O.K., Kenny." She looked at Soong and Won Ju. "Sorry I screamed so loud, but he stepped on my hand. Kenny, watch where you're going next time."

Kenny smiled, feigning embarrassment. He felt uncomfortable pulling off this look, too. "I will, I will." He yawned. "Well, I'm tired." He walked to Won Ju. "Let's go to bed."

Soong walked back into her room. Won Ju walked into hers. Kenny smiled and followed his wife. Crystal backed him. Maybe she wanted him? Maybe she was just shocked that he wanted her and couldn't hold in her scream?

The lights went off. The doors closed. Brandon closed his eyes. Crystal closed hers. "I thought it was you," she whispered.

--9--

SO IN WORLD *Civ. Mr. Andrews told us that there are now officially six billion people in the world. Who counts this? How can anyone count to six billion? Where are all of the graves going to go? You always see these things on TV that count stuff. The numbers are always digital, and are usually going up so fast that you only see the ten thousand column change. The thousand, hundred, ten, and one column is just moving too fast. People being born, people dying because they smoke, women who get sexually assaulted by men. All of this is happening by the thousands as I sit in Mr. Andrew's class for an hour listening to how Hitler killed, like, millions of Jews. It makes me feel kind of, I don't know, I guess tiny and a little bit sad, but mostly tired. It's times like this that I think about playing Everquest. I'm a kick-ass druid in Everquest, not a flashing red digital single-digit number that flashes so fast on the display that no one even really sees it. But sometimes I'm even too tired to play when I think about this. Mom and Dad think that all I do in my room is play with my computer, but sometimes I just leave it on and stare at it from bed and think. I get so tired I don't* want to move. I feel like my chest is trying to sink me through my bed. Sometimes I feel like my hollowed-out chest will sink me through every floor of our apartment, but I'm too tired to stop it. It's weird, it's like two thousand pounds of emptiness. Then I feel like crying, but I'm even too tired to do that. It's weird how crying and throwing up is the same when I'm like this. I get crying dry heaves.

Dad once told me he doesn't like to see me get so obsessed over things. He also gets on me to get my driver's permit, but I'm not really interested. He's right about the obsession thing, though. Like now it's the computer games, and I guess before that, it was comics. When I was in the fourth grade, Dad bought me my first X-Men. For about three years, I collected comics. I still have them, and most of the are in pretty cherry condition. I think I could sell them for about a thousand dollars. Everyone loves Wolverine the most. And I guess he's cool. He's definitely the one that seems to like to kill people. All the rest of them just want to defeat evil, but Wolverine, man, with his adamantium claws, he wants to kill evil. Plus, he had all that ninja training in Japan, and he smokes cigars when out of costume, and calls people "bub." No question, he's cool.

And I guess I always told my two comic friends that he was my favorite, too. I didn't want to tell them the truth. I didn't want to tell them that a chick was my favorite X-Man. That would have been gay. But my favorite X-Man, without a doubt, was Rogue. And I'm not talking about Rogue in the old-school X-Men, not Rogue in X-Men #173, where she looks all lesbo with her mean face and short hair, when she was a bad guy. I'm talking about the new and improved Rogue, the one with the skin-tight green and yellow costume (God, what a body), and the long, curlyish, dark hair, with that one streak of white. All of that and she can fly and has superhuman strength (even though she stole both powers from Carol Danvers). She may be the toughest X-Man. And the hottest. But it's not all good being Rogue. Her mutant power is kind of sad. If she touches anybody skin-to-skin, she steals their powers and their memories. In other words, now that she's a good guy, she can't touch anyone. When she was a bad guy, she really fucked up Carol Danvers; she took everything. So now that she's good, she can't even really kiss anybody or anything like that. I was really into Rogue, had a poster of her in my room and everything. She was untouchable.

I guess Crystal reminds me of Rogue, especially when she first moved in. At first, I was like completely stoked, especially when I found out she had to sleep in the living room with me because Grandma is in my room. That definitely pissed me off at first because it cut into my Everquest time, but it was all good when I found out that I'd be sleeping in the same room as Crystal. When she came over that first night, and I acted like I was sleeping, and when Mom told her where she had to sleep, I thought, fuck Brian Kelsey, who got to spend so much time with Mary Keller because of the fact that their last names started with the same letter so they were in homeroom together, and I thought fuck Mary Keller, who was killer for a freshman, but no Crystal. I had a girl with a superhero body sleeping in the same room as me. Now how many of the six billion have that. There must only be like one million girls in the world with superhero bodies, and one of them was in my living room.

But that first night, after Mom went to her room and all the lights were off, I started to get like, nervous. I don't know why; it wasn't like I even dreamed of doing anything. Maybe it wasn't nervous, maybe, I don't know, after I stared at the back of her head for an hour or so, it didn't seem like such a big deal because I was just staring at some untouchable girl's hair. I mean, I might as well have been staring at my old poster of Rogue. There was nothing to do but stare, and I guess when I thought about that, I got uncomfortable. So I couldn't sleep, and Crystal didn't even move. I guess I was still a little glad, I mean, it was like inevitable that she'd leave the loser, but I'm like fifteen. That automatically makes me a loser, too. The fact that I was into comics and am into computer games doesn't help either.

But then after about two hours, something scary and wonderful happened. I think she was still sleeping, but suddenly she threw off the blanket that Mom gave her and started tossing and turning. It was weird at first because she was throwing up her arm like she was trying to get someone off of her, and I was kind of scared, because even though I wasn't near her, I thought she meant me. Like in her sleep she telepathically knew that I wanted to jump her bones. Well, I don't know if I wanted to jump her bones. I guess a part of me did.

But she kept doing it. I think she was having a bad dream or something. I wanted to wake her up, but I didn't know how to do it. At first I was going to touch her arm or something, but then I had all of that Rogue issue stuff going on, so I froze. Then I thought about whispering her name, but I was afraid that I wouldn't be able to control my voice and I'd say it too loud and wake everyone up or something. I even thought about throwing one of my pillows at her, but that seemed kinda rude. So I just watched, wanting to help her, but not being able to.

Then it happened. First she suddenly stopped moving. Then after being still for about a minute, she started taking off her T-shirt. It was kind of gradual. I guess you're kind of uncord in your sleep. It took like six tries and a minute and a half to get it off. Needless to say, I had like the woody from hell. Those breasts. Perfect. Just like a superhero's.

Then she went downstairs. I don't know what I was thinking at this point. Actually, I don't think I was even thinking, I was just watching. It's like my brain turned off or something. But not really because I was concentrating really hard. I had to; it was dark. But she started taking off her panties, and I think, and I hate this word; I don't know why, it just kind of sounds funny to me; but it was the most beautiful thing I ever saw. I'm not saying that her pussy was the most beautiful thing I saw, I mean it was the first time I saw a pussy in real life, and I didn't even really see it; it was dark, but, I don't know, I guess I mean just her getting totally naked was like the most beautiful thing I ever saw. And I had the mother of all woodies. It was like so hard, it hurt. But I didn't want to touch her. It was like the last thing I wanted to do was touch her. I don't know, it's like if you see like a really nice car, you don't want to touch it; no, that's not right, I guess it's more like if you're in the same room as a nuclear missile and you don't want to touch it. The last thing you want to do is touch it. But it was more than that because missiles aren't beautiful, but she was. I would've touched a nuke in an instant before I would've touched her.

Then she woke up. She didn't sit up or anything, her eyes just opened. If it were possible for people to actually jump up from the lying position, I would've done it. God, I was embarrassed. She saw me looking. So I turned and pressed down on my woody praying that it would go away. I felt like *complete shit. I wanted to cry even. But then I thought about World Civ. I thought about the six billion. I thought if there's a digital counter counting the amount of fifteen-year-old kids who just went through what I went through, I bet the numbers move up pretty slow. I was thinking that you could see the one column move even.*

HIGH CLASS REFUGEE

chapter six

JUN JANG. WAR. Is a country ever the same afterwards? Even in some countries that almost never have wars at home, like America, where it's almost only young men, mostly poor, who die, countries are not the same. But when the war is at home, things do not merely change; they transform. Park Soong Nan considered, in large part, the Korean War an American War. And all one had to do was live in Seoul in the 1960's to see that.

The Americans called it industrialism. To Soong Nan, industrialism meant steel, glass, newspapers, movies, leather wallets, paper money, and doing whatever it took to make everyone believe that you were O.K. Maybe not O.K., but good even. Seoul needed to look good. The city worked furiously to paint dirt mountains green, replace short, cement buildings with steel skyscrapers, build roads with smooth asphalt, and fill these new roads with cars. Lots of cars. Soong Nan remembered the cars she'd seen made out of American beer cans when she first arrived in Seoul a decade before. She knew she would never see one again.

The city stopped worrying about death and started to worry about money. How do I get money? Why can't I get more of it? How much will it take to make me happy? How much will it take to make me look happy? To Soong Nan it seemed that there was not a city in this world, not even Tokyo, that pondered these questions more than Seoul did. And she pondered them, too. She was a woman in a growth industry, and during the war, when hundreds of thousands of women unwillingly learned how to make money in the most ruthless fashion, and then the war ended, these women decided that not only were they going to hold on to what they had, but they, along with Soong Nan, were going to make even more. But you cannot simply erase five thousand years of history. Not even Americans, though they have been trying ever since they became the United States of America to do so everywhere they go.

In 1962, at the age of twenty-four, Park Soong Nan, widowed and a mother of two, began her fight for more. More for her, more for her children. Soong Nan had seen many books trying to explain why human beings behave they way they do, but to her it was one-word simple. More. Keep what you have and make more. So after her husband's death, she had to work to keep the house. She had to work to keep the car. She had to work to keep the servants. Later, she had to work to keep her children in boarding school. But she was a woman. More was not coming so easily. She did not produce movies, only children; she did not direct films, only households. At work, she acted. And she didn't get paid like the men. She didn't have power like the men. The paths that men took to success were not open to her. So she always kept her eyes open for a man who would help clear the path for her. Another Dong Jin. But at the same time, she often felt herself wish that she'd never find him.

Sometimes she felt like that little girl again, the one who walked from North to South Korea. But she knew she was being silly. She was no longer barefoot and ignorant. But on the other hand, she now carried two children with her whom she decided she'd live and work for. Yes, five thousand, or for that matter, a million years of history doesn't simply vanish after war.

The offers came after two years had passed since her husband's death. Politicians, actors, producers, and directors. Members of the renowned Rider's Club. On weekends the members, who included the head of the Cum Chul Jung (Korean Central Intelligence), and the heads of the two political parties (the Yau Dong and Ya Dong), would take in an early-morning ride, then eat lunch at the clubhouse. She was often invited. And subtle propositions would be given. These were powerful, married men who wanted mistresses. And on top of many of their lists was Mul Ui Yau Wang. The Queen of Tears.

Soong did not want to be a mistress. But at the same time she knew for these men, men who could set her children up for life, there were no other options. The fact that she was a widow with two children counted against her. The fact that they were married made the situation more impossible. So she slowly convinced herself that being a mistress was not that bad a thing. She started an affair with Moon Chung Han, one of the heads of the Yau Dong party, and one of the most powerful men in South Korea.

Between the affair and her hectic work schedule, Soong had almost no time for her children. They would come back from school and spend vacations, not with her, but the nannies that cared for them when they were babies. Sometimes, out of guilt, she'd bring them to a movie set. And while the little girl Won Ju remained quiet and watched things carefully, Chung Yun would pout, cry, and scream every time the director said, "action." It became so bad that several directors, none of them either woman or mothers, had the small boy banned from the set. In fact, they even began to resent her little girl. "Too quiet," they'd say. "It makes me nervous. She looks like she's judging."

And Soong started hearing a lot of such things about her daughter. Even her teachers would mention it after going on a tirade about Chung Yun. "And your daughter. She shouldn't stare so quietly. It's not only the teachers, but the other students do not like it. They call her conceited. They say it's because you are her mother."

Rubbish. Soong knew her daughter was intelligent, shy, and polite, maybe even to a fault. Maybe when people see humble goodness, it makes them uncomfortable because it makes them feel guilty. As far as Soong was concerned, the comments about her daughter were made by people insecure about their own goodness or their inability to keep their mouths shut. She didn't know how to respond against the criticism of her son, though.

Both children posed a difficult problem for Soong. The simple fact of the matter was that she did not have the time to be a mother.

Won Ju and Chung Yun were brought up in a world of rotating nannies and schools, and each time it was time for a change, like the time Chung Yun got kicked out of the second-most-prestigious children's boarding school (he had already been kicked out of the first) for stabbing a teacher in the leg with his scissors, the only thing his older sister said was, "Mother, send me to the same school as Chung Yun. He needs me." Soong complied and threw her hard-earned money at the problem. And the entire time she would blame herself for the condition of her son, knowing that she didn't even find the time to feed him grapes, like she did with her daughter, when he was growing in her womb. The fact that he'd been born with a shallow crater in the middle of his chest confirmed it for her. The guilt would be overwhelming after each incident, but she had no one to turn to. She had no friends, only employees and business associates. And Moon Chung Han, her lover, made it quite clear in the beginning that he did not want to discuss children that weren't his own.

It was in this condition, in the summer of 1968, after Chung Yun got kicked out of the last prestigious children's school in South Korea that Soong met the American soldier, Captain Henry Lee. It was at a private, exclusive dinner party in Seoul, and he was the guest of the head of the Cum Chul Jung, Korean Central Intelligence. She was escorted by Moon Chung Han and had her party face on, despite her worries, when the bold American soldier of Korean ancestry introduced himself after dinner.

He was not built like the other men attending the party. Though he was obviously older than Soong, like just about every other male in the ballroom, the soldier lacked the balding head and bulging stomach of the rest. His shiny black hair was combed back. And his tight neck worked up to a strong muscular jowl. Soong could tell that under the tuxedo, this man of about forty probably had the wiry build of a swimmer. His tanned face and clear eyes also hinted at activeness. But perhaps the biggest thing that separated him from the rest of the men was that he seemed to be the only one not picking his teeth with a toothpick, rubbing his stomach, or wearing a rolled-up sleeve so everyone could see his Rolex. When he approached her, he spoke in perhaps the worst Korean she had ever heard, and though she couldn't see it at first, he wore the cheapest Timex watch money could buy. "Hi, woman," he said, "I saw your movies and thought that they were awful."

She had heard about the captain before at the Rider's Club. Since it had been powerful men who had spoken his name, she tried to shrug off the bold insult. "What don't you like about my films, sir?"

He shook his head. "Sorry, my Korean's pretty not O.K. What I meant to say was that your movies don't do you credit or justice or whatever."

Soong smiled. "Thank you, sir. Can I get you something to drink?"

Henry smiled. "Yes. I drink Scotch. Get me one."

Soong understood his rudeness. He was trying to learn the nuances of the Korean language, which were based on a hierarchical structure. Children and women were spoken down to by men, and there were subtle differences; however, Henry was obviously mixing them up. "So, how long have you been studying our complex language sir?"

Henry laughed. "I still don't have it, do I, child? The American military taught me language, but only me how to speak the Korean you speak talking to those superior to you. The formal one. When some of my new friends heard me speak to children as warlords, they laughed and tried to teach me proper way."

Soong nodded. "Well, sir, allow me to get your drink."

Henry smiled and nodded. Soong walked across the burgundy carpet of the ballroom. She looked up at the chandeliers. She was beginning to feel accustomed to Western things. It seemed ages since she had first seen the Western possessions her first husband had. The years that followed brought so many Western things into Seoul that one could not keep one's eyes open and not see the influence. The ballroom was filled with tuxedos and gowns. Louis Armstrong, whom she had actually met a few years back, was being played by the house orchestra. She stepped in front of the Western bar and asked the bartender, who wore a white shirt, black bow tie, and black vest, for a Scotch on the rocks. Just then Moon Chung Han stepped to her side and asked, "How are you, my child?"

She took the drink from the bartender. She looked at Chung Han. He wore the face of a hardened soldier masked with a layer of baby fat. Sometime, in the past, the face must've been muscled and hard, like the captain's. But it was growing softer as the years of newfound comfort passed. A toothpick hung from his mouth. "I just met that interesting American captain. His Korean is quite terrible."

Chung Han laughed and ordered a Scotch. "Don't let his ignorance fool you, child. He is a very dangerous man."

Soong Nan looked at Henry. "Really? What is it that he does that makes him so dangerous?"

Chung Han sipped his drink. "You know better than to ask me."

Soong shrugged. "I apologize."

Chung Han glanced around the room. "Well, if you must know, he is a warlord in the American CIA. He deals with unhappy Communists in the North."

Soong, keeping a straight face, asked, "He really goes to the North?"

Chung Han smiled. "All of the time. I have seen the type many times before. He is an adventurer. He fears little. He probably watches too many American movies. Or too much, who was that, Daniel Boone as a child. It is often a pity to see this type of man grow old."

Soong looked up into Chung Han's middle-aged face that was not growing old very gracefully. "Why so?"

"These men cannot cope with getting older. They are not businessmen or politicians. As I said, they're adventurers. They are better off dying young, so that they do not have to see that life in the real world is not adventure. It is monotony."

She wanted to ask him how he knew this so well, but knew it was inappropriate. "Well, I better be getting back to him. I have his drink."

As a couple of men passed him, Chung Han rubbed his stomach and checked his watch. "Do not stray far," he said.

Soong walked back to Henry. He took his drink and smiled. "So, what did old Moon have to say about me?"

"That you're an adventurer."

"One getting too old for the adventure. He thinks I think that I am Peter Pan."

"Petera Pahn?"

"A boy in Western stories. Never grow up."

Soong waited for at least a rub of the stomach by the lean man. As if reading her mind, he said, "Korean men are so funny. Look. Picking teeth, rubbing stomachs. They want each other know that they had good meal. They want each other know they afford good meal. A Korean man spend two month pay to buy a watch he cannot afford. Look, they even roll up sleeve to show they watch."

"This is not so in America?" Soong asked.

Henry smiled. "With some. But not like this. No one roll up sleeve of tuxedo to show off watch. Koreans, so proud. Too proud."

"What kind of watch do you wear?"

Henry laughed and rolled up his sleeve. "Timex. $5.95."

Soong laughed back. "So what will you do after your adventure is over?"

Henry smiled. "I thought I marry Korean actress, take her and her family to America, and make million dollars."

Soong, so conscious of maintaining control of her face, involuntarily blushed. This man was way too rude and presumptuous. He was way too American. She consciously decided that she'd never be one of those sad, pathetic women who fall for American soldiers. It was so unoriginal and boring. The American soldier's dream.

-2-

THEIR VERY PRIVATE wedding followed three months after. The courtship consisted of Korean language lessons, and the fact that Henry was such a quick learner was one of the main reasons that Soong fell in love with him. Actually, Soong knew that this was only a small part of it. Soong was learning about the dynamics of love. It seemed to her that this type of love was almost like the Big Bang. Everything, like mass, temperature, the presence of key elements, and time, had to happen exactly how it did in order for this thing to exist. It wasn't so much that if one of these things didn't happen, it would've been dead rocks floating in space. It was more like these things were the things in Henry, and every aspect of him seemed perfect to her, even his imperfections. He was unabashedly human. He was never trying to trick her into believing that he was anything more than this. Though Soong often tried to articulate this love in her head, she was constantly making amendments and retractions. So finally she came to the conclusion that when he was around she felt very happy, and when he was not around, she was miserable. Maybe it was that simple.

Disaster followed the day of her wedding. Someone had done a close investigation of Soong's past and found out that she was not a distant relative of the late and great film producer Park Dong Jin. The papers released a story, saying that not only was Soong a peasant girl but a peasant girl with possible Japanese ancestry. It had been discovered that her mother was a comfort woman during the Japanese occupation. The scandal was not that she was what she was, the scandal was rooted in the attempted deception. Who does not despise a person caught in a lie?

In a more minor story that day, it was discovered that an unidentified American Army captain was running a black market. He was selling goods to the Communist North. The Korean government demanded that he leave South Korea forever.

Soong knew that Moon Chung Han's anger would be fierce, but she did not imagine this. That such a powerful man could act like such a child scared her, not only for herself, but also for her country. She dropped the paper in front of Henry, who was sipping his coffee and looking out of the window of her house, the same great house which was once Dong Jin's. He seemed to be admiring the green mountain. He looked down at the paper and smiled. "It would take me hours figure out what this says." He paused. "But I see the picture of you. You look beautiful."

She found his ignorance charming. She smiled despite herself. "You do not understand. We are ruined."

He picked up the paper and squinted at it. "What you mean?"

She sighed. "It's Chung Han. He has ruined us. He says you run a black market. They will make you go back to America."

Henry put down the paper. He wrapped his hand around his coffee mug and the wiry muscles and veins in his forearm bulged. He frowned, then smiled. The grip he had on the mug loosened. His muscles amazed Soong. Their response to stress reminded Soong of a cobra hood. He pulled her onto his lap. "So, I go back to America. Wasn't that the plan?"

She knew he was trying to make her feel better, but his initial reaction to the news betrayed concern. Then an unpleasant thought popped into her mind. "What will your Army do to you?"

He smiled. But this smile was of a more wicked nature. "End my adventure."

At first she'd thought that the black-market accusations were either false, or his involvement was sanctioned by either the Korean or American government, or both. But now she realized that Henry had been operating illegally, and perhaps both the head of Korean Central Intelligence and Chung Han were his partners. Chung Han, out of jealousy, had blown the whistle. He had threatened her the last time she'd seen him. "You leave me for that American, and you'll regret it. Perhaps even all of South Korea will regret it. Do you not realize the power, not I, but you possess?"

She had left frightened, but perhaps because Henry was American, or because he was so brave, the fear faded into a bothersome worry. But now, sitting with her second husband in the kitchen, she knew what Chung Han was capable of. For the first time since she had known him, she knew now how much he actually loved her. Only pure love could bear such wild and risky jealousy. Perhaps true love mixed with the endangerment of an aging and powerful man's pride. Henry patted her leg. "Don't worry, we will all go America and be rid all this foolishness."

She thought about her children. She would have to send for them. They would leave with Henry as soon as possible. She needed to stay for a while to liquidate her assets. The thought of money led Soong's mind to something Henry had said that first night they'd met. She brushed her fingers through his straight black hair. "And your million dollars?"

It was a week before Soong understood what he said next. But she remembered the sound of it so that she could translate it later. He said, "Shot to hell, baby. Shot to fuckin' hell."

■ ■ ■

They spent the morning packing Henry's suitcase. The embassy called and required his presence. He knew he'd be shipped out the next day, then dishonorably discharged. He agreed that he'd take Won Ju and Chung Yun with him. He had only seen the children twice before, and Soong liked the way he was with them. When Chung Yun had thrown a tantrum at the second meeting, Henry just laughed hard. Chung Yun, embarrassed, had quickly closed his mouth. This, among many other things, had drawn Soong even closer to Henry. So while they packed, she felt sure that Henry would be able to handle her children while she caught up to them.

The doorbell rang while Henry and Soong were finishing packing the last suitcase. Soong stood up and walked downstairs. She had already dismissed the servants, and gave them a handsome compensatory check, so she had to answer the door. Passing the window, towards the door, she saw a taxi accelerate quickly on the gravel driveway. It kicked up a pebble that hit the window and made Soong jump. Before she could even say anything, the taxi was replaced by a trail of dust. The piece of gravel left a ding on the window. Annoyed, Soong walked to the door and opened it.

Standing at the open door were two pathetic-looking children. The older one, the girl, wore a torn, dark blue schoolgirl skirt, a white shirt missing a few buttons; she stood in front of a tattered and hastily packed suitcase which was not even completely closed. Her round, pre-pubescent face wore drying tears. Clear mucus dripped from her nose. The boy was an even more pitiful sight. His hair had been chopped up. He had a black eye. His shirt was almost completely ripped off. The remnants of it hung from his pants. He had only one shoe on and didn't have a suitcase. Before she could say anything, the girl asked, "Are we really Japanese, Mother?"

Soong bit her lip. Her arms were shaking. From the looks of things, someone had tried to rape the twelve-year-old Won Ju. As for Chung Yun, he had obviously been teased, demoralized, and beaten. Soong fell to her knees and opened her arms. Won Ju approached slowly, then hugged her mother. Chung Yun, not even looking at either of them, walked through the door and headed straight for his room. Won Ju whispered in Soong's ear. "They tried, but I didn't let them. They tried, but I didn't let them. They said they were going to do to me what the Japanese did to Korea. They said they were going to do to me what the Americans and Russians did to Korea. They were going to rip me in half."

Soong knew they didn't like her in the first place. All they needed was a reason, no matter how stupid, to make her scream. To them, Won Ju was like a broken car horn. They instinctively wanted to pound it to hear the sound instead of finding out why it did not work. She pulled her daughter in front of her. "I will never let them try again. Do you hear me? I will never let them try again. We are all going to America where they cannot touch you."

She hugged her daughter and heard her son slam the door five times before finally leaving it shut. She took Won Ju to her bedroom and sat her on the bed while she dug in her bureau. Under her neatly folded silk slips, she pulled out a cherry-colored wooden box. She rubbed her hand over the dragons carved of mother-of-pearl. She knelt before her daughter and handed her the box. Won Ju opened it. "It was a gift from your father a long time ago. It is for protection. I cannot go with you to America yet, but this will watch over you until I can catch up. Keep it with you at all times."

Won Ju unsheathed the silver blade. The girl seemed disgusted by it. She quickly slid the sheath back on and put it in the box. "I could never," she said.

Soong shook her head. "But you must keep it on you. It will protect you."

"How can it protect me when I know I could never use it?"

"Please just keep it. For me. It will make me feel better."

Won Ju shrugged. She stood up and walked towards the doorway. She stopped, seeming as if she wanted to say something, but then she walked out of the room. Soong despised and admired her daughter at that moment. She despised her squeamishness, but admired her morality. But then perhaps it wasn't morality. Perhaps it was innocence. Perhaps she was like the swell that doesn't know it must become a wave.

-3-

AT THE AIRPORT, Soong watched the American military plane take off with her new husband and two children. She prayed to God that the plane would take them to America safely. Right after she did so, she laughed. Her praying to God revealed how long she had come from 1952, the year she had walked from North to South Korea. She had been a cynical child then. Now as the huge plane climbed in the air, she wondered how something so enormous could stay in the air for so long. She smiled. Yes, she had been a cynical fourteen-year-old who would never have prayed to a god she didn't think existed. But now, sixteen years later, she knew there was no room for cynicism for a wife and mother. As the plane shot to dangerous heights, she prayed to herself unabashedly.

When the plane disappeared, Soong turned around to hurry back to the bank and start settling her financial affairs. A black limousine was approaching the runway. She recognized the car immediately. It was a car she had ridden in many times. When the car finally stopped in front of her, the door opened. No one stepped out. Soong shrugged and stepped through the open door.

Moon Chung Yan was wearing a gray Western business suit with a white shirt and yellow tie. His black shoes were off, revealing thin black socks. Soong crossed her legs and smoothed out her dress as the car drove off. She then took a pin out of her purse, wrapped her hair in a bun, and pinned it up. She rolled down the window. "You know, I have a history with black cars. I was re-born when one hit me, then took me in. I am in one now. I suppose when I die, I will be put in one, too."

Chung Han leaned forward and sighed. "I had to do it. I had to hurt you."

The wind was blowing at his thin web of hair. His eyes had dark, sleepless circles under them. "Yes, men and their pride."

"Yes, men and their pride, and their love."

Soong refused to look at him, focusing on the passing landscape through the open window. She knew if she looked at him, she'd betray fear. "My daughter was almost raped. I had to take her to an American military nurse to make sure."

He sighed. "I am truly sorry. But I could not be the laughingstock of the entire nation. You *knew* that. Not a man in my position, not a man with my power."

It was strange how he talked about power. It was like a possession of his that people were always evidently trying to steal. Maybe at one time power had not been as important to him. But she supposed that if others are trying to just take one thing from you, that one thing becomes the most valuable thing in the world to you. "I suppose so. Where are we going?"

"If I were to run for President... It would have been impossible."

"Telling them that I was a whore you threw away was not enough?"

He laughed. "No one would believe I threw away the Queen of Tears."

The car seemed to be heading back to her house. She was puzzled. She thought for sure Chung Han was going to take her to some dreadful prison where she'd be raped and killed. But she always had an overactive imagination about these things. She always thought death was always trying to steal from her. Just as she had refused to show fear, she refused to show any kind of relief. "My country hates me now."

"It is no longer your country."

"I no longer have the power you claimed I possessed?"

"Why do you love him? The great Park Dong Jin would reject this nonsense."

He always spoke as if he were giving a speech. Vague words with multiple meanings, or melodramatic words always concerning the past, the future, fear, and exaggerated relevance. "You did not know Dong Jin. The shame would have been greater if he saw me become someone's mistress, rather than an American's wife. Besides, he was more concerned about my happiness than any other person I had ever known."

"Are you happy?"

"I was on my wedding day. Not so much anymore."

"Do you love him?"

She turned her head towards Chung Han. His tired face waited eagerly for an answer. "He is my romantic love. Do you know what this means? Even though I know I shouldn't, I love him more than I loved Dong Jin himself."

Chung Han turned his head towards the open window. Soong also looked out and saw the car approach her house. She was reminded of the first drive she had taken to the house, how the little fourteen-year-old she once was feigned unconsciousness the entire ride. But she was conscious now. When the car pulled up to the house, she didn't fight the tears. Somehow she knew this might be the last time she would see the house. "Why do you cry?" Chung Han asked.

"I am saying goodbye."

He opened his briefcase as the car stopped in front of the house. He pulled out a folder and handed it to Soong. He cleared his throat and suddenly a colder, businesslike voice came out. "The car will take you to a hotel. You will stay in your room under an assumed name. While you are there, you will not leave the hotel for any reason. Your first-class flight for America is scheduled in two days. This car will pick you up and take you to the airport. Here," he handed her the folder. "This is your itinerary, your copy of receipts, and the information you need to access your new bank account in America. I am buying you out. This will be my house now. But the trade is more than fair. Generous, in fact. In America, you will find your account balance at five hundred thousand dollars, American. You can start your new life comfortably."

The deal was indeed generous. Not only would Soong walk away with more cash than she would have selling everything herself, but now she also did not have to deal with getting all of her affairs in order, which could take weeks. The fact that Chung Han didn't consult with her did not annoy her. He never did. She looked at him while blotting the tears on her face with a handkerchief. "Chung Han, thank you."

His voice turned soft again. "On one condition. If you ever need anything, if you ever need to return, you talk to me. I am just keeping this house for you. It will always be your house."

She thought about the garden, the fishpond, and especially the grapes in the back. Yes, it was better if she did not see them right now. A clean break. She grabbed Chung Han's hand, sure she would never return. "I will call only you if things do not work out."

He smiled and stepped out of the car. "Remember what I said about the adventurous man. But I should not remind you. You will remember soon enough. You are my romantic love."

The car drove off. Soong did not look back.

■ ■ ■

When Soong arrived in Hawaii three days later after a stormy flight that scared her to death, she called Henry from the airport. Henry and the two children were in Fresno, California waiting for her arrival. After she hung up the phone, she couldn't really remember what had just been said. She faintly remembered complaining about the flight, asking about the children, and telling Henry how much she loved and missed him, but the last several days had left her so tired and disoriented that her mind was terribly cloudy. She had to focus. She was in a foreign airport with foreign symbols she could not understand. As she aimlessly looked for the gate for her connecting flight to California, something that Henry had said over the phone suddenly popped into her head. "I have this great idea for a business," he said. "Let's invest in the farming industry. Food will be a great investment. Everyone has to eat, right?"

He had also told her about all the grapes in Fresno. Grapes. If she and Henry had children, she would be glad to be around a city of grapes. Yes, investing in grapes would be a great idea. So there she was, conscious of the fact that she simply and perhaps falsely assumed, like millions before her, most of whom had been way worse off than her, so they had been more susceptible to the illusion, that life got simpler on American soil.

TURBULENCE

chapter seven

WHEN HENRY AND Soong had gone on their third secret date, Henry had told her about how he was in the second wave that invaded Normandy Beach. He never once described himself as brave or courageous, instead he used the word "lucky" at least a dozen times. Through the sides of his eyes, he'd seen his companions fall, each one shooting or oozing fluids where no fluids should come out. One of his friends, a Private Jonah Smiley, whom they called "Rabbit" because he was the quickest, fastest, and most athletic in the company during basic, had his head disintegrated. There were no lasers or space weapons in the 1940s, but Henry had seen it. His friend's head disintegrated, leaving behind nothing but a shattered helmet and Army fatigues stuffed with dead flesh. Not even a mist of blood was left, or at least Henry hadn't seen one.

Now, thirty years after this first date, Soong thought about the story again. In fact, whenever she was not satisfied with how her life was going, she thought about poor Private Smiley, the unlucky rabbit. To make matters worse, Private Smiley had a pregnant wife waiting for him back in Idaho. Henry had shaken his head when he told the young Soong the story, and the older Soong shook her head now as she thought about it.

Life was unfair. It was unfair to her because she had been born poor, her first husband died, she hadn't had the time to raise her children, she was practically exiled from her country, she lost a half a million dollars in bad investments, her children, especially her daughter, suffered in her absence, her second husband died, and her children continued to suffer perhaps because of the unfairness that had plagued her life years before. Life was unfair, but not as unfair as it was to "Rabbit" and his wife and child back home. No, she knew she was luckier than that. And besides, what was fair? Everyone hopes that their lives will turn out like a fairy tale or movie, and if it falls short of that, then life is unfair. Yes, Soong thought, hope makes life unfair.

As Soong unpacked in her new apartment, she looked out the window. Her heart went out to the Smiley family. She thought about the unborn Smiley child, who would be in his fifties now, and it made her sad. But she also missed Henry Lee; she missed her husband. He'd had a way of making her feel better with his tragic stories and his unbending refusal to take life seriously. She missed his irresponsibility. She was all about responsibility, and so she lacked balance without him.

Things were looking bad for her family. Her son, Chung Yun, or "Donny," as everyone else called him, was still estranged from his wife. He was drinking heavily, and sometimes he would pick her up ten minutes before their shift would start, so they would arrive at W & D late. Her crazy daughter-in-law, Crystal, was still staying with Won Ju, Kenny, and Brandon. Soong wasn't fooled. She knew Kenny lusted for Crystal, as she knew most men would. Won Ju, also aware of this, was coming closer and closer to separating from her husband. Brandon was becoming even more quiet and distant, reminding Soong of a young, hating Chung Yun. It was ironic. The more Brandon hated his uncle, the more he was becoming like him.

As for Darian, the girl who had once been Soong's hope, she rarely showed up. Instead she sat around drinking coffee all day, talking about working, talking about school, talking about living, but evidently doing none of these things.

Since her husband's death, Soong obsessed over her own mortality, and as she thought about her legacy, she felt as if she'd failed. It could've all gone better. Unlike young "Rabbit," she was given a chance, but perhaps because she had not been around when her children were young, they never grew up, especially her son.

There was still so much to do. Stacks of brown boxes waited to be opened. Suitcases filled with clothes waited to be hung. And bags of groceries waited to be unpacked. She looked around the small, one-bedroom apartment, and was painfully reminded of that big, brown house in Korea with the garden, fishpond, and grapevines in the back, wondering if even today Chung Han waited for her return.

She had gone back once. Just once. It had been 1973: The Year of the Ox. Her daughter Darian had just been born in a sea of green grapes. She was born in Fresno, California, where acres of grape vineyards lined up in rows. So many grapes. Too many grapes. It had been an unwise investment. So almost a half a million dollars poorer, Soong Lee returned to South Korea because it was the only place where she knew how to make money. And again, in her quest for fortune she felt was necessary, her children were left behind.

Surprisingly, her decision to return had been met with little resistance from the dishonorably discharged ex-Army captain, Henry Lee. He didn't want her to go, but he knew she needed to go. Henry Lee was never the type of man to keep people away from their needs. It was because he'd kill before anyone could keep his from him. Henry always had that kind of open-mindedness, that objectivity which would've driven lesser women crazy. But Soong loved that easy-going way about him, perhaps because it was so unfamiliar to her, and perhaps because she was confident that he'd always love her, but didn't need to flex his jealousy muscles to show it.

Stripping open one of the many brown boxes, Soong came across a picture of Henry. It was a black-and-white eight-by-twelve, framed with tarnished gold trimming. He was wearing his dress uniform, hat and all, and wearing that look of easy confidence. He looked completely happy with himself, but didn't pose with an arrogant smile to prove it. Soong sighed and pulled out the photo albums beneath the picture.

If he had known her plan, he probably would have put up more of a fight. She told him a half-truth. She'd said that she had a friend in South Korea who was going to invest in a high-class restaurant in Seoul and that friend wanted her to run it. She also planned to do some acting. This was true. However, she did not tell him who the friend was, and Henry being Henry, he didn't ask. Maybe he knew, but didn't want to hear it. His years in Military Intelligence had probably taught him how to put away information that would make him emotionally involved. But Soong didn't know if he knew her friend was her ex-lover, Moon Chung Han.

She looked in the albums. They were filled with pictures of the children when they were young. Most of the photos had been taken by someone else besides her. She closed the albums and put them back in the box. She stepped away from the boxes and walked to the small kitchen. She unloaded the groceries into the refrigerator. She thought about her grandson Brandon as she loaded wonbok kimchee, hotdogs, ketchup, dijon mustard, two Japanese pears, and a papaya into the refreshingly cold box. She would never get used to Hawaii's humidity.

■ ■ ■

After unpacking her groceries, Soong decided to go three floors down to see if her grandson was back from school. He was a high-schooler now, attending the same high school as his father did. Punahou, the expensive private school that Won Ju hated. It was almost the end of his first year, and he didn't talk about it much. He seemed almost suspicious of his family, like they were trying to catch him doing something wrong.

Soong waited for the elevator. She hated elevators. In heaven, which she did not believe in, elevator doors opened as soon as you pressed the button. Her awareness that her mortality clock was ticking, and there were things to fix, gave her little patience for waiting for elevators. Just as she felt she would scream, the little orange light went off, and the doors opened.

Soong entered the elevator and stood uncomfortably as two local teenagers, a girl wearing denim shorts and a red halter-top and a boy wearing a blue tank top and red surf shorts stood in an embrace. The colors of clothing pressed together with the bodies, but did not mix. The color purple was once again elusive for Soong. When the doors opened to her daughter's floor, she gratefully stepped out of the elevator, and headed for the apartment, knowing that no one was home. Won Ju was at work with Crystal. Kenny was also at work. It was only two o'clock, and school didn't get out for another half an hour, so Brandon was also not home. But she still had the key. She could wait. Donny wouldn't pick her up for work for another two and a half hours, if he'd actually be on time. She knew her grandson avoided her too, but she couldn't help herself. She wanted to make sure the child was not hungry. Food concerning her grandchild had become a fixation with her. She always felt that the tall, lanky boy was not getting enough to eat. She disliked hotdogs, ketchup, and dijon mustard, but Brandon liked these things, and they sat in the refrigerator on the unlikely chance that she'd be able to prod him up to her new apartment once in a while.

Soong looked for the appropriate key on her key chain. So many keys. One for her new apartment, one for her daughter's apartment, one to get into the apartment building, three for the restaurant, and one small one for her jewelry box upstairs. She found the key and opened the door.

Someone had closed all the windows and drapes. The heat was stifling, but she heard the air conditioning. Like when she had gotten off the airplane months before, the humidity slapped her in the face. She swore under her breath and gently closed the door. As she walked towards the windows, she heard music coming from the door of Won Ju and Kenny's bedroom. She listened closely. It was that new, infuriating music: rap. She hated rap. So much anger, and absolutely no melodic quality. But she didn't suppose the music was made for sixty-year-old Korean women.

She walked to the windows, thinking it odd that either Won Ju or Kenny was home. The air conditioner must've just been turned on, she thought. The cool air jetted out of the vents on the ceiling, but the only cold pocket was directly underneath the vent. She walked to the pocket and stood there, despite her hatred for air conditioners.

Not finding the cool, chemical air satisfying, Soong walked again to the windows. After opening the windows and drapes, she stuck her head out the window to feel a breeze. No breeze came. The air was unmoving atmosphere which seemed to hold heated moisture in every atom. The trees way down on the sidewalks stood unflinching. No leaves seemed to be moving. As Soong tortured her fear of heights by looking down at the trees, she heard laughter. The laugh was unrecognizable to her. For a moment she stood still in terror, imagining a rap-listening young man behind the door looting the room. Then she heard another laugh. It was the laugh of a woman she recognized. She could recognize Crystal's laugh easily, because it seemed to her that the silly girl was always laughing. It was a throaty, unbridled laugh that was loud but not oppressive. She didn't hate the laugh, just that it came out too often. But this laugh was a little bit different. It was a sex laugh. Soong frowned and walked to the phone.

She dialed the number for W & D. Darian answered the phone. "Darian," she asked in Korean, "where's your sister?"

"Mom, she's in the back grilling meat. Do you want me to get her?"

"Where's Crystal?"

"She called in sick. I'm here for her. Do you want me to get Won Ju?"

"No, I'll call back later."

Soong hung up the phone. It was that whore Crystal. She'd brought someone over. Did marriage mean nothing to that girl, despite the lack of love or flawed reasons for getting into it? You don't have to like marriage, Soong thought, but you have to respect it. You must always respect promises no matter how ill-advised. Crystal's disrespect for marriage went so far as to use her hosts', a married couple's, bed, for her sordid affairs. The heat in the room somehow got into her, and she decided to go back to her apartment.

There was little she could do. Besides, a part of her was glad it seemed to be ending so quickly. The slow death of a thing is very troubling to watch.

But as she reached for the doorknob, another thought occurred to her. Why here? Was Crystal that insane? Surely she would go to the man's place. Unless the man was married. It wouldn't surprise her. Could a married man take his mistress to his house? Well, anything seemed possible to Soong; many American wives worked too now. In her day, in her circle, it had been done more appropriately. Maybe two restaurants that the wives never went to, then a hotel. She never would've dreamed of going to Moon Chung Yun's wife's home. That's right, she thought, I had an affair with a married man.

Then her ears began to throb with heat. Her ears were so hot that even the hot air in the apartment seemed to cool them a little, keeping them from bursting into flames. It was a married man, and they were at his home. His wife's home. It was Crystal and Won Ju's no-good husband. Won Ju would hear about this. Soong walked towards the door to return to her apartment. Before she could open it, images of her daughter raced through her mind. The unborn fetus in her womb that she'd never seen, but had imagined eating plump, purple grapes. The quiet little round-faced girl who'd used to watch things patiently, waiting as if a plot twist in seemingly insignificant events were always about to occur. The angry teenager, who'd yelled at her mother for the first and last time when she'd found out that Soong was leaving Fresno and returning to Korea alone. The broken young woman in Las Vegas, whose quiet state scared Soong far worse than any hateful yelling she could hear from any soul on earth. The young bride, who seemed recovered, but not fully so. The young mother, who, after the birth of her son, seemed glued together by the process. No, Soong would not walk out of that door. She would find Kenny and Crystal behind it in bed and kill them with her shrieking voice. They would shatter like glass.

Soong walked to Brandon's bedroom. She wanted to make sure he wasn't home. Finding his room empty, his bed neatly made, she walked to the master bedroom. The music, which sounded like pulsating gibberish to Soong, still played. She gripped the doorknob and sighed. She waited a few seconds, preparing, it seemed to her, for an acting scene, then she opened the door and stormed in. Crystal was dancing naked at the foot of the bed while Brandon lay on his stomach with his hands resting under his chin. Soong ran out of the room, slamming the door behind her.

-2-

WHEN WON JU got home, she was surprised to see that no one was there. Crystal had said she was sick earlier in the morning, and several hours later, Punahou had called to inform her that Brandon was going home sick and he was being picked up by his aunt. She didn't expect Kenny home yet. He'd been coming home later and later over the last few weeks, saying it was work or telling her he was taking Donny out. Maybe a few years before, this would have caused suspicion, but at this point in their marriage, Won Ju found herself not even caring. Often, she'd rush to bed early, just so she could enjoy the bigger area of cold sheets, and think about how many thousands of generations it took to produce Kenny Akana, and how it was such a waste of time.

Won Ju walked to the bedroom and found the pillows and blankets in disarray. She shrugged. Crystal, being sick, must have slept on the bed after everyone had left. A feeling of invasion should have come, but it didn't. Won Ju just thought about how nice it was of Crystal, being sick and all, to pick Brandon up from school. She suspected that Brandon had a crush on his aunt, but it was probably harmless. Crystal was a man's woman, despite her marriage to Donny, and Brandon was still just a boy.

She fixed the bed, turned on the air conditioner, then took a shower. The restaurant had a way of letting her know she had been there all day, especially in the shower. Water beaded on her forearms.

She thoroughly scrubbed the grease from her body. Satisfied that all remnants from the day of cooking were gone, Won Ju got out and dried herself off. She looked at her face closely in the mirror. New signs of age seemed to be popping up every day, and she had a row of containers on the basin to combat them. There were tubes, jars filled with cream. But she knew these products were effective only to a certain point. Like sweeping rubbish under a chair, slowly the accumulation would be too much to hide. The funny thing was that she didn't know why she was fighting age. She didn't feel like it really bothered her, but fighting it seemed like the proper thing to do. She had come a long way from being the pretty and ignorant cocktail waitress at the California Hotel in Las Vegas. Won Ju sighed and applied one of the creams to her face.

At about six-thirty, before anyone got home, Won Ju went to bed. Before she fell asleep, she found herself rolling from her side of the bed to Kenny's side. Then after Kenny's side warmed up, she rolled back to hers. After most of the coolness was used up and the air conditioner finally cooled the entire room, she fell asleep and curled up like a fetus on one of the corners of the mattress. One wrong move during R.E.M., and she'd find herself on the floor.

■ ■ ■

Her eyes shot open at ten-thirty. She looked around, disoriented from the suddenness of consciousness. It was strange being in the dark apartment alone. There was no noise, little light, and a strong awareness of loneliness. She didn't really feel lonely, instead loneliness was like a big, strange thing floating outside of her. Maybe it wasn't her, but the apartment that felt lonely. She felt a sudden urge to keep it company.

Won Ju went through the apartment turning all the lights on. Not satisfied, and without any intention of watching it, she turned on the television, too. She even went to the fish tank, which she hated and had purposely neglected for the last couple of months, to turn the fluorescent light on. Moss covered a large area of the glass, and the Oscars slowly rose to the surface waiting to be fed. They looked a bit pale. The clown loach on the bottom frantically vacuumed the moss on the glass. But there was too much. She felt sorry for the loach and decided she needed to clean the tank. After two months, it was obvious that no one else would. But then she felt like cooking. The tank could wait, and despite the fact that there was no one home to eat, she took out a bag of chicken wings anyway and decided to fry them up. It was strange, after spending the entire day cooking at the restaurant, Won Ju prepared food eagerly. Then the thought finally occurred to her. Where the hell was Brandon?

After she cooked the rice, heated up two cans of corn, and was finishing up the last batch of fried chicken wings frying in a wok full of vegetable oil, Brandon came walking through the door. He stopped at the kitchen and stared at his mother. She knew he was waiting to get yelled at for being home so late. "Where were you?" she asked. "I thought you were sick?"

Brandon shrugged then cast his eyes down. "Hiding."

He thought she knew something. It was something beyond her knowing that he'd feigned sickness. At first, she didn't want to play the game because she was just happy that the apartment wasn't lonely anymore. But then the motherly curiosity kicked in. She wanted to know what kind of minor trouble her quiet, mild-mannered son got himself into. As the chicken fried, she began to fish out errant bits of clumped burnt flour, putting then in a small bowl. "You can't hide forever, Brandon."

He put his hands in the pockets of his shorts. "So I guess Grandma told you."

Now Won Ju was really curious. The noise from the game filled the once-empty home like a pinball machine. How would her mother know anything before she did? He hardly talked to his grandmother. She continued to remove the bits, careful not to let them touch the frying chicken. "And what do you have to say for yourself?"

He stood silent. Won Ju became worried. This thing moved from being minor to being something he couldn't even say. She had to test it. "Don't worry about it. We all make mistakes."

Brandon's head shot up and his eyes widened. "Really? You aren't mad? But you should be mad, right?"

"Why? I probably wanted to do the same thing sometime in the past. I'm not that old."

"Don't be sick, Mom. You're teasing me, right?"

Won Ju kept her face still with little effort. "No. You think you're the only one to get urges to do something bad?"

"But what about Dad?"

Dad, bad. It was about a girl. He was fifteen. She wasn't surprised, but why did he think he was in trouble? Pregnancy. Won Ju put the tongs down, walked to the table, and sat down. But why would he think she knew about it? Was it someone she knew? But she didn't know anybody. He'd never brought friends over in the last year since he started going to Punahou. And she never saw him around girls. "We really need to talk about this," was all she could think of saying.

Brandon sat down and sighed. It was the sigh of an adult with adult problems, not a bored or disappointed child. Won Ju stood up to take the chicken wings out of the oil-filled wok. As she removed each piece with tongs, she asked, "So what are you going to do now?"

"I guess I have to stop, right?"

"Right."

She put a plate full of chicken on the table in front of him. "Here, eat." She walked back to the stove and turned off the burners, and continued to remove burnt bits of chicken and flour. There were only several pieces left.

"So did you tell her she had to move out?"

Crystal?

Brandon turned around and walked into the bathroom. Won Ju grabbed the keys from her purse and walked out of the now crowded, overstuffed apartment before it suffocated her.

Walking into Soong's apartment, Won Ju threw her keys on the counter, ready to yell at her mother. It was the first time she was actually ready to yell at Soong. Soong was sitting cross-legged on the white carpet in front of the brown boxes. Besides the boxes and a few pieces of furniture, the room was empty. Won Ju wondered how a woman who lived over a half a century could have so little to show for it. As feelings of pity were about to overwhelm Won Ju, Soong's strong Korean voice emerged from her bird-like body. "Look. I have pictures of you when you were a baby."

Instead of sitting by her mother and looking, Won Ju asked, "What is this about Brandon and Crystal?"

Soong sighed and stood up. "I caught them."

"Why didn't you tell me?"

"I had to go to work. How could I?"

"Did you tell Donny?"

"No."

Won Ju didn't know what to say next. In fact, she wasn't sure how she felt. She wasn't angry, but she wasn't calm. She kind of felt like she was in a crashing plane, thinking, wow, this is really happening. Except the fear that should have been there wasn't. "What do I feel about this?"

Soong frowned. "I don't know about you, but I'm mortified."

"I haven't known many women who could keep this in, and go to work mortified."

"You should get to know older women."

Won Ju sat on the small love seat that still had plastic covering on it. "What did you do?"

"I walked out."

"So where is Crystal?"

"I don't know. Hopefully gone forever."

"Do I tell Kenny?"

"Of course; he is the father. He is the very one who should speak to your son about this."

Won Ju noticed the change. In the past, every time Soong referred to Brandon, she'd say, "my grandson." But now Brandon was "your son." "What about Donny? He is the husband."

"He will hate me even more for not telling him. He will think I'm glad that it happened."

"So why did you not tell him?"

"How could I?"

"So I have to?"

"You don't have to. I won't. Besides, he would not hate you for it."

"Even though Brandon is my son?"

"Chung Yun could never hate you. This is, how do the Americans say? His 'saving grace.' I cannot give up on him as long as he could never hate you."

Won Ju knew she was right. To Donny, Brandon was this thing that he didn't really like or care to understand. He never considered his nephew a part of Won Ju. Instead, Brandon was just an inconvenience to him, like a cracked step he had to step over in order to see his sister. And Won Ju did not feel badly towards Donny because of it. Suddenly, Won Ju needed a cigarette very badly. "I have to go back down. Hopefully Kenny will be home."

As Won Ju walked towards the door, she heard her mother mumble, "I guess I can't die yet."

■　■　■

Before Won Ju walked through her apartment doorway, she hoped the place was no longer overcrowded. She longed for it to be lonely again. She sighed and opened it. The lights were still on, but Brandon's door was closed. She put the food away, turned off the lights, and grabbed her cigarettes. She stood by the window and blew out smoke. There was no wind, so the clouds from her mouth shot out and slowly rose, then disappeared.

She looked at the fish tank. She decided to clean it. She went to the kitchen and grabbed a small beige bucket from under the seat. She went back to the tank, turned the light off, and put the cover and light to the side. She turned off the pump. The fish, even the slow-moving ocsars, became frantic. Won Ju reluctantly put her hand in the mossy water, and began taking out the decorative rock and plastic plants. When she lifted each object out, she noticed that a brown cloud would rise from the spot where the object was sitting. She went to the kitchen, dripping water on the carpet from her right hand, to get a sponge to scrub the glass.

When she began to scrub the glass, the water became so cloudy that she could hardly see the fish. But it was nothing compared to the undergravel filter. When she buried her hand beneath the gravel and pulled at the white plastic grating under it, the entire tank turned brown. Disgusted, Won Ju pulled her hand out of the water, and decided that the only thing that would get all of that filth out would be a complete change of water and gravel. But even if she were to take most of the water out, she wasn't confident that she could carry the tank to the tub, or toilet, to dump everything out. Besides, what would she do with the gravel? She decided to wait for Kenny to get home.

■ ■ ■

It was a little past midnight when Kenny arrived. Won Ju had nearly scalded her arm with a hot-water washing and finished her pack of cigarettes when she saw him come through the door. His curly brown hair was messy, and he wore a big grin on his face. His eyes were red. He was drunk. Her suspicions were confirmed when he walked to her and kissed her on the cheek. "Hi, baby," he said, as invisible alcohol fumes escaped his mouth. "Hey, what happened to the fish tank?"

She looked at the tank. The brown cloud had settled, but the cover and light were still off to the side, the decorative rocks and plants were still in the bucket, and the gravel was pushed to one side of the tank. She knew the filth was still there, under the white grating of the filter. It was hiding, which irritated her. She turned back to Kenny. "Where were you?"

"At the club. We paddled till late tonight and the boys wanted to have a few beers."

"Was it the boys or the girls?"

Kenny frowned. "What are you talking about?"

She didn't know. She just felt like unleashing at him. "Never mind. Do you know what happened with your son today?" She said it in a tone that suggested he was in an accident or something.

Kenny's face turned serious. Won Ju knew, despite everything, Kenny loved his son dearly. "What happened?"

"Are you sure you want to know? I mean, you could sleep it off first."

"Won Ju, stop fucking around and tell me what happened."

"Evidently Crystal's fucking our son."

Kenny's face, for a split second, flickered with relief. Then Won Ju read anger. No jealousy. Then, his next split-second twitch shocked her. He smirked. Not enough for anyone else to notice, but as a woman who had been married to this man for over fourteen years, as a woman who could see more than anyone else she knew, she swore she saw a smirk. Why would he smirk? Was it insignificant to him? No, it was something else. It was pride. It was an overwhelming pride that his fifteen-year-old son was screwing a beautiful twenty-something stripper. That time he'd stepped on Crystal and woke up the entire house, he probably didn't step on her at all. He'd probably caught Crystal and Brandon, so she screamed. But he lied. He was so proud of his son that he let the relationship continue. Won Ju walked to the kitchen and pulled a gallon bottle of Clorox out from under the sink. There was still about a third left. As she walked back to the living room, she heard Kenny ask, "You're gonna do laundry now?"

She stopped at the fish tank and twisted off the blue cap from the bottle. The smell jolted her, sending a burning sensation up her nostrils. It really woke her up. She tilted the mouth of the bottle over the edge of the tank. "I'm taking Brandon and leaving you," she said, as she poured the contents of the bottle into the tank. First the oscars twitched, then floated to the surface. The clown loach lasted a bit longer, swimming rapidly, to and fro at the bottom, but soon it was floating too. She felt bad about killing the fish, but felt satisfied after the loach floated to the surface. Suddenly her favorite fish was the one she wanted to see die the most. She put the cap back on the bottle and placed it in the tank. Now all four objects were floating on the surface.

Kenny was quiet throughout the entire process. And when she looked at him, she sensed a bit of fear, and it made her feel good. She imagined it was the first time in her life that anyone feared her. She didn't see him as being petrified or anything like that, nor did he seem like he was afraid of bodily harm. Perhaps it was the cruelty of it; knowing for the first time that she could be cruel. She just found out herself and it scared her. Or maybe it wasn't even the action, instead it was the words, "I'm taking Brandon and leaving you." Her question may have been answered when he asked, standing very still, "Why? He was the one fucking her, not me."

The answer to her was perfectly clear. "He got it from you."

"What?"

"He got it from you."

Kenny sighed. "Fine. Leave. Cool off. Go run to mama."

Won Ju walked to the bedroom and quickly packed a suitcase. When she carried it out, Kenny was sitting at the dining-room table drinking a bottle of water. She turned around to wake Brandon up. She sat at the edge of his bed and shook him. "C'mon," she said, "we're leaving."

With his eyes half-closed, he said, "What?"

"We're leaving. Get some clothes. We can come back and get the rest tomorrow."

"Where are we going?"

Won Ju wasn't sure. All she knew was the apartment got that crowded feeling again, only worse than before. She felt like she'd burst if she and her son didn't get out of there soon. "Just grab some stuff."

He sat up and scratched his head. After sitting for a few seconds, he stood up, put on a shirt and pair of jeans, and grabbed his shoes. "That's good enough," Won Ju said.

When they walked out of Brandon's bedroom, Kenny was still sitting at the table. "Son, you know you can stay," he said. "She's being crazy right now. Look at the fish, for Christsakes." He pointed at the four floating objects. "It makes no sense for you to leave tonight."

Brandon looked at the tank, then his father, then Won Ju. "No, Dad. I better go with Mom."

Brandon walked to the door and waited for his mother. She knew his guilt made it easier for her to get him to do what she wanted. As she walked by Kenny, she heard him mumble, "I'm not going to wait for you forever."

She paused in front of him. Then she walked quickly to the door. She wanted to get out of the room that seemed to be overcrowded with dead things to her.

When she closed the door, she put down her suitcase. Brandon looked at her, obviously wondering about their destination. "We'll go to Grandma's," she said.

"I don't want to go there."

"We'll go to Uncle Donny's."

"I definitely do not want to go there."

"O.K., wait downstairs. I'll call Aunty Darian from Grandma's and she can pick us up."

"Mom, when are you going to yell at me?"

"Later. Hopefully tomorrow."

They both walked to the elevator. Won Ju pressed the button and sighed. When the doors opened and they both got in, Won Ju inhaled deeply. She momentarily held her breath while the box descended. After she exhaled, she felt relaxed. Standing in the elevator alone with her son felt right to her. Both the loneliness and overcrowdedness she'd experienced earlier in the evening dissipated. Her and her son, it was all that she needed. She wanted to hug

Brandon, but knew he would have none of that. When was the last time she hugged or kissed her son? She couldn't remember.

-3-

IT TOOK DARIAN an hour to get to town. The beat-up Nissan Sentra had sped from the far west coast of the island. She was shocked and curious by Won Ju's call. She knew that Won Ju and Kenny had a fight, but she wondered what it was about. It had to be bad. She could never have imagined Won Ju leaving her husband. The good little Asian wife. When Darian finally pulled into the condo parking lot, Brandon was sitting on the curb half-asleep while Won Ju stood frozen, looking out into space.

They put the suitcase in the trunk. Brandon got in the back and lay down. He put his forearm over his eyes and went to sleep. Won Ju got in the passenger side and asked for a cigarette. Darian gave her one and said in Korean, "Sorry I took so long."

"I was going to say. Where did you drive from? Waianae?"

"As a matter of fact, yes."

Won Ju rolled down the window and took hard, greedy drags from the cigarette. "What were you doing in Waianae?"

"I live there."

Won Ju ashed her cigarette. Instead of floating into the wind, the ashes blew back up into the car. Won Ju brushed her shirt. "I thought you lived in town with some college people?"

"I moved out about a month ago."

"Why?"

Darian had been waiting to say it. She wasn't anxious because of fear; instead she looked forward to the outraged, class-driven reactions she felt she rightfully deserved. She loved throwing pies at snobby faces. But then it was Won Ju sitting next to her. There would probably be no physical reaction. "Don't tell Mom, but I'm living with Kaipo," she said.

Won Ju smiled. Darian was having a difficult time switching her eyes back and forth from the road to her sister. "Crystal's brother Kaipo?"

Darian focused on the car in front of her, trying to read the license-plate number just to test her eyes. "Yes," she said. "God, he's so McMurphy." It had been his tattoo that did it. When she saw the tattoo on the left side of his chest while he'd been changing his shirt at the restaurant, she saw the two hands pressed together in prayer, the wrists bound together by handcuffs. After she saw the tattoo, that was it.

Won Ju was quiet, but Darian knew she was harboring disapproving thoughts. It wasn't that Won Ju was a snob, but she was probably upset that Darian was doing something that was sure to upset her mother. It often surprised Darian how different from, yet protective of Soong Won Ju was. Suddenly, Darian felt defensive. Who were they to approve or disapprove? "I guess I figured I'd follow in yours and Donny's footsteps. It's my turn to rock Mom's boat."

Won Ju threw the cigarette out the window. "So you're not going back to school?"

"I don't know."

"It seems like a waste of money if you don't."

"It could be a waste of money if I continue."

"Good. You can work with me tomorrow."

"Is Crystal sick again?"

"Yes, she's definitely sick."

Little was said after this, but Darian expected the silence. She knew she was bound to Won Ju and Donny because they were family, but she knew they didn't really approve of her. They were real Koreans. Darian was an American. Darian had heard the stories from her father. How Soong had to go back to Korea for a while right after she was born. How Won Ju took care of her for about a year and then split to Vegas with Donny. Won Ju and Donny never really got along with her father after this. She resented this along with the fact that Won Ju had abandoned her. It was weird. She felt no resentment towards her mother for going back to Korea when she'd been an infant, but she resented Won Ju for leaving her for Vegas. Of course, as an infant, she had no resentment, no consciousness really. It wasn't until she got to know her older half-sister a little better, as a teenager, that she began resenting her for it. Thinking about it, she wondered to herself, why am I rescuing her now? What has she ever done for me? She knew why she resented Won Ju for it. Because Won Ju would never have left Donny, her real sibling. She thought about pulling the car over and dumping her sister and nephew off at the side of the road, but she believed it was an American thought, and bit her lip because of it. Besides, they were on the freeway.

■ ■ ■

When they finally got to the house, Darian pulled the car onto the front lawn. Since the little town of Waianae had no sidewalks, it was common for the residents to do this. Darian had found this to be a charming detail when she'd first arrived. The lights in the little house went on. Kaipo opened the screen door and walked toward the car, wearing boxers and rubber slippers. His gut hung over the elastic waistband. His stomach was very different from the washboard that Kenny liked showing off. In fact, his entire body was completely different. Though flabby in some areas, the body seemed to have a natural strength, while much of Kenny's apparent strength looked manufactured. Like he walked into a drug store and asked, "Could I get tennis balls for biceps, a couple of teflon frying pans for my chest, and a stack of strongly spined telephone books for my stomach?" His body was like those barbarians she'd see airbrushed on lowriders in Latino communities. Everyone got it so wrong. Barbarians didn't watch their carb intake, their form on the bench press, nor were they conscious of tanlines. In fact they were barbarians because they could care less about such things. Darian liked Kaipo's body better. It seemed more real to her, the kind of body you can hang on to. She supposed her sister never thought about how a body like Kenny's had no elasticity. It was probably like trying to keep a grip on a polished and oiled wooden tiki.

Darian waited for Won Ju and Brandon to enter the house before her. When they passed, she closed the door behind her. Won Ju asked where Brandon could sleep, and after Kaipo directed him to a room, Won Ju told her son to get to bed. He tried to ask how he was going to get to school the next day, but Won Ju put up her hand. Brandon went to bed without another word.

Darian directed Won Ju to the kitchen and opened her a beer. Kaipo came in a few seconds later and offered Won Ju a seat at the small kitchen table. Won Ju sat in one of the rusting, metal-legged chairs and took a long drink from the Miller Lite can. Kaipo pulled two more beers out of the fridge and both he and Darian sat down. "So what happened?" Kaipo asked.

"I think your sister is fucking my son."

Darian laughed. She couldn't help it. She tried to picture her young nephew screwing Crystal, and the image just couldn't appear. But then, trying to imagine her nephew naked, she saw the similarity in body structure of the father and son. Brandon was like Kenny, pre-canoe paddling and lifting weights. She looked at Kaipo, shook her head, and smiled. The praying hands in handcuffs had freckles on them. He wasn't much of a tanner. But then, he didn't seem to get sunburned either. He just turned more and more freckly with exposure to the sun, and the hairs on his forearms turned blond. The red hair on his head was Lucille Ball red. The sun never had an effect on it. He was the most amazing thing Darian had ever seen. A red-headed Hawaiian. Who would've thought? All of his features seemed Hawaiian except for his color. She loved looking at him. She turned to Won Ju. "Are you serious?" she asked.

Won Ju took another drink from her beer. "Guess who caught them."

"You?" Darian asked.

"Mom."

When she said it, Darian was taking a swig of beer. All of that beer in her mouth immediately came gushing out. Kaipo grabbed a dishtowel to wipe up the mess. Darian held her hand to her mouth for a second before saying, "I'm sorry."

Kaipo wiped up the beer. He was so nice to her. It was weird, watching this man, who was bigger than most bouncers she'd seen, and had prison tattoos to boot, clean up after her. In fact, he was meticulously neat. Each room in this tiny three-bedroom house with walls separated by a mere seven paces, with its thirty-year-old furniture, was neat. She was a slob compared to him, but he'd never got on her about it. In fact, she had her suspicions that the reason he did all of the cleaning was that he didn't trust her with it. It was fine with her. Kaipo turned to Won Ju and asked, "Dey was, like, doing um right dere?"

"From what I understand," Won Ju said, " your sister was, uh, performing in front of him."

"That's fucked up," Darian said, smiling. Her sister seemed so calm about it. But then again, she'd decided to leave her husband right then and there.

"I'm sorry," Kaipo said. "My sista, she was always funny kine. Eva since high school. She do whateva she like. Den she get in trouble. She no learn."

Darian smiled. She loved his pidgin, or technically creole. What was it? Yes, Hawaiian Creole English. It was so authentic because that was the way he'd always talked. It was his first and only language. Some locals she'd met over the years attempted to hide the creole. Not Kaipo. Darian spoke, "And what about you, ex-con? I guess it runs in the family."

"Yeah," he said. "But I feel mo' sorry fo' her. Me, I no care. But her, she get all guilty all da time."

Won Ju shook her head. "I let her into my house. I gave her a place to stay. Both women and men can't go around doing whatever they want. Sooner or later someone close will get hurt."

Kaipo shrugged. Darian didn't like the tone her sister was using with Kaipo. It was filled with that condescending tone her mother sometimes used, and it was said with that accent that drove Darian mad. Since Darian had learned Korean as her first language from her mother, she fought hard to keep the accent absent from her English. She was always scared that it would creep up one day, which was why she was always aware of the sounds coming out of her mouth. How could her half-sister and half-brother not shake the accent? They'd been in the States longer than she'd been alive. "Listen, Won Ju. Kaipo's not condoning her actions. He's just trying to tell you why it happened. As for me, I'm curious about what this Crystal and Brandon thing has to do with you leaving your husband. It doesn't seem to have anything to do with him."

"It has everything to do with him," Won Ju said. "He's proud of his son. I saw it on his face. I will not raise another Kenny. But Kenny wants to raise another Kenny. I feel like Kenny is just waiting for Brandon to reach eighteen, so that they can go whoring together."

Darian laughed. Kaipo grabbed Won Ju's hand. "You get one place hea as long as you like. I no like talk stink about your husband or my sista, so I goin' go bed now. But you need anyting, you let me know."

Kaipo finished his beer, threw away the empty can, and walked towards the bedroom. Won Ju smiled. "He is so...what's the word?"

"Hospitable."

"Yes."

Darian smiled and reverted back to Korean. "It's called the 'aloha spirit.' It's the reason why the Hawaiians got their nation taken away from them so easily. They should've cut off the heads of Cook and his boys and put them on stakes on the beach."

"Too bad."

"Tragic."

"So," Won Ju said, "how did this happen with you?"

She smiled and lit a cigarette. He'd been so reserved. She practically had to attack him. She'd kissed him first at the restaurant.

It was an awkward kiss. To reach his mouth, she had to climb him as if he were a tree. "I chased him. Mom would have been disgusted."

Won Ju laughed. "You have always been very pretty. Like Mom. It must have been a short chase."

Darian shook her head, remembering the puzzled look Kaipo gave her after she'd kissed him and climbed back down. She'd felt so humiliated. "Actually, it took a while. I went about it the wrong way at first. I'd tell him how I've been reading this and that about the Hawaiians, how they totally got screwed over by white people. You know what he'd say?"

"What?"

"He'd say, 'I no need one book fo' tell me dat'."

Won Ju laughed. "Well, I guess it's turn white or live in poor towns without any sidewalks. So what about you? Are you through turning white?"

Darian took a sip of beer before responding. Bitch. "No, are you?"

"What do you mean? I never tried to turn white."

Darian was surprised Won Ju couldn't see it. "You live in, or lived in a condo with a Hawaiian who might as well be white. You send your son to a preppy private school with a bunch of spoiled white kids. You're trying to be white, only you're not as good at it as me."

Won Ju shook her head. She asked Darian for a cigarette, then lit it. After taking a long drag, she said, "Brandon going to Punahou was Kenny's demand. The condo is, or was, a nice place to live. You don't get it, do you? I was never trying to be white, I was trying to be Mom."

Darian lit a cigarette of her own. "We'd all fail. Not only in our own eyes, but hers, too. Besides, I don't think that's what she wants."

"Maybe it's not trying to be Mom, but trying to be what Mom wants me to be."

Darian took a long drag from her cigarette. "And what's that?"

"A tolerant wife and a perfect mother."

"Yes, she wants me to be a successful American. Which of course means a rich American."

Won Ju sighed. "So we will both fail?"

"It's not about failure, Won Ju. It's about finding our own way. There is no success or failure. It's just finding your own path to your grave at midnight. Don't try to follow someone else's footsteps in the dark, Won Ju. You'll just spend most of the journey walking in circles."

Won Ju smiled. "Not the happiest thought. But it makes sense. Thanks. I like you for saying it."

Darian got the message. She knew her sister loved her, but didn't really like her. It seemed that for the first time, Won Ju liked Darian. It was as if they were two scared people walking around the boneyard in the dark, and for a moment, they ran into each other. For that second, the fear was gone, and they looked at each other with comfort. Darian smiled, "So what about Mom?"

"I don't know," Won Ju said. "By the way, what does Kaipo do for money? He doesn't work enough hours at the restaurant to make a living?"

Darian sighed. "You didn't hear him? He does whatever he wants."

"What's that?"

"He breaks his parole."

"Drugs?"

"Steals and sells."

"I can't imagine him climbing out of a window. He isn't afraid of jail?"

"He had a funny response when I asked him that. He said, 'Well, da haoles and Japs may run jus' about everyting. But I tell you one ting, dey no run da jails. Hawaiians run da jails.' So, no, he's not afraid of prison."

Won Ju finished her beer and put her cigarette in the empty can. The cherry sizzled as it hit the liquid at the bottom of the can. "I think I miss him," Won Ju said.

Darian didn't know how to respond, so she asked, "How is Brandon going to get to school? The bus?"

"I don't know."

"Won Ju," Darian said as she put her cigarette in the same beer can, "you really need to learn how to drive."

Won Ju sighed. "I know."

-4-

SOONG SAT IN the dark apartment and wished she were a heavy drinker. She wanted an anesthetic to ease the pain. She thought about the state of her family, how it seemed to be spiraling downward out of control.

She'd called her daughter's apartment. Kenny told her both son and wife had left him. At first she tried to tell herself that Won Ju just lost her temper, but then she remembered Won Ju mentioning several times that she wanted to leave Kenny. She knew her daughter was the kind of person who didn't make important decisions so suddenly. It just appeared suddenly to most because she kept her thoughts to herself. Soong knew Won Ju was serious.

After finding out her daughter had left, Soong had tried to call Donny. He was home, but extremely drunk. He spent most of the conversation slurring insults towards Crystal, but after about five minutes of this, he told Soong something very interesting. He'd said, "And perfect Darian, she's living with that criminal Kaipo. See, Mother, I'm not the only child of yours ruining your life."

Soong had hung up the phone. Was it true? Was Darian living with Kaipo? Soong shook her head. She walked to the open window and looked down. She deliberately scared herself. Then she thought about it. Perhaps the reason she was afraid of heights was because a part of her always wanted to jump? She went back to the boxes.

Soong sat in the dark. The Hawaiians...Kenny, Crystal, Kaipo... Why did her children choose them? Kenny had been a fine man at first. He exercised, he dressed well, he had a good job. And he was good with money. He did not spend extravagantly. He saved and did not take risks. Soong admired that about him. She knew it would provide her daughter with security and stability. And that was all she wanted for her daughter, especially after Las Vegas, security and stability. Yes, she had judged Kenny so fine that she'd felt comfortable leaving her daughter in Hawaii and moving to Long Island with her husband. And why not? Won Ju had found a man who reminded Soong of her first husband, Dong Jin. Only now did she realize there may have been a flaw in the comparison.

Then there was Crystal. Crystal. When she'd first seen that girl teasing her grandchild in the restaurant, she knew what she was immediately. A whore. Only a whore would dress like that. She'd seen women like Crystal years before when she'd first walked into Seoul. Fake, painted women standing on street corners, not waiting, but chasing men for their money. The lowest class of street trash. When she'd moved from Fresno and back to Seoul, she'd met a woman, Chung Yun's friend, who ran a geisha house, and her girls were way above that. For them, satisfying a man was an art. And it was not purely sexual. She respected that. But Crystal, she oozed just one thing: sex.

And now possibly Darian and Kaipo. Soong shook her head. Why? She'd expected Darian to be her rebellious American daughter, but this she did not see coming. He represented, like his sister, everything Soong hated about Hawaiians. She knew the story. She knew many of the stories. The foreigners came. The foreigners colonized. The foreigners killed. The indigenous people died. The foreigners became the indigenous. It was a sad, but common story. It was also the story of Korea. It was the story of the human race. But does tragedy give license to idleness and wickedness? Soong did not think so. She thought of people like Crystal and Kaipo as fools who wallowed in their birthright of poverty. It had been her birthright, too. But she rose above it. She made the effort to rise above it. When she walked over a hundred miles from North Korea to South, she wasn't walking down, she was walking up. And if she'd failed? She knew she'd been lucky, but if she'd failed, she at least had tried. She would have died dirty and starving, with flies probably buzzing over her rotten corpse, but she would've died with dignity, flies and all. To Soong, Crystal and Kaipo didn't even try, so their deaths, like their lives, would be a waste.

Soong stood up and turned on the lights. The sudden brightness made her lose her train of thought. She wanted to dull the light so she opened a bottle of sake. She searched for a ceramic kettle in one of the brown boxes, pulled it out, and prepared the drink. After the sake was warmed up, she poured herself a small serving. She sipped the small ceramic cup.

Her children...they were in many ways a disappointment. Chung Yun, or Donny, was the most obvious example. Whose child was he? She did not see any of herself in her son in appearance or personality. His face was broad, his eyes small and dark. His nose was rather flat and his mouth was too small for his face. Perhaps his ears looked like hers, but now she couldn't imagine what they looked like. In appearance, he took more after his father, she supposed, but he acted nothing like Dong Jin. Her first husband was sweet and not condescending, whereas Donny seemed to always want to hurt people and he'd even hurt himself to do it. Ah, but the restaurant, Soong thought. He'd finally shown promise. W & D Korean Restaurant was still a successful business, and it was a family business. A family business. She'd been glad. But the joy disappeared once her son's marriage fell apart, not because she liked Crystal, but because she knew it probably hurt her son, and she was ashamed because a part of her hoped it did. The best way for a child to learn not to stick his finger into an electrical socket is to stick his finger into an electrical socket. What was wrong with her son? He was weak. There were millions of weak people in the world. How can a parent so blindly assume that their child will be one of the strong ones?

Soong poured herself another serving of sake when her thoughts turned to Darian. Darian was the child she saw as a perfect half of herself and Henry Lee. Darian looked like a young "Queen of Tears" without the tears. She was slight and light-skinned like her mother. She was pretty and had Soong's dark eyes. And best of all, her life was easy. She was born in America, in Fresno, California, in a sea of grapes. Unlike Soong, her childhood was filled with memories of toys, birthday parties, and her parents' affectionate love. Soong remembered especially how her father doted on her. And it made sense. Her personality was very much like his. She was stubborn, fiery, and adventurous. Like the true American child, Darian longed for independence. She did things to satisfy herself and not others. Though Soong was sometimes annoyed by her selfishness, she also respected and envied it. And most of all, she was happy for Darian for having it. Ahh, to worry about yourself before others. It was a feeling Soong longed for, but could never bring herself to indulge in.

Soong reached for the kettle of sake and found it empty. Her head was spinning slightly, and her thinking about Darian's freedom combined with the alcohol made her feel slightly euphoric. Darian's freedom. That was why she may have involved herself with Kaipo. It was simple. She did it because she wanted to do it. Soong took comfort in this. Darian would never become that man's wife. It would mean that she'd toil in poverty and people like Darian, people like Soong refused to toil in poverty. In fact, Darian refused to toil at all. She was very much unlike her half-sister Won Ju.

Won Ju... Perhaps she was the child Soong loved the most. Won Ju was her first. Won Ju gave her a beautiful grandson. Won Ju suffered. Won Ju, unlike her siblings, was giving and sweet, two qualities which are misconstrued as stupidity by selfish people. Soong knew Won Ju was not dumb. When she was ten, she scored at the top of her class in IQ. But Won Ju was Soong's Korean daughter, and although she'd been proud of the test score, she was more happy to see how much Won Ju cared for her brother. She'd probably been more of a mother to Donny than Soong. Won Ju's life should have been easy, but it turned out and was continuing to be so hard.

Soong's euphoria turned to depression when she thought about Won Ju. She cursed the sake and put the ceramic kettle and cup in the sink. As she washed them, she remembered getting the phone call from Las Vegas. She remembered it had been late in Seoul that night, and she was just about to turn in when the phone rang. It was a long-distance call from her daughter. Her daughter had been viciously attacked and raped.

Soong dropped the delicate cup and it shattered in the sink. The broken pieces of lacquered white were being washed down toward the drain. Soong's hand shot towards the jagged pieces. She tried to save them.

"Mother, it's Won Ju."

"Won Ju? I haven't heard from you since you left Henry and Darian. Why did you leave them? I told you that I was depending on you."

"I'm sorry I yelled at you when you left."

"We need the money."

Soong turned off the faucet and put her hand in the garbage disposal. As she tried to retrieve the pieces of broken ceramic, she cut herself. She pulled her hand out and ran cold water under it. After the blood stopped running from her index finger, she reached her hand back down the drain. She carefully tried to retrieve every piece. Luckily, the cup seemed to only break into about eight pieces.

"It was wrong for you to leave. Henry is your husband, Darian your daughter."

"But the money. We need the money."

"I don't need money. I need you."

"Don't talk like a little girl. Since you were a little girl, you've never talked like a little girl. That's how I knew I could always depend on you."

"Nothing good has ever happened when you weren't with us."

"I work for you. Where are you?"

"Nothing ever."

"You're scaring me. Where are you?"

"Do you remember the day we left for America? Do you remember how Chung Yun and I returned from school beaten and humiliated?"

"Yes."

"Do you remember what you said?"

"Yes."

"You said, 'I will never let them try again. We are all going to America where they cannot touch you.'"

Silence.

"I'm in Las Vegas. I'm in the hospital. I need you."

■ ■ ■

After Soong was sure that all of the pieces were out, she collected the broken cup and carefully wrapped it in newspaper. Just as she was about to throw it away, she paused. She placed the wadded newspaper on the counter. Then she walked to one of the boxes, each marked with a list in black ink indicating the contents of each box. She found the box she was looking for and rummaged through it. She pulled out a small tube of Crazy Glue and walked back to the kitchen counter. After she opened the wad of newspaper, she counted the pieces. There were eight of varying size. Did she want to do this? It was three in the morning, and she was very tired. She was struck by a sudden desire to go to bed. She yawned. It sucked even more energy out of her. Then she sighed. She knew she would never be able to fall asleep knowing that this cup was sitting on her counter unrepaired. It was why she had trouble sleeping most of her life. She could never leave things undone. When she'd acted, she rarely slept until the final scene was shot. Why did everything have to be finished with her? She stared at the pieces and shook her head. Then she began to meticulously put the cup back together, all the while thinking about how nice it was going to be when she finished and could have the longest night of sleep of her life.

-5-

NORMALLY, I HATE *PE. It's so stupid. Jumping jacks in the gym. All of the cool kids, both guys and girls, with their gray gym T-shirt sleeves rolled up to the tops of their shoulders. It's like a rule. You can only do it if you're cool. Then picking the teams for basketball. I'm actually not bad, but do I get picked first or second? Nope. Even though I'm better than most of them in here, even though Coach Randy, our PE teacher, keeps trying to get me to try out for JV next season, I get picked like third or fourth. The cool guys (the ones who say, "It's like Cube says, 'Life ain't nothing but bitches an' money.'") are always captains, and they pick their friends or the girls (the ones who read Cosmo and put highlighted streaks in their hair) they want to get with first and second. It's so stupid. Usually, all I want to do is get out of there, go home, and play Everquest.*

But today I don't give a shit about any of that. Who cares? I have other things on my mind. Big things. Besides, I'm tired. Can't sleep. I have to wake up at five in the morning and catch the bus all the way from Waianae. It takes like years to get to school. Kaipo doesn't have a computer. But I'm not even sure if I want to play computer games anymore. It's like I don't want to do anything. I'm tired all the time now. That's why I didn't bring my gym clothes to school on purpose today. That's why I'm laying on the bleachers right now with my arm over my eyes. The last thing I want to do is fuckin' jumping jacks right now.

I think I'm in love. I'm talkin' Disney in love, Little Mermaid, Beauty and the Beast in love, only with crazy sex and stuff. But I don't know what she's doing or where she is. That's all I think about now. I think, any day now, she's going to come and pick me up from school. Then she'll take me to her place, and we'll live there. I can drop out of school and get a job. I don't even like school anyway. I could work at Safeway or something. That'd be unbelievably cool. I think any day now she's going to come. I don't know where to find her, but she knows where to find me. She'll come. But it's been over a week. Why didn't she come yet? I mean, I know I'm a kid and all, but she told me so much stuff. It was like we could tell each other anything.

She told me about her fucked-up childhood. I felt so bad for her. All I did was ask about the scar on the lower part of her stomach and she told me.

She told me how she got hit by a car running away from her dad, who was raping her for like years. She told me how when she woke up in the hospital the doctors told her that she had been four months pregnant, but she wasn't anymore and that she probably wouldn't be again. She told me how she moved in with her cousin after that and never saw her dad again. She told me how Kaipo had to go to the boys' home because when he was finally big enough to kick their father's ass, it was the first thing he did. Broke their dad's nose, both cheekbones, and his own hands on his father's face. She told me that the problem with Kaipo was that when he first started hitting their dad, it was like he couldn't stop. He had to hit everybody. She told me how she would visit him every weekend. She told me how her dad finally died of a heart attack, and it was like the happiest day of her life. She told me that her mother's still alive, apparently, but she hasn't seen her in years. She said even though her mother lived in the same house for years, the same one Kaipo lives at now, and she still lives there to this day, the last time she remembered seeing her mother was when she was like twelve years old. I've been there for a week now, and I still haven't seen her.

She told me she used to fuck a lot of guys in high school, and at the same time she was taking Kaipo's liver pills because she wanted to be bigger than all of them. She told me how Kaipo graduated from the boys' home to prison, and how she still visited him on weekends. She told me that the stuff she was telling me was stuff she never told anyone before.

But I don't know what's going on. I'm stuck out in Waianae with Mom, Aunty Darian, and Kaipo. I dig Kaipo. I mean Crystal thinks he's the coolest, so I dig him. And she's right. He's cool. I wanted to ask him if he'd heard from Crystal, but I chickened out. He doesn't really work, so he takes me to places after he picks me up from school. He even bought a dog like the day after we moved to Waianae. It's a half-pit bull, half-Akita puppy. It had like a lot of fleas. When Mom and Darian started complaining about the fleas, Kaipo laughed and started walking around the living room while dragging his right foot behind. He looked weird, like he was hurt, but then he showed me how all of the fleas jumped on his leg. "Trolling fo' fleas," he said. That afternoon me and him trolled for fleas. We caught like twenty of them.

Last Saturday, he took me surfing. But it wasn't like surfing with Dad. When I'm out there with Dad, it's like he wants to turn me into a pro or something. But Kaipo doesn't even say anything. We just surf. That's when I almost asked him about Crystal.

But he's not always quiet. He talks a lot when we drive. But he's not like the others. It's not like I'm getting the full interrogation with him. "How's school?" Actually, that's the only question they seem to ask, but they ask it constantly, like when I say, "O.K.," they don't believe me. But Kaipo doesn't even ask me anything. He just points out mountains, beaches, and roads that I've seen a thousand times before, and tells me what went on there like hundreds of years ago. His favorite is the Pali Lookout. We pass it every day to pick up Mom and Aunty Darian, and he always points it out. It's either the Kamehameha story, where the king pitched a bunch of Hawaiians off the cliff like two hundred years ago, or the whiffle ball story, where Hawaiians used to jump off on windy days, and get gently blown back up. They did it for fun, those crazy bastards. We stop up there sometimes. Kaipo jumps on the wall, wets his finger, and tests the wind. Then he shakes his head. "Not windy enough," he says. There would have to be like a hurricane to blow him back up. Me, on the other hand, as small as I am, it might work. I stood on the wall a couple of times with him. It scared me, but I felt that sinking feeling, like I wouldn't just drop, but I'd float. It was neat looking down and feeling the wind fill my T-shirt like a balloon. It was a good scared feeling. It was weird thinking that if I just took one leap something would happen, and it would happen fast. Sometimes things don't happen fast enough, and it hurts. I guess that's why people who know people who died are all thankful if he or she "went quickly." I guess velocity is kind of neat. Suddenly, I got nervous, and Kaipo must've seen it because he laughed. Then he asked me the first question I remember him ever asking me. "What kind Hawaiian you?" It was a good question. I still don't know.

Mom doesn't even talk about her or Dad. Nobody does. After Kaipo picks me up, and we go cruise and stuff, and we have to pick up Mom and Aunty Darian from the restaurant in Kailua, it's like the quietest ride in the car. And Waianae is far. They sit in the back and talk about work and Grandma. Apparently, Grandma isn't showing up for work, so the dumb *fuck works by himself in the mornings. Good for him. But it's only been a week. I think everyone is worried about Grandma. I'm kinda worried, too. She's like old. What if something happened to her?*

But they don't talk about that, either. They talk about how maybe they should give up the restaurant. How there's too much work for just three people. How any day now, the dumb ass isn't going to show up and open. How, even though they're shocked that he's made it a week, that it can't last long. They're probably right. So it's like the car is already crowded with the four of us, but there's like all of these other people in there sitting with us, too. And for me the ones that they don't talk about take up the most space. It's like a clown car and Crystal and Dad are wearing the biggest clown shoes.

A couple of times I daydreamed that I told them in the car how much I love Crystal. They all started laughing. Even when I try to force to dream them up as being like sympathetic to my deal, I just can't imagine it. I'm just a dumb kid. I don't even know what love is. Blah, blah, blah. Like they do.

When is the bell going to ring? There they are, playing basketball. Back and forth, back and forth. Put the ball into the basket, then run the other way. I remember during the first week of the basketball part of the class, Coach Randy tried to teach us the weave. It's so stupid. The weave. I never saw anyone do the weave in a basketball game on TV before. It like looks pretty and all, but nobody ever does it in game situations.

It's like sex in the movies. The first time me and Crystal were about to do it, I was trying to make all smooth, like Leonardo DiCaprio in Titanic, which was a pretty shitty movie with great special effects. But then I thought, the first time me and Crystal were about to do it, that I was glad I sat through the like forty hours of the movie, because at least I had an idea now how to kiss. Boy, was I wrong. I didn't see any tongue action in that movie, but Crystal was giving me all kind of tongue action. So Titanic ended up being a complete waste of time.

But me downloading porn was not as much of a waste. That's kind of how sex is. I didn't feel like this kind of corny, tingling love thing when we were doing it. That came after. When we were doing it, I just thought it was the coolest thing in the world. And when she started making noises, boy, that was it. I guess I don't know how it is for other people, but for me it was like *sex was sex, and all of the other stuff was kind of separate. Or maybe it was that all of that stuff is like after-sex stuff. The post-game show. But that's not right. The post-game is shitty compared to the game. The other stuff wasn't shitty. Maybe it's like science. Maybe sex is the catalyst.*

God, I miss her. I can't wait for the bell to ring. Last period. I'm going to force myself to get up and go to the parking lot, and I hope she comes. I don't think she will, though. How could she? Everyone hates her except me. Mom and Grandma probably want to kill her. Of course the dumb ass does. But I don't know if he knows what happened between me and Crystal. Dad's probably pissed. I'm supposed to stay with him this weekend, so I guess I'll feel that out. It's weird, I don't really miss him, but I think I'd probably miss Mom, even though she pisses me off more than he does. But with all of this, there's no way I'm ever going to see Crystal again. Besides, I'm just a kid. Besides, even if I got a job at Safeway, what kind of chick would want a guy who works at Safeway? Besides, I don't think she loves me. It's funny, all that time, after I heard about how there's six billion people in the world and thought about that plus how we're on a planet, in a solar system, in a galaxy, in a universe, I was kind of sad that I was just one of them. Now I want to take it back. I want to just be a number again. I want to lie in bed and sink into my mattress. Being like a person is too hard.

Well, all of them, Mom, Aunty Darian, Kaipo, Grandma, Dad, and the dumb ass, they'll all start talking about her again. They'll start talking all right. Because if she doesn't show up today after school, I'm going to tell them that Crystal is pregnant, and she's keeping the baby. Me, the kid, is going to be a father. And pretty soon it's going to be time to see what kind of Hawaiian I really am. Will I float or sink like a stone?

SILVER KNIFE

chapter eight

IN 1974, WHEN Won Ju was nineteen, she left Fresno, California with her sixteen-year-old brother and moved to Las Vegas. She was sick of playing nursemaid to her stepfather and one-year-old half-sister. She was sick of assuming the role that her mother left her when she had fled back to Korea. She was nineteen, and the last thing she wanted to do was take care of a middle-aged ex-military man and his constantly crying infant daughter. Besides, she hated the city of Fresno itself. There was nothing but stuck-up whites, crazy Mexicans, and grape vineyards farther than the eye could see. She grew to hate grapes, and almost gagged just at the sight of them. She was no farm girl. She craved the city life. Besides, Elvis Presley performed in Vegas. She'd always wanted to see an Elvis show.

Her mother had just upped and left. Soong'd had another conversation with Henry about money, then fled to Korea the next day. Won Ju told herself she could do the same. She took care of the baby Darian by day, and bagged groceries at Safeway by night, earning enough money for the move. And she would have left alone, had her brother not been awakened by the fight she had with her stepfather and begged her to take him with her. She was used to taking care of Chung Yun, and felt sorry for him because he took weekly beatings at his high school for being a Korean with a bad accent. She remembered her own beatings had forced her to drop out, so, feeling empathy for her younger brother, she decided to take him with her.

Won Ju and Chung Yun took a cab to the Fresno Air Terminal. It was nine at night and the taxi whizzed by rows of grape vineyards.

Passing the grapes by car always left Won Ju with an unsettling feeling. They looked like stilts walking rapidly, always keeping up with the vehicle. She felt like the grapes were chasing her. This night was no different. She tried not to look outside.

Chung Yun's head leaned against the closed window. His thin body seemed too weak to hold up his round head. When she looked at him, he smiled. He seemed even happier to be leaving. Won Ju guessed why.

"Hey gook."

"Hey jap."

"Hey chink."

Won Ju had heard it on a daily basis before. The only thing was Won Ju and Chung Yun were neither Vietnamese, Japanese, or Chinese. They were, for the most part, Korean. But to both the Mexicans and whites, it didn't matter. All Asians looked the same. Won Ju shook her head. Ignorant farmers. Did they not know Asia, like Europe, like America, was filled with different nations that were not only different, but had despised each other for centuries? Their calling her and her brother "gooks" was just as stupid as calling a Frenchman a "kraut," or calling an Apache a "wetback." But to them, it didn't matter. Once she or her brother opened their mouths and spoke their rotten English, it was like the ringing of the Pavlov bell for the other students.

"What are you, a retarded jap?"

"Why don't you learn our language, you fuckin' chink."

"My father died in Vietnam, gook. Now I'm going to take it out on your ass. It was probably your commie dad that killed my pops."

Won Ju checked the window. The grape stilts were still following her. She imagined them whispering, "Where are you going, you chink? You can't hide from us." She turned her attention back to her brother, who was still glowing. She spoke in Korean. "Don't look so happy, brother. Las Vegas is still America. Las Vegas has a high school. And I expect you to go to that high school."

Chung Yun's smile didn't break. "I don't care."

"Then why are you so happy?"

Chung Yun looked at his sister. "I don't know, but I am."

Won Ju was curious. She fully understood that this new life they were beginning was not going to be easy. They would have to find a place to stay; she would have to find a job which would hire her despite her bad English. And Chung Yun would have to enroll in school. All of this would have to happen in the first week, or the money she'd saved would not be enough. "You're scaring me."

"Maybe I am happy because I think I will never see Mother again."

"Why should that make you happy?"

Chung Yun's smile disappeared. "I hate her."

"You shouldn't say that."

"She left us like she always did. Career first. Money first. She does not care about us. I say I hate her not to hurt you or her. I say I hate her because I do."

Won Ju turned back to the window. Beyond and above the horizon was a dark empty place. The Fresno sky was empty. There were no clouds, no stars. It was often like this. It was like the city itself. There was nothing bright, nothing moving. To the nineteen-year-old Won Ju, it was limbo. And her mother had taken her to this place and left. Perhaps she hated her mother, too.

■ ■ ■

When they emerged from the grapes, and entered what Won Ju considered a pathetic joke of an airport, she paid the Mexican cab driver and unloaded her suitcases. She and Chung Yun carried the suitcases to the one-story terminal and approached the ticket purchasing line. A few men wearing cowboy hats and flannel shirts stood in front of them. When she got to the counter, Won Ju reached into her purse to pull out her checkbook. A folded piece of paper flew out and landed on the ground. Won Ju knew what it was. Her stepfather Henry had made her take it with her. It was her mother's phone number in Korea. She decided to leave it where it fell. Now came the part that Won Ju dreaded. She cleared her throat and prayed she'd get it right. "Two going Las Vegas?"

She realized she did not request it, but asked for it. She cursed herself. Americans did not ask for things they were going to pay for. The blue-haired Caucasian woman behind the counter gave forms for Won Ju to fill out. This part Won Ju did not mind. Her writing in English was better than some of the people she had gone to high school with. She was born with a fit mind, but unathletic tongue. She rapidly filled out the forms, trying to make up for her verbal mistake, and handed them to the older, red-scarfed woman. The woman smiled. "You know, you are very pretty. You're Chinese, right?"

Won Ju smiled while writing the check. "No. Korean."

"Is that your brother?"

Chung Yun was sitting on a suitcase a few feet away from her. Won Ju felt herself nod rapidly and subserviently. She hated herself for it. "Yes. He my younger brudder."

The ticket lady smiled. "Such a handsome boy."

Won Ju smiled so hard she thought her cheeks would pop. "Tank you, tank you."

As the woman processed the paperwork, Won Ju wondered at her inability to control herself when talking to Americans, especially older white ones. Here was this over-painted, overweight white woman serving her, and yet Won Ju could not help but to look for her permission and approval. When the woman handed her the tickets Won Ju smiled and waited. Finally the lady said, "Oh. Check in your luggage, then you can go. Gate four is that way."

Won Ju bowed slightly. She bowed! Even after six years in America, she bowed. At this point, she despised herself. She motioned for Chung Yun to bring the suitcases. He stood up and dragged them to the counter. He stopped to pick up the piece of paper that had fallen out of Won Ju's purse. The edges of his palms were red from the weight of the luggage. "Here," he said.

Won Ju just wanted to get out of there. She stuffed the phone number into her purse and rushed with her brother to the gate.

Won Ju noticed that he kept looking back towards the counter where they'd checked in their luggage. "Why do you look back?" she asked.

He laughed. Then in English he said, "Seem stupid, yeah?"

She smiled, then replied in English. "Yeah, no look back. Fuck dis place."

She was proud that she could pronounce the word "fuck" perfectly. For her, "fuck" was easy, along with "shit," but "asshole" sometimes came out "assahole." She figured she'd better learn how to cuss well considering they were going to Sin City. "Chung Yun," she said in Korean, "perhaps we should try to only speak English to each other. I think we will learn the nuances of the language a lot quicker that way, even with my clumsy tongue."

Chung Yun put his carry-on down in front of the gate. He sat down and sighed. "Yes," he said. "Once we get on the plane, no more Korean. And also, I want to change my name."

Won Ju sat next to him and frowned. It was the last flight out, and the gate was empty except for them and a group of quiet older gentlemen in suits. She was glad about that. She turned to her brother and, thinking about his name-change proposal, she asked, "To what?"

"Something American."

She thought about it. "What about Henry? Henry like our stepfather."

"No thanks."

"Well every name should have significance, American or not. And everything that has been important to us, besides our stepfather, has been Korean."

"What about Don?"

"Why Don?"

"I don't know. It seems like the American version of 'Dong Jin.' You remember, our real father."

"I like it." Won Ju smiled. Chung Yun was still a baby when their father died, and she only remembered bits and pieces. She remembered waking up and seeing him one night, and after that, never seeing him again. It was strange to think that the death of a man she could hardly remember completely changed the course of her life. She also thought about an American film that she'd taken Chung Yun to a couple of years earlier. There was that dignified man that everyone in the film referred to as "The Don." It seemed like such an adult name. Then she remembered an American song that she used to hum at school constantly called, "Where is the Love?" It was a brother and sister. She thought the brother was gorgeous and remembered his name. "That sounds like a fine idea. But maybe 'Donny' instead. Like Donny and Marie."

Chung Yun frowned. "I don't like him."

"Girls like him."

"In that case 'Donny' it is."

They laughed. Then Chung Yun asked, "So what about you?"

Won Ju thought about it. She'd been teased enough about her name in high school to despise it at times, but trying to remember her father made her feel guilty about changing it. It had been one of the only things he had a chance to give her. "I'll stick to 'Won Ju,'" she said. "I'm afraid if I change it, and someone calls me by my new name, I won't answer. It wouldn't be a good way to start a new job. People will think I'm stupid enough because of my poor English."

Chung Yun laughed. "Remember, once we get on the plane."

When they finally boarded, they spent the flight trying to get through conversations in English. They were laughing so hard, tears welled in their eyes. Watching each other fumble with the language was like watching children run down grassy hills, falling and tumbling down. They watched each other tumble and tumble until the plane descended over the neon-lit city. They both stopped tumbling to watch the artificial shine of their new home. The vastness and density of the lights intimidated Won Ju. Chung Yun leaned over her to look out the window. "Cool," he said.

She smiled. His new name matched him perfectly.

-2-

WON JU HAD left California only to find herself working in the California Hotel and Casino several months later. After working in some of the worst dives in downtown, gaining waitress experience, she was glad to get the job. When the new casino opened, she was one of the first to apply. But spending these months in Vegas brought her to the conclusion that besides the neon lights and all-night gambling, it was as if she hadn't left the state of California in the first place. There were the same hick whites and Mexicans all around her. There were the same racist comments and ogling eyes of men looking for a little geisha. She had never considered herself attractive because she knew her mother was beautiful and she did not look like her. And she had felt even uglier when boys in high school catcalled to her because no truly beautiful woman was treated that way. Her mother was never treated that way. Only trash was treated that way.

But the best job she could find was cocktailing at the California. The name itself made her shudder and think of the grape stilts following her all the way to Nevada. And when she'd seen the uniform—black pumps, fishnet stockings, a bathing-suit bottom, and a white tuxedo shirt—she felt the sudden urge to feed the baby Darian. Better a surrogate mother for your baby half-sister than bait for men who thought of you as foreign trash. But she'd taken the job. She decided she would not go crawling back to Fresno, no matter what.

Besides, Donny, formally Chung Yun, seemed to like Vegas a lot. His English was improving day by day, he made friends at school, other kids who were either dragged or escaped from Southeast Asia, and he seemed to have money to throw around. A couple of times, Won Ju wanted to ask him where he got the money, but he seemed happy for the first time in his life, so she stopped herself from looking into it. Besides, she wasn't his mother.

So she worked graveyard shifts and slept during the day when Donny was at school. As she walked through the aisles between "Blazing Seven" dollar slots where the blue-haired ladies sat and pushed buttons like hungry rats hoping a pellet would drop, and the blackjack tables where men with cowboy hats and big bellies held two cards in one hand and sipped whiskey with the other, she envied her sleeping brother. When she walked past the spinning roulette wheel with her round tray, and a young man would slap her on the butt and wink, she envied her male brother. Some of these young men were like the old ladies in that they were mindlessly pushing buttons in hope that a pellet would come out. This was the second place that she'd lived in America, and her opinion of Americans was continuously spiraling downwards.

Occasionally, there would be tourists from Hawaii. These were the best customers. Some Hawaiian, some Japanese, these guys from paradise were always politely joking around and always tipping well. Sure, they hit on her, but it was usually not a hands-on approach. They would smile and joke in their peculiar style of speaking, and they would whisper in each other's ears when she walked away with their orders, but they would rarely touch. Besides, they actually looked like they had fun gambling. Their hope of winning seemed more optimistic. Cigarettes dangling from their lips, lame jokes for the dealers, these guys were actually having fun even when they were losing their shirts. Won Ju appreciated this optimism and wondered, even dreamed, what this place Hawaii must be like. She knew her stepfather was from there, but she figured that time in Korea and Fresno must've simply jaded him. Who could be unhappy when they lived in a place surrounded by white sandy beaches and crystal-blue oceans? Even though Won Ju didn't know how to swim, she wanted to go to this place. Surfers and hula girls, even a potential drowning victim could appreciate it.

But there weren't enough Hawaiians to make the job a good one. The ones who pushed her buttons weren't limited to the customers. The button-pushers, the arm-pullers, extended to her fellow employees.

A couple of bartenders who she knew kept track of how many cocktail waitresses they slept with would put their hands on her when she'd be dropping off empty glasses. Middle-aged pit bosses would slide her obscene notes with a hundred-dollar chip and scowl when she gave it back to them. Dealers who would be joking around with the customers would slap her on the butt and laugh as she went to get another round of drinks. Sometimes they would say, "Gotta love Asians. Best servers in the business. And they know their role."

Customers would laugh along with the dealer. Won Ju was beginning to understand what was wrong with Americans. They thought they deserved. The land of milk and honey. Even those blue-haired ladies playing the Blazing Sevens thought they deserved. So they waited. Pushed buttons and waited. But she blamed herself too. She never fought back. She knew it was her fault for not fighting back. She would remember the airport in Fresno. She could not help but think that they were better than her.

Coming home at five-thirty in the morning, showering, then cooking breakfast for her brother was routine. She didn't mind. First she went to the bathroom and removed her makeup and false eyelashes. Then the shower, followed by the application of creams and moisturizers. She then went to the kitchen in her silk bathrobe, wearing a towel on her head. She cooked rice, scrambled three eggs, and fried bacon. Kimchee seemed impossible to come by in Las Vegas, so she made her own and added it to the breakfast menu. She woke her brother up at six-thirty. He usually didn't get up right away, so she shook him again at six-forty-five. After taking at least thirty minutes to get ready and do his hair, he emerged every day facing the challenge of finishing off more food than his stomach could fit. Three eggs, five pieces of bacon, a huge pile of rice, kimchee, a glass of orange juice, a glass of milk, and a Hostess powdered sugar donut. Won Ju watched as the sweat beaded on his forehead, his cheeks puffed up, and his face gave off a look of determination. She shook her head while writing the usual tardy note for him. He was almost never on time for school.

When he left, she cleared the table and was happy that he did not vomit that time. Sometimes he ate himself sick. She suspected why he did it. He was small. He was about five-seven and a hundred thirty pounds. Many of the other boys at school must've dwarfed him. She imagined the sight of six-foot-two adolescents driving him crazy. He wanted to be an American, and that not only meant you had to speak grammatically incorrect, accent-free English, but it also meant being big. To be a good American, you had to be big. Robert Redford, Paul Newman, they were big and tough. Elvis was so big it showed even in his hair and stomach. Sean Connery, even though he wasn't really American, was huge. Her brother didn't want to look like some bellhop in a James Bond movie, he wanted to be James Bond. Even Americans accepted that James Bond was cooler than all Americans. Won Ju knew it was only a matter of time before her brother began puking out martinis, shaken, not stirred. He was already smoking cigarettes with that between-the-index-and-middle-finger style that indicated that he was in absolutely no hurry to finish.

Won Ju smiled while making her brother's bed. She walked to his dresser and pulled out an open pack of Marlboros. Cowboy smokes. She pulled one out. She looked at his John Lennon poster. She liked his hair shorter. She walked to the small kitchen. She looked over her shoulder. Still looking for her mother. She lit the cigarette on the gas stove. She walked to her own room and looked in the mirror while smoking. She didn't like the way she smoked. Her face scrunched up, fighting against the white plumes slowly attacking her face. She smoked quickly and too efficiently, like she was a blue-collar worker who only had a couple of minutes to devour the cigarette. She smoked like she ate. She put out the cigarette and went to the kitchen, where she made herself a small portion of kimchee and rice. It took her fifteen minutes to prepare her food, eat it, and wash her dishes. Twenty minutes later, after taking the towel off of her head, she was fighting to get some sleep.

She could never sleep. Though her body was often weary, her mind was constantly racing. About five to ten minutes were spent in calculator mode, trying to figure out if rent for the two-bedroom walk-up, grocery, and clothes bills were going to be covered with a hundred to spare for her savings. This thinking about money brought about thoughts on her mother. She wondered, sometimes for over an hour, what her mother was doing in Korea, why she left, was she ever going to return. Then she struggled with the guilt of leaving her stepfather and her baby half-sister alone in Fresno. The guilt was fought by thoughts on how her brother seemed so happy living in Las Vegas.

Her mother. Everything started from there. She left because of money, she'd said. Won Ju didn't believe her because ever since she'd known what money was, her mother had had a lot of it. How could one of the most celebrated actresses in Korea not have it? The marriage must've been falling apart. What did her mother expect? Her mother could not have forgotten what she could have been, what she was. Fresno had to have reminded her mother that in America, she was nothing.

Won Ju got out of bed and walked to her bureau mirror. She'd do it often whenever she thought about her mother. Tanned, roundish face. Tanned roundish face. Why did her mother not take her with her?

She did not hate Henry Lee. She did not hate baby Darian. She knew that the reason she had been the housekeeper there was because no one else would do it. Henry would not do it. Donny would definitely not do it. And even her mother had been bad at it when she was around. Well, if no one else was going to do it, why should she? Besides, she was just as unqualified; there were servants in Korea. She was the only one that tried to do it, and that was simply not fair. A girl should find a husband before she becomes a wife and mother. And when Henry had asked if it would be possible to iron his boxer underwear, that was the last straw. Won Ju walked back to the kitchen and ran water over the lit cigarette. The red glow became a black sludge. She went to bed knowing she was right, but feeling the guilt shake her every time she was about to fall asleep.

She woke up when her brother's key entered the door. Her eyes opened and Donny peeked into her bedroom. He smiled slyly. She waved him in. He walked in with a couple of school books and looked around the room. "You should put poster on walls. Your room look like hotel room, not home."

His English was always improving. She replied in Korean, "I have no idols."

His round face combined smile and frown. He said in English: "Then who you want to be?"

She thought about that and couldn't come up with anything. She said in Korean, "I don't know, who's famous for doing something good?"

His smile disappeared as he thought. Won Ju wanted to tease him about his futile attempts at growing a mustache and sideburns, but she knew she would hurt his feelings. Finally, he laughed. "I don't know. Richard Nixon?"

Won Ju had tried to understand what exactly what Watergate was about, but couldn't. But she always thought that America must've known something was going to happen by just looking at that man. She wondered if Americans would learn their lesson from this, but then what if someone just tried to put a handsome actor up there? Americans would surely be fooled by it. The impatient look her brother gave her broke her out of her mental rambling. "I don't know what to say," she said.

Donny switched to Korean. "You never know what to say. You should speak more English, sister. Thinking in two languages broadens the mind. I feel like I'm getting smarter. I want you to have the same feeling."

Won Ju sat up. "It's confusing. Besides, I hear enough English at work. 'Nice ass, honey.' 'I could use a geisha girl.' 'Nice hooters.' There's a lot of English, but not much thinking going on there."

Donny walked to her dresser and sat on it. "Those are compliments. You know what? You need a boyfriend. That might help."

She wanted a boyfriend. It wasn't that she was that lonely; she often liked being alone with her thoughts, but she was curious as to what it would be like. Of course she saw boyfriends and girlfriends on TV's *General Hospital*. Who killed Phil? Howe's vasectomy. Lesley buying her newly found daughter, Laura, everything her heart desired. But she suspected that that wasn't really what it was like. She wasn't sure, but she suspected. "I don't want one," she said. "I'm too busy."

"I found a girlfriend."

She was surprised. "Really?"

"You don't look surprised."

"I'm not. What's she like?"

Donny sighed. "Well, she makes me think of all of these wonderful things."

"That sounds good. Is she pretty?"

Donny frowned. "Not really. But she looks better and better the more I'm around her. She also makes me hungry."

"For food?"

"Yah."

Donny slowly opened one of his books. He pulled out a joint. It was the first one Won Ju had ever seen. She wanted to demand that he flush it down the toilet, but she stopped herself. "You are crazy. You could go to jail."

Donny laughed. "Nobody goes to jail for pot. This is America. The government knows this is fun, harmless stuff. Besides, don't worry about the police, the paranoia comes afterwards."

Won Ju stood up. "I'm not smoking that."

"Don't be such an old woman, sister. It's fun. I brought this home especially for you. It's a thank-you gift."

"Where did you get the money to pay for that? For that matter, where do you get your money, period?"

"I'll tell you if you smoke this with me."

Won Ju was definitely curious, but more about the marijuana than the money. Like her thoughts on having a boyfriend, marijuana was something that she heard about, but never experienced. It was supposed to be really good, but again she was skeptical. Besides, she had to work that night. "What else is in it for me?" she asked.

"I'll cook you dinner for an entire week."

She knew he'd never follow through with it, but she nodded anyway. She said in English, "Let's geta high, den."

Donny jumped off the dresser and cheered.

-3-

AS SHE SUSPECTED, weed, she called it "weed" now, was overrated. But it was still good. It certainly helped her sleep. It also made her job easier. She didn't feel as self-conscious; she didn't feel as guilty. She was a joint-a-day smoker, half when she got home, half before she went to work. Because it wasn't dangerous, and it did not affect her performance, she didn't see any problems with it, except that it provided her with information that she'd rather have not known.

Donny had stolen from their mother. Jewelry and a curious silver knife, the stuff that their mother left behind, it all went to a local pawn shop. Two thousand dollars worth. Won Ju had been extremely upset when she first found out. Not even the weed helped, but after Donny calmed her down and explained it to her, it kind of made sense. The funny thing about it was that it really only took him one sentence to make sense out it for her. In fact, the sentence wasn't even declarative, or imperative, it was interrogative. "Do you think she's coming back?"

Of course not. She wasn't coming back. Who would? If Won Ju were her mother, would she come back? Seoul or Fresno? A city with hundreds of years of rich history versus a new city filled with farmers? The only thing that would bring her back was her children, and if her children were that important to her she wouldn't have left in the first place. No, Won Ju thought, the great actress Soong Nan Lee was not going to return to America.

Won Ju knew that her mother had left the silver knife behind. The night before she'd left, she told Won Ju to keep the knife close to her until her mother returned. Won Ju thought of it as a going-away gift, so she didn't want anything to do with it and left it in Fresno. But now here was her brother, who'd brought it with them and sold it, a priceless antique, for two hundred dollars at a pawn shop. He sold it to someone who would obviously not know its value, not that her brother did. But Won Ju wasn't angry. She didn't miss it. And in a way she was glad that it didn't go to waste. Besides, the knife only brought back bad memories. It reminded her of the first time she'd seen it, the day she came home from school tattered and beaten in Korea because of her Japanese ancestry. The image of her mother showing it to her was not a happy memory. She'd wanted her mother to hold her quietly that day, instead her mother showed her a side of the great actress that petrified her. She knew her mother could do practically anything, walk from North to South Korea barefooted over shrapnel, make an entire nation adore her, but it never occurred to Won Ju that her mother could kill. And just by looking at her that day, talking about the ancient knife meant to be wielded by virgins for protection, she knew that her mother could indeed kill. She'd wanted to kill. Not out of hurt pride or revenge, but it looked like Soong felt like killing was sometimes a necessity, and she'd be able to do it in a blink of an eye.

That afternoon years ago planted some extraordinary scenarios in Won Ju's mind. She knew they were ridiculous, but thought them anyway. How did her father, Dong Jin, really die? Had her mother met and fell in love with Henry Lee in secrecy, years before they supposedly met, and plotted his death? They certainly both had the connections. She knew her mother made great men in Korea fall to their knees. She knew that Henry Lee was considered a dangerous and powerful man in Korea. They could have gotten it done. A simple drop in a cup of tea or a glass of scotch. Some kind of top-secret American poison. They could have done it.

But Won Ju knew she was inventing things in her mind, but she never had control over her mind's inventions. So she'd laugh at herself and shrug it off. But she'd found out that afternoon that her mother could kill. It was something that awed Won Ju because she knew she never could. But then what could she do that her mother could?

Great people rarely have great children. Won Ju knew that. She was not destined for greatness. Greatness was not something handed to a person, like a birthday present handed from a parent; greatness was something earned. It was part tirelessness, part luck, part brilliance; it was to be tested by a puzzle impossible to solve. It was rarely obtained, rarely sustained, and never something given, but always something taken. Parents constantly try to give their children this, but it's like trying to hand someone a cloud from the sky. It is impossible enough to hold on to a cloud, much less place it in another's grasp. Won Ju was a cocktail waitress in one of the many gaudy casinos in the middle of a North American desert. It was a dry place with hardly a cloud in the sky. Won Ju thought this as she put out her joint and got ready for work.

Getting drugs in Las Vegas in the 1970s was hardly a problem. Won Ju had known she could've approached just about any one of her fellow employees and they would've happily obliged, despite their surprise. She'd chosen Andy Martinez, "Chief" to the employees and patrons who were his friends, not because he was the biggest reputed bartender/drug dealer in the casino, but because of the way he looked. Andy was a half-Cherokee/half-Mexican, who, though dark, had eyes that seemed familiar to Won Ju. Indian eyes. Asian eyes. Some of her ancestors had once walked the Bering Strait, and Andy, though she thought it extremely corny, could have been a cousin eight thousand times removed.

After Won Ju clocked in, she picked up her round tray from behind the bar and began working tables. She emptied and replaced ashtrays, went back and forth from the bar to serve whiskey sours, gin and tonics, and Marlboro Reds. Sometimes she noticed that she didn't even hear the customers anymore. The screams of anger or delight that had once made her jump were as quiet to her as role of the dice on the felt surface of a crap table or the shuffling of cards in skilled hands. This alarmed her a bit. She thought it might be the weed, but then realized that no matter what the cause, it was a good thing. Deafness was sometimes a good thing.

The smiles appeared on her face, and she realized this no longer took conscious effort. Half the time she didn't even know what the customers said to her, not because of the language barrier—she understood English quite well—but because she no longer cared what they were saying. She walked through the flirtations, the lewd comments as if they were cigarette smoke. She kept on smiling. This was her lot in life. Did her mother even try to give her greatness?

About halfway through her shift, Won Ju took her first break. As she was quickly smoking her cigarette in the break room, Andy approached her. "Slow night," he said as he lit a cigarette.

He wasn't very tall, but he was wide. Perhaps his most impressive feature was his neck. His neck looked broader than his head. She wondered how long the strap for his bow tie must be. "Yeah," she said.

"Hey, did you see that guy at the bar? The one with the blue pinstriped suit?"

Won Ju often saw him at the bar. He was a quiet man, and a terrific tipper, an ideal customer. "Yes," she said," he seem very nice man."

Andy leaned his head back and laughed. His neck expanded as air left his lungs. She expected the top button of his tuxedo shirt to pop off. "Not to everybody." He leaned towards Won Ju and whispered, "He's a mob guy."

Won Ju shrugged. "But don't worry," Andy said, "he's a friend. That's my supplier."

Won Ju wondered why Andy was telling her this. She was hardly a prized customer. She only bought joints from him a few at a time. So she just nodded. "Listen," he said. "I'm actually pretty connected. If you need anything, just let me know. These guys take care of me."

She put out her cigarette in the ashtray. "I go back now."

Andy gently grabbed her arm. "Wait," he said. "Hold on. Listen, I know you don't really talk to anyone here because of the language thing, but everybody needs friends. I mean, some of the other bartenders and waitresses think you're stuck up, but I know it's just because you're shy. Let me be your friend."

He let go of her arm and put out his cigarette. Won Ju didn't know whether she should respond or walk back to the floor. She looked at her watch, then looked at Andy. He was smiling. He seemed very nice, and it was the first time someone tried to make friends with her since she'd been to America. Actually, she guessed there were others that had tried to be friendly with her, but she never knew what to do. This was the first time someone had actually come out and asked for friendship using the word "friend." So after thinking about it, she felt like she at least owed him a response. "O.K.," she said.

He laughed. "So we're friends?"

"Yes," she said as she walked back out to the floor.

■ ■ ■

A week later, Won Ju was preparing for the first date. Not only was it her and Andy's first date, but it was the first date of her life. Donny watched as she meticulously glued on her false eyelashes in front of the bathroom mirror. He seemed just as excited as she was, and he teased her relentlessly. "Sis has a hot date. Is Sis going to get lucky tonight? Wait until the lucky guy sees her beautiful eyelashes flutter. He won't be able to control himself."

Won Ju carefully picked up her cigarette, which was balancing at the edge of the basin. She took a drag and looked into the mirror at her brother. "Shut up before I put this cigarette out on you."

Donny laughed and took the cigarette from her. He took a drag and blew the smoke in her face. She playfully grabbed his earlobe and pulled it. "So, Brother," she said as she returned to her eyelashes, "do you have any tips?"

"Yeah, when you make out with him, remember to cram your tongue into his mouth immediately. He'll like that."

"You are disgusting."

"Also, grab his behind firmly. Dig those fingernails in. Just pretend you are a lion devouring prey."

She did not feel like the predator in this situation. After she'd consented to the friendship with Andy, she'd thought that was that. She'd also never really had a friend before, and she assumed that all it meant was that when she'd see him, she'd just smile and say "hi." Maybe they'd smoke cigarettes together during breaks, or maybe they'd have a drink after work, but what else did you do with friends? In Korea, she'd seen friends on the playground, joking around, playing sports, and in high school she'd seen girls hanging out after school, smoking cigarettes and flirting with boys, but she really did not know what adult friends did together. In Korea, her mother had "associates," not really friends, and her stepfather had seemed perfectly content in isolation in the middle of all of those grape vineyards in Fresno, so she had no idea what adult friends did together. On TV in *General Hospital*, she'd seen adult friends, but all they seemed to do was withhold information from each other. What did one do if they did not have any information on their friend? She did not even know anything about Andy except he was a bartender who sold drugs on the side, he apparently had mafia connections, and his neck was enormous. Was it typical to know so little about a friend? "Chung Yun," she said, "we're just friends."

"English, sister, English. We've been cheating long enough. I think you need the practice for tonight."

She thought carefully before she spoke. "Friends. Not boyfriend-girlfriend." That was the other thing that disturbed Won Ju. Why did her first friend have to be a man? It made her feel uncomfortable. She'd always felt uncomfortable around all people, except for her mother and brother, but adult men made her feel especially uncomfortable. They were so big. And Andy was no exception. And over the last week, he'd pursued her relentlessly until she finally consented in going out with him. She definitely did not feel like a predator. If she were a predator, she would not feel startled every time his neck expanded to unleash a deep roaring laugh. "So, Sister," Donny said, "make sure you wear high heel. Nice, sexy. He like."

Won Ju palmed her brother's face and pushed it away. She put on lipstick and closely inspected her hair one last time. It felt heavy with hairspray. The doorbell rang. Donny excitedly went to answer it. She put away her cosmetics and washed her hands. She dried them and tugged on the skirt of her newly purchased white dress. It was too tight, but he was already there. Before walking out the door, she kissed her brother on the cheek. Donny seemed disturbed by the appearance of her date. She left wondering what he was thinking; sure that it was some sort of criticism. Perhaps he was expecting Sean Connery.

The date started with a fine, candlelight dinner in a quiet, muted-light restaurant. It seemed that Andy too watched his share of television, because it was one of those scenes out of a soap opera. However, usually, on TV the couple seemed perfectly comfortable. Won Ju was terrified. The quiet bothered her especially. Every time, no matter how careful she was, she put her polished, silver fork on the plate, she heard a conspicuous clang. Whenever she took a sip of wine, she heard herself swallow. Her chewing seemed the loudest to her. She wondered if Andy was as conscious of the sound her jaws were making when chewing food as she was. He didn't seem to notice, but perhaps he was just being polite. She barely touched her swordfish as Andy devoured his twenty-two-ounce T-bone steak.

He ate quickly, yet neatly, careful not to get any food on his silk shirt, which was buttoned a little too far down for Won Ju's taste. He was wearing a thick gold rope chain. Won Ju wondered if that was why he left the top two buttons undone. He didn't talk very much when he ate, and Won Ju had no problem with that. She had enough problems trying to keep the noise down at her side of the table.

When they finished dinner, and were walking back to the car, Andy politely asked, "So, where to next? Your choice."

Won Ju had no idea how to answer. She wanted to go home, but knew it would be impolite to say that. Besides, she did not know where to go anyway. Her life was spent only at work and home. She thought about what the proper answer would be, but couldn't come up with anything specific. So she simply said, "Someplace not too quiet."

Andy clapped his hands together and smiled as if he knew exactly what she meant. This puzzled her because she did not know what she'd meant. She got a little nervous about their next destination.

■ ■ ■

He took her to the loudest place she'd ever been to before: a disco. It was dark, much like the restaurant, but the music blared out of the speakers with so much power that when she concentrated, she could feel the floor shake beneath her high heels. All of the faces around her contorted as the people tried to communicate with each other. She and Andy were standing at the bar. He was attempting to order a gin and tonic for himself, and a glass of white wine for her. She already felt tipsy from the wine they drank at the restaurant, so she promised herself that this would be her last glass. Andy handed her the glass of chardonnay, and yelled in her ear, "Do you want to dance?"

She could barely hear him. She'd never danced before. The dance floor was filled with people who were basically involved in the same movements, but skill levels definitely varied. It seemed, overall, that the women were better at it than the men. This made her more nervous about dancing, so she politely declined. "Maybe later," she said.

While she and Andy were standing at the bar, sipping their drinks, Won Ju once again became aware of the quiet. Although there was noise, as well as bodies, constantly passing the space between them, neither was contributing. She did not want to talk mostly because she was hesitant to enter the onramp of noise between them; it was intimidating, yet she was surprised that Andy was so quiet. It was as if he were waiting for something. Finally, his voice entered the steam of sound and traveled to her ear. "Are you bored?" he asked.

She shook her head. He smiled, looked around, then reached into his pocket. He pulled out two tiny slips of paper. He put one in his mouth and gave the other to her. "Here, take this."

She took the tiny slip of paper and asked, "What this?"

"It's kind of like weed. You'll like it. Just stick it under your tongue."

She did not want to take it, but again, she also didn't want to be impolite. Besides, she watched him slip it into his mouth, and he seemed fine. She decided to wait several minutes before taking it, just in case it started to make him act crazy. After a few minutes, Andy seemed fine; in fact he was less jittery. He'd said it was like weed, which she found very calming, and because he looked so calm, she shrugged and put the tiny slip of paper under her tongue.

At first, she thought the drug a fraud. She felt nothing. She should've known that something so small could hardly affect her. She was still bored and longed to go home. Andy kept trying to convince her to dance, but each time she refused politely. Then, as she almost finished her glass of wine, things started to look fuzzy. She thought it was the wine, but as her vision and sense of sound seemed to get progressively worse, she knew it was the drug. When she looked at the dance floor, she no longer saw groups of two spinning, instead she saw each couple turn into something that to her looked like a pulsating egg. All of these eggs seemed to contract with the beat of the music, which Won Ju enjoyed watching, but when the music first slowed, then became nothing but the sound of an enormous, two-story heart beating, Won Ju began to feel very sick. She felt as if she were in a gigantic human body, in a huge womb, and the oppressive, pulsating noise was driving her outside.

But she couldn't find the way out. She fell to her knees. Suddenly, she felt something tugging on her and dragging her out of this place that seemed familiar, but very ugly. Won Ju was grateful. "Take me home, please," she said. It was the clearest, phonetically most concise sentence she'd ever spoken in English.

■ ■ ■

When Won Ju woke up, she was lying on a loveseat in an unfamiliar living room. She sat up slowly, and saw Andy straddling a chair, smiling at her. "You had a bad trip," he said.

Won Ju's vision was still blurred, but she knew she wasn't home. "Take me home, please," she said, again.

"Not yet," he said.

Andy stood up and walked to his turntable. He pulled out a record and put it on. The sudden sound made Won Ju jump. It was a song she'd remembered. It was the Four Tops, "Can't Help Myself." She liked the song, but she was still hearing things in slow motion. It sounded like the song was being played at half-speed, and though the voices started crisper, they slowed until the sound became grotesque. It was as if the singers were melting. They were no longer professing love. They were moaning like dying animals.

That's when she noticed Andy. He was sitting right next to her, putting his mouth on hers. She felt his tongue slide into her mouth. The slimy texture disgusted Won Ju, so she tried to push away. But one of his hands was palming the back of her head, while the other was moving up her white dress. She put both her hands on Andy's head and pushed with all her might. Finally she managed to get a half a foot of distance between their faces, and said, "Take me home, please." The tension in her throat told her that she'd screamed it, but it sounded like a whisper to her. Andy smiled and tore her underwear off with the hand under her dress. The sound of moaning animals became unbearable for her, and she knew she had to get out or she would be driven mad. As his face neared hers, she took close notice of his left eyeball. It looked so vulnerable, almost like a grape. She wanted to pop it, so she jammed her thumb into it. The head flew back, then a horrible scream followed. Just as she got up to scramble for the door, a fist came flying towards her. It didn't hurt. But she found herself dazed on the other side of the room.

She tried to get up, but the screaming was getting closer and closer, so she instinctively crumbled into the fetal position. She felt another stunning blow on her face, and her cheek hit the floor hard. It was linoleum, she noticed. Then there was a weight on her. She fought hard against it, but she felt like she was drowning in the middle of the ocean. Despite how hard she tried to get the water off of her, it was impossible. Before she blacked out, she noticed another voice joined the quartet in the painful moaning. She wondered who it was as her face was being pushed into the sticky linoleum floor.

■ ■ ■

When she woke up, she was curled up in the passenger seat of Andy's car. They were parked outside of her apartment. It was still dark. Her entire body ached. She looked down. There was blood all over her dress. Andy leaned over her. She flinched. He opened the door. "Now remember," he said, "don't say a goddamn word. You remember my friend in the casino? I could have you and your brother killed," he snapped his fingers, "just like that. Buried out in the desert."

Won Ju scurried out of the car, ignoring the pain. She ran up the stairs, breaking a heel. She didn't stop to pick it up. She opened the door and headed straight for the bathroom. Turning on the shower, and looking at the bruises on her arms, legs, and face, she asked herself, how am I going to go to work tonight? She entered the shower and sat down. She fell asleep and felt like she didn't want to wake up again.

The frantic knocking on the door woke her up. "C'mon, Sis, I really have to piss bad. By the way, where's breakfast?"

She didn't answer and closed her eyes, trying to go back to sleep. The water was cold by then, but she didn't care. The knocking continued. "Are you O.K.?"

It was an interesting question. She felt O.K. as long as she didn't move. She would be fine if she never had to stand up, open her eyes, and talk ever again. She stayed perfectly still and listened to Donny attempt to break the door down. After several tries, he stopped. Then about a minute later, she heard someone tinkering with the lock. Won Ju opened her eyes. Donny came in holding his shoulder with one hand and a butter knife in the other. He stood over her. "I'm calling an ambulance," he said, as he ran out of the bathroom. Won Ju couldn't bear it anymore. She closed her eyes, hoping Donny wouldn't trip and stab himself with the knife. Then she noticed something peculiar. She was grinding her teeth. She tried to stop, but couldn't. It was a weak effort, though. Especially after she realized that the slow, methodical, pendulum that was her lower jaw was her only comfort.

-4-

When Soong's first husband had been brought back to her home, cold and already dead, she hated what she later considered the primitiveness of South Korea during that time. What if there had been ambulances? What if there had been emergency rooms? Who knows? Her husband may have lived for another twenty years. When Soong had first arrived in the United States, that was one of the things about her new country that appealed to her. People could be saved here.

However, when her second husband took permanent residence in a Long Island hospital, she began to consider her first husband's death a merciful one. It had been then that she'd realized hospitals and emergency care did not prolong life; they prolonged death. They also cost a fortune. Medicare covered eighty percent of her second husband's medical bill, but even with that, as the bills came piling in, it was as if they were staying at the Ritz Carlton. After her second husband died, and the bills continued to roll in, Soong realized that things needed to be liquidated. The store had to go. The house had to go. By the time she'd been ready to fly to Hawaii, she only had four bags of belongings. It seemed to Soong that in America, death was not only a black-hooded figure holding a scythe, he had a calculator hidden somewhere in that robe, too: the patron saint of repossession.

But she'd learned to hate hospitals years before that. When Soong arrived in Las Vegas, she hated the hospital before she even saw it. She did not even want to be in the country. Things had been good in Korea. She ran a restaurant that practically ran itself; she appeared in several movies in supporting roles; her star power, which she told herself she never liked anyway, was long gone because of the fickleness of audiences and the army of younger actresses that rose after her time. Chung Han was supportive, never oppressive. And she kept up her responsibilities. She sent money to Henry bimonthly. It was enough to keep the farm aboveground and support Darian. Why would she come back? Her two eldest children were adults, at least she'd been an adult at their age, and her American daughter was being taken care of by her American husband. What could she contribute to the life of that child but money? Darian had the adoring and everpresent love of one parent and the financial support of the other. Soong supposed that this would be enough for her. It was more than she'd ever had. It was more than her two eldest children ever had. Soong had begun telling herself that she did not need to return. They were all better off with her in a place where she could make money.

But with one phone call, she'd been boarding a plane in Seoul. Now, two days later, she was in Las Vegas, dodging the merciless sun rays, attempting to find a shaded path to the entrance of the hospital, where her daughter needed her. And when she located the room, which she would later realize was in the psychiatric ward, and saw her skinny son with huge hair, making a ridiculous and futile attempt to grow sideburns, leaning against the bed where her broken daughter lay, she knew that she would probably not get back to Seoul ever again.

Donny stood up, "I think she was mugged," he said. Then he shrugged, not looking at his mother. "I don't know why she's like this. She has only spoken once since I found her. She asked for her purse, and that's when she called you."

Nobody had told Donny what had happened. Soong took a chair and dragged it next to the bed. "They only let me visit an hour a day," Donny said.

She sat down. "Leave," she said.

Donny quickly responded. "You have your nerve. You leave us and go back home. Now you come back and think you can tell me what to do. I'm surprised Won Ju even called you. You have been dead to us. We were doing just fine without you. You should leave. We do not need you."

It sounded rehearsed. Soong wondered how much time her son had spent thinking about what he was going to say to her. He'd probably also spent a lot of time thinking about whether or not he was going to say it at all. She was glad that he'd said it. It demonstrated strength to her. She turned to him. "Please, son. Just wait outside. I need to talk to your sister alone."

Donny was about to say something else, but seemed to change his mind. As he walked out, he said, "Hurry up. The nurse will kick us out soon. This is a crazy ward. We cannot stay here too long."

Soong turned to her daughter. She was curled in a fetal position with her back facing her mother. Her hair was sprawled out on the pillow. The strands looked so stiff, like fossils on the white pillowcase. She had an IV tube running from her arm. Soong knew that she probably wasn't eating, and she was overcome by one feeling: rage. She stood up and walked to the other side of the bed. Won Ju was staring vacantly at the wall. "Who?" Soong asked.

Soong was surprised that her daughter responded immediately. Still keeping her eyes focused on an empty portion of the white wall, she said, "Andy Martinez. He works with me at the California. I don't know how I am going to go back to work. I have to go pretty soon, though, or they will fire me."

"I will call the police."

Won Ju's eyes rolled up at Soong. "Please, don't. Please, don't. Just take me home, please."

"I will kill him."

Won Ju didn't say anything. She closed her eyes. Then she said, "If you call the police, he will kill us. He said so. He knows some important people."

She was like a child. Soong was shaking. She fought with herself to maintain control. She wanted to rip the entire world apart, even her curled-up daughter. She closed her eyes. Then she realized that she'd been holding her breath since she last spoke. She let out a powerful breath. "You and your brother will go back to California. I will take care of things here, and meet you there."

Won Ju's eyes remained closed. "Why can't we go and live someplace nice. I want to live someplace nice. Like maybe Hawaii."

"Wherever you want to go. We will all pack our things, me, you, Chung Yun, your stepfather and Darian. And we will go wherever you want to go."

"Hawaii."

Soong bit her lip. She remembered something. It wasn't a thing that could have possibly prevented this, but it suddenly became very important to her. "Now you have to listen to me carefully. Years ago, I gave you something. It was a silver knife. Do you remember? I left it at your stepfather's house for you."

"I remember."

"Where is it?"

"You have to promise me you won't get mad."

"I promise."

"I mean it."

"I promise."

"ChungYun brought it here with us.Then he sold it.We needed the money…"

Soong was heading out the door. She pushed it open and saw her son sitting on the floor. She began to kick him as hard as she could. He curled up, yelling, "What did I do?"

One of her heels broke on his head. She continued to kick violently. She was screaming, "You did this! You did this!"

The nurses came running, attempting to restrain her. Despite the fact that these nurses were experts in restraining, and twice her size, it took three of them to get her off her son. She heard her daughter screaming from behind the door, "You promised! You promised!"

The voice was hoarse and a lot softer than Soong's. It took a couple of seconds for Soong to soak in her daughter's words. Suddenly, they sent a chill through her. She had promised. She had promised years ago that she would not let this happen to her daughter. She had lied. A feeling of crushing self-hatred filled her. She felt faint, but managed to remain standing, with the help of the nurses. Donny stood up. He glared at his mother. "I didn't do this, you did. And you know it.You know it."

Soong looked at the nurses who held her against the wall. They were obviously disoriented because they couldn't understand a word the three of them were saying. For all they knew, Soong, Donny, and Won Ju could have been threatening to kill each other. Donny shook his head. Blood was trickling down his forehead. One of the nurses approached him. "I hate you," he said.

"Where did you sell it? Where?"

Donny smiled. "You are mad because I sold some of your jewelry and old trinkets.You greedy bitch.Always money." He reached into his back pocket.The nurse approaching him paused. He pulled out his wallet. He threw a slip of paper at Soong. Despite the fact that he seemed to throw it as hard as he could, the slip only traveled a foot from his hand, then floated downward like a feather. "Take it.

Your daughter is sick in there and all you care about is your stuff. I hate you."

Soong broke loose from the nurses, limped toward the slip on her one broken heel, and picked up the slip. She walked back into her daughter's room, while the nurses gently tried to restrain her. She picked up her purse, looked at her daughter who was now sitting up and staring at her. Soong walked out. "I'll be back for you," she said.

Donny was holding gauze on his head. She shook her head. She wanted to say something, but couldn't. She began to walk out of the hospital, with the nurses following her. She ignored them and made it to the exit. She marched out into the sun, calling the first taxi she saw. She gave the cab driver the slip of paper. "Right away, ma'am," he said.

■ ■ ■

By the time she'd gotten the silver knife back, and was back at the hospital, Soong had cooled down. She was glad that she only had to pay two hundred dollars for it. It didn't really surprise her, though. How could he know that he had sold a priceless Korean antique older than this country for two hundred dollars? It wasn't a neoclassical painting, nor was it a doubloon from a sunken pirate ship, it was a slightly tarnished, unassuming silver knife, worn down by time.

After regaining most of her composure back, she was also amazed at the need she felt in getting the knife back. Why? she asked herself. She felt like a child awakened in the middle of the night, looking frantically for that doll or blanket that had been with her all of her life. Soong considered it very pathetic. An old woman feeling the need to have a symbol of security in her hands when security had already been decimated by a rude awakening, a nightmare that did not disappear with the arrival of consciousness. But despite the fact that she knew she was being irrational, she could not help but be comforted by the knife in her purse as she sat in the hospital lobby.

Cold rage was a funny feeling to her. It seemed like a contradiction. She was sitting there knowing that her mind was not clouded. It was sharp. In fact, she felt as if it were sharper than usual. The heat on the rims of her ears was gone, and she could calculate. What now? She would get her daughter out of this place. Police? No, her daughter would never forgive her. How could she make it up? She never could. But something had to be done; her rage demanded it. Kill him. It was the only option Soong had been thinking about since she'd received the phone call from her daughter. But her energy had to go elsewhere. It had to be spent putting her daughter back together.

There were at least a hundred and fifty Martinezes in the phone book. More than twenty started with some form of the letter "A." "A." "A." "A." "A D." "A E." "A R." "Abraham." "Al." "Albert." "Alfred." "Alex." "Alma." "Andrew." "Ann" "Anthony." "Arlo…" She looked back up at "Andrew." There was an address. Soong took out her address book and wrote it down. She closed the book and walked back to the chairs in the lobby. She curled up, hugging her purse. She suddenly felt very tired, and was soon learning that there were two places she could never fall asleep: hospitals and planes. She'd been up for two days, and was sure that her daughter had been awake longer than she had.

-5-

THE DOCTORS WOULDN'T release her. Soong was the only person that Won Ju would talk to, which the doctors decided was insane. Soong moved out of the hospital and got a room at the California Hotel and Casino. And though she wasn't a big drinker, she found herself at the bar every evening, sipping a scotch on the rocks, her husband's drink, peering at the thick-necked bartender whom Soong found intolerably loud, obnoxious, and unrepentant.

She committed his schedule to memory. Monday, Wednesday, Friday, and Saturday, 11 PM to 5 AM. She wondered whether this is what her husband had done as an American military intelligence officer in Korea. Spy. Spy with detachment, caution, and thoroughness. She still hadn't called her husband since she'd been back in the States; in fact she talked to no one except Won Ju. She didn't even talk to her son, whom she also saw at the hospital every day. She was proud of him. He loved his sister. But she didn't know what to say to him. He hated her, but right now, she could not be concerned with that. She could not be concerned with any of her children except the first now. Soong realized then that she had only so much room in her heart, as if it could only concentrate on one thing at a time. How can one actively love more than one person at a time? She did not feel that it was possible.

At that moment, she was loving her daughter, and watching very closely the man that might have destroyed her. Immediately she knew why he'd won his daughter's confidence. He was friendly, outgoing, in fact, charming. He genuinely cared about those around him. It took Soong a half an hour of surveillance to discover his true talent: he was an actor. He was one of the millions walking the world with the talent, but not the luck. Besides, he was not handsome enough. He was dark, thick, and brutish. To Soong, he was disgusting. He lacked class. He looked to her like one of the lazy Mexican field hands that worked on her husband's grape farm, disguised in a coatless tuxedo. She was aware of her racism, but it didn't shame her. It was funny to her that she had to come and live in the United States to become a racist. Looking at the man who had nearly killed her daughter, Soong decided that all of Mexico could be wiped out in nuclear holocaust, and she would not care one bit.

She never spoke to him, except to order her drink. He'd tried to start up a conversation a couple of times, but she just looked at him blankly, communicating to him that she spoke no English. On this night, like every other night, Soong finished her drink, thought about it, reached for her wallet instead of her knife, and looked at him one last time before walking through the dullards that populated the casino who were hoping for luck trying to force luck, which to Soong was as pointless as trying to force gravity to allow you to fly. She looked at him for the last time that night and smiled. She looked around the casino, listening to the promises made by the sirens and the sound of coins falling on stainless steel. Does he know how close to death he is? Does he know, as the Americans love to say, that his luck is about to run out?

■ ■ ■

Andy Martinez' luck ran out the next day, the moment Soong found out that Won Ju was pregnant, and that she'd already decided to have an abortion. It amazed Soong that the same doctors who were proclaiming her daughter insane consented to the abortion immediately. When Won Ju told her, still curled up in the fetal position, Soong sat in the chair, shocked. Was anybody more unlucky than her daughter? A grandchild. Or as Won Ju called it, "An abomination."

She saw hate for the first time in her daughter. It made Soong glad. She knew that her daughter would find strength enough in her hatred to leave the hospital. But the child had to go. Soong understood it. She understood that in order for her daughter to live, the child must die. An abomination. Soong herself was an abomination. She was an unwanted child of rape. Perhaps that was why the mother she'd never known died. In a situation like this, one often had to go. If Won Ju had decided to choose as Soong's own mother might have done, Soong would've begged her daughter to reconsider. Yes, the child had to go. There would be other grandchildren. Soong and Won Ju would feed these future grandchildren with love as great as the rage they felt now. They would make up for it. But this one had to go. Soong looked at her daughter. They were thinking the same thing. Without saying goodbye, Soong walked away knowing that one would not be enough. Two had to pay the price for this. Because, though Soong was sure it would sound irrational to others, it made perfect sense to her. The one who created her grandchild also destroyed it. The destruction came before the conception. Time, for Soong at that moment, became a very complex, but very clear thing. Why not destruction before birth? The lack of the linear made perfect sense to her.

■ ■ ■

She had been sitting on the porch for hours. After the hospital visit, after the unceremonious death of her first grandchild, after she'd watched her daughter sit up and eat solid food for the first time since she'd been in Las Vegas, after she'd gone back to her hotel room and stared at the address of the near, undearly departed, after she'd showered and dressed as she would on any day, after she'd gone to the bar marching past the slot machines that were in soldier formation and watched Andy Martinez enjoy his final day of work, after she took a taxi to the latest address scribbled in her address book, she 'd been sitting on the second step of the porch of the small, unassuming white house, staring at the neatly cut, dying light-brown grass on the tiny lawn divided in perfect halves by flat, cement walkway, waiting for that time of day when it was not quite day, but not quite night either, when she knew Andy Martinez would walk up, shoes clicking on the hard, gray path, past the dead grass, the shoes clicking like a crisp heartbeat, stopping when they reached her. She imagined it without passion, glee, or fear. In fact, to her, it was not imagination, really, it was the clairvoyance she'd felt when she realized that time was not only linear, that it did have more than one dimension. This was going to happen as if it had happened already.

At five-thirty five, the grass had no residue. It was the first thing Soong noticed as Andy pulled up to the curb in front of his house. It was odd to her, the lack of morning dew. It was like the beer bottles she'd noticed in the casino. They didn't sweat. The entire city seemed to lack condensation. She, herself, was not sweating one bit.

The second thing she'd noticed was the color of the sky. The sun was not visible, but present. The blue-black of night was being bleached by the approach of the star. Soong saw purple. It was a brilliant, cloudless, windless, starless purple that was all around her. These are the times when things happen, she thought. Sometimes you see it, and sometimes you don't but these are the times, the times of transition, the times when two giant forces such as day and night, heat and cold grate together, when things happen below.

Andy approached her frowning and without apprehension. "Who the hell are you? Oh, you're a guest at the hotel? But what the hell are you doing here?" He was obviously both irritated and shocked, though he tried to hide it with shoddy acting.

Soong stood up and gave him her most radiant smile. One hand was in her coat pocket while the other waved him in closer, like she wanted to whisper a secret into his ear. Andy shrugged, leaned over, and moved in closer. He wasn't that tall, but he was a lot taller than her. He casually moved the left side of his head to her mouth. His neck bulged like ripe fruit.

Soong was a little surprised by the fragility of human flesh. She'd cut open rotten oranges that had given more resistance to the blade.

-6-

IN HIGH SCHOOL, in English, Donny had to read *The Great Gatsby*. It was not as difficult for him as it was with other books in English. He couldn't even get through one page of Shakespeare. But he finished *The Great Gatsby*. It was the first book he read in English in its entirety.

But when the teacher, an old white-haired woman who talked in whispers, told the class what the book was about, it was as if he hadn't even read it. To her, it was a book about the danger of dreaming falsely, the danger of dreaming of money and beautiful girls, the danger of dreaming of becoming American. He knew better. The book was about the danger of being a big man and not having the gate locked to your swimming pool. In America, you must protect what is yours, and your own life is cluttered with the rest of your possessions. Lock them all in a closet. That was what *The Great Gatsby* was about.

They were not staying in Las Vegas, and he didn't have any say about it. He never had any say about anything. Did he want to go to those snotty private schools in Korea? No. Did he want to have that old, bent-back servant woman raising him, the one who would eat chicken legs with one foot perched on the rim of a garbage can, looking ridiculous, like she was a warlord enjoying her booty? No. Did he want to come to America? No. Now, he did not want to leave Las Vegas, but his mother was taking control again. She was talking about Hawaii. It was crazy. She was packing up her belongings, which included her children, neatly folding them into a suitcase, locking everything up, and taking only what she wanted. Sometimes she wanted the kids, sometimes she didn't. Donny thought of himself as one of her pets. He only went for the permanent moves.

And what happened when she'd left the last time, and like Jay Gatsby, didn't lock the gate? His sister was hurt. And since she had been here, had she even spoken to him? No. She'd kicked him in the head instead. He was treated like a dog who urinated on the carpet one too many times. In public, no less.

He thought they could've had a happy life in Korea. His mother was a star. He would have been the child of a star. He could have been Tom Buchanan, the rich, well-respected man with the beautiful wife. Instead he felt like Jay Gatsby, or actually Jimmy Gatz. He was a tourist and had to fight on his own for everything he felt he should have had already. How can one be expected to do such a thing? How can you create a closet of your own when you yourself are locked in a closet?

Yes, Donny thought, he stole from his own mother. Yes, it was wrong. But did she not owe him that much? Did she still not owe him? It was like she kept borrowing and borrowing from him, and he didn't have anything. It was like she kept borrowing, and he believed they both knew she would never be able to pay him back.

But I will get it back, Donny thought. He would squeeze and squeeze and squeeze until that rag of a woman would be so dry that she'd be stiffer than she was already. He would have his own closet with things locked away safely. In America, he supposed, considering what he'd read about and see on TV, these things are possible. A beautiful wife that others envy, a beautiful car that others envy, a beautiful life that others envy. He would become a big man. And he would lock the gate. Is it wrong to hate your mother? Probably. Is it relevant? He did not think so. Become a big man by any means necessary. He would do it, no matter how much it cost her. And as the Americans say, he mused, "So sue me."

LEARNING TO FLY

chapter nine

ARE MOTHERS BORN? Soong thought about this as she sat in the white, black, and yellow city bus that was taking her to Waianae. She felt safest on the bus; its size and lack of speed eased her fears of traffic fatalities. But it was top-heavy. She could tell that busses had a high center of gravity, especially when she would take the bus up the Ko'olau Mountains, down the windy roads, and into Kailua town to the restaurant. When the bus accelerated down the Pali Highway, she was aware of the high center of gravity, and felt as if the bus, when taking a sharp turn down the mountain, would topple over the low cement railing and fall off the cliff. If that didn't get her, she would fear the tunnel. A hole through a mountain felt unnatural to her. All of that earth pressing the round arch of the hollow. She anticipated the tunnel deflating every time the bus would pass through it. She knew something bad was going to happen whether caused by pressure or gravity, and the Pali Highway had both.

But today, she was heading towards the west side of the island, not the east, and this trip was almost all freeway. There were no mountains. And Soong was aware of how the landscape she passed turned from wet to dry. She thought about motherhood and wondered if she'd ever been cut out for it. Are women born to be mothers? She supposed that this notion could be challenged by the logical follow-up question. Are men born to be fathers? She supposed not everybody, no matter what gender, was up to the task. She'd never felt up to it. But she tried; she knew she tried.

Won Ju had told her to meet her at Safeway in Waianae. When Soong asked how she was supposed to know which Safeway to meet her at, Won Ju laughed and said, "There's only one. You can't miss it."

Soong did not think that it was an odd place to meet her daughter. She knew that Won Ju had an affinity for supermarkets. She was not a shopper, not even a window shopper, but for years, since the first time the entire family had moved to Hawaii, Soong remembered her daughter's desire to always go to a supermarket. Back then Soong had been keeping a close eye on her daughter, and she immediately noticed that Won Ju rarely bought anything. When she'd asked Won Ju about it, she said, "I don't know, it's therapy. I just look at all of that stuff, and I feel better. It's like I stop thinking when I look at meats and produce. There is nothing that stops my brain more than looking at a rack of pork short ribs."

Soong thought she had really gone mad. But over the years, she'd noticed that her daughter only did it in times of crisis. She did it before she got married, then when she was pregnant with Brandon. She did not abuse her therapy. So Soong thought that it was eccentric, but perfectly healthy. In fact, Soong envied the fact that she had a haven from herself.

It was a long bus ride, over an hour, and it gave Soong time to reflect on her family. She was tired of thinking about them, but it was all very astronomical to her. She was simply a planet revolving around a star, compelled by something as uninteresting and powerful as gravity, moving around and around, in a slow oval orbit. Sometimes she would be closer to it than other times, but she was never far enough away to break the monotony of gravity. And the star always burned. She felt like a dead planet, a moon. There was no cause, just carousel motion. Around and around and around.

She found it funny in a very unfunny way that when people have children, they have such high hopes. Parents think success when there is weakness and failure all around them. Soong felt that indeed most people were failures and weak. And it took her years to learn that her children, as chances would have it, were among them. Chung Yun, born with a dent in his baby chest, failing to fill it; Won Ju, who only just discovered anger in her forties. Did she only just realize that anger and strength are tied together?

As the bus neared Waianae, Soong became very interested in the passing landscape. It amazed her that on such a tiny speck of an island like Oahu, there was such variety in climate and vegetation. Kailua, on the east side of Oahu, was brilliantly green and often rainy. It was also very humid. Honolulu, on the south, was more moderate. It rained, but not too much. It was often hot, but not too hot. At least it was not as uncomfortable as the restaurant in Kailua. Now, nearing the west side of the island, Waianae, for the first time in her life, she noticed it was very dry. Sun-baked branches, probably good for fire-building. Long shafts of dried vines and grass. It looked like North Korea. How could that be? It never snowed here; there was no Siberian winter pushing from the north. Soong imagined what she saw was an anomaly, like some sort of tropical glacier.

The people also piqued her interest as the bus entered Waianae town. Hawaiians. Then for the first time in the hour-long bus ride, she looked closely at the people on the bus. The overweight woman wearing an old purple tank top, holding her sleeping infant. A white, crumpled Longs Drugs translucent plastic bag filled with what appeared to be two baby bottles, a few diapers, and a big leather wallet leaned against her dry feet. An old man, his cracked skin sagging off from bones, hunched over, his hands folded on the handle of his stainless-steel cane. The three teenage girls, all three wearing denim shorts and rubber slippers, holding their wicker purses, using their beach towels as pillows. But she felt that the observation was forced. She laughed to herself, knowing that she'd never been good at it. She'd never been good at seeing things. Doing, she did brilliantly, efficiently, and quickly. But seeing things was an entirely different thing.

Could she see her grandson? She didn't even know the awkward, quiet, gangly boy whom she would do anything for, did she? Did she have to? If he were on this bus right now, would she even notice him? Probably not, she conceded to herself. He would've fit in on this bus. He was part-Hawaiian, as almost all Hawaiians were, and he would have blended in on this bus with the now-different colors of Hawaiian people. She was coming to Waianae for him. The phone call she'd received from her daughter earlier that morning was distressed. Meet at the supermarket? Soong knew that there was big trouble. She was on the bus thirty-three minutes later.

Speculating on what could be wrong with her grandson, Soong missed the bus stop in front of the shopping center. She'd just missed it. Swearing to herself, she rang for the next stop. After she got off, she shook her head. How could she have missed it? The shopping center, with its Safeway and Blockbuster video store, contrasted sharply with the rest of the neighborhood. She imagined that this is what it must look like when the Americans start pushing themselves into foreign countries now. Colonel Sanders is the new missionary.

Soong walked quickly to Safeway. She swore under her breath at the heat. There was no path of shade to the store, so she was forced to weather sun exposure. When she got to the entrance, Won Ju was standing by the front door smoking a cigarette. Soong looked down at her feet. There were five cigarette butts, all the same brand, flattened in front of her. They nodded to each other. Won Ju threw down her cigarette while stepping towards the automatic door. She tried to step on it, but missed. Soong quickly stepped on the lit butt.

Won Ju didn't grab a shopping cart or basket. She slowly walked to the right, towards the produce section. Soong patiently followed her. Won Ju stopped in front of the grapes. She picked up a bunch and seemed to be inspecting them. Some of the purple orbs had a white film on them. "Crystal is pregnant," Won Ju said.

Soong sighed. Won Ju put down the bunch of grapes. "Donny is not the father. Brandon is."

Soong closed her eyes. She realized that she should be shocked, but she no longer had the ability to be shocked. When did she lose it? She shook her head. "Are you sure?"

"Brandon has no doubt."

"It could be anybody, couldn't it?"

Won Ju began walking. "Don't start, Mother."

They walked to the end of the produce section and turned left. Milk and eggs. Won Ju stopped at the orange juice. "What do I do?"

Soong paused. It amazed her that she was feeling so numb. She did not feel excited at all. She was just tired. She didn't know what Won Ju should do, and at the moment she wasn't sure if she cared, though she knew it was her duty to care. "Where is Crystal?"

"Nobody has heard from her, not even her brother."

"Who is living with you? You, Crystal's brother, Darian, and Brandon?"

"You knew about Darian and Kaipo?"

"Well, it was obvious, wasn't it? Why else would you move here? Your sister picked you up."

Won Ju began walking again. They turned up the next aisle. Diapers and baby food. A teenage mother pushing a stroller, a beautiful girl, grotesquely dressed and made-up, was reading the label of a jar of mashed peas. Her long brown hair was streaked with blond highlights, and her shorts were so short that the crease on the bottom of her buttocks showed. There were a few faint bruises on her smooth thighs. "Kaipo's mother still lives at the house, but I've only seen her once," Won Ju said.

"Is it a big house?"

"No, it's only three bedrooms. And the only time I saw her was in the middle of the night. I couldn't sleep, so I sat in the kitchen smoking. She came out of nowhere. I thought she was a ghost. And as soon as she saw me, she disappeared. It was, I don't know, sad. She's almost invisible. When I asked Kaipo about her the next day, he said that it wasn't a ghost, and his mother was still alive. I didn't believe him."

"When are you going back to your husband? You son needs a father."

"I don't think I am going back. Besides, what does he have to teach?"

Soong noticed the music for the first time. It was very mellow and sedate, careful not to offend. The sound did not seem manmade. Soong imagined that there must be some kind of computerized machine that makes supermarket music. It was very soulless; very sad. It seemed as artificial as the bright fluorescent lights. For the first time, Soong noticed the similarities between supermarkets and hospitals. "Why do you hate him so much?"

Won Ju began walking. They skipped a couple of aisles before coming to the next. Frozen foods. A man with bushy hair, a large stomach, and baggy jeans was looking at Tombstone pizzas. Two for nine dollars with your Safeway Club Card. Everything was big on the man, except for his rear. The back of his jeans looked like an empty pouch. Won Ju stopped and looked at TV dinners. "I hate his feet."

"That sounds very stupid."

"He has enormous feet. They did not bother me at first, in fact I liked them, but now I hate them. They never stop moving. When he is watching TV, and he drops the remote control, he tries to pick it up with his toes. If he doesn't have anything to pick up, he's poking at the nearest thing, whether it's the coffee table, magazines on the coffee table. In bed, he used to pinch me with his toes, and think it was all very cute. He is constantly knocking things down with his feet. Or trying to grab things with his feet. If I were to go back, I would not be able to help myself. I would saw off his feet."

"What about Brandon? How is he?"

They walked a few aisles down. Alcohol. It was the first time Won Ju actually grabbed something. It was a box of white zinfandel with a plastic spout. Won Ju looked at her mother. "I know, it's terrible. But it does the job affordably."

"Do not become Chung Yun on me. Once you start speaking about alcohol in terms of affordability, you are drinking too much. I asked you how Brandon was."

"Did you know that Donny has been at the restaurant, working by himself, every day? Something inside of him broke or something. Have you spoken to him? He's very sullen, but I'm so proud of him. You should go see him."

"I plan to. How is Brandon?"

Won Ju sighed. "Let's go. This is all I'm going to buy."

Normally, Soong hated grocery-market store lines more than any other type of line. It was a place that was permeated with lack of human consideration. Why did people demand to write checks? Why did people go to the nine-items-or-less line when it was apparent to everyone that they had more than nine items? Why did people argue over the price of a pound and a half of yellow onions when, first of all, yellow onions were usually only about sixty-nine cents a pound, and second of all, when most of these people could not comprehend mathematics beyond the third-grade level? The supermarket line was a place of evil to Soong, because it was a place of inconsiderateness. Wasn't that what evil was? Soong was feeling all of this frustration standing in the express line with her daughter, but she was even more upset because Won Ju would not tell her how her grandson was. "Now tell me," she said, aware of heightened volume of her voice, "how is Brandon?"

The checkout girl looked toward the back of the line at Soong. Soong wondered if she would've gotten the same look if she asked the question in perfect English. "He's not good. He's scaring me."

"Why? What is he doing?"

"That's just it. He's not doing anything. He doesn't talk, he doesn't eat much. He never mentions his computer. Before any of this happened, I had to fight him to spend less than six hours a night on that computer. Now, he doesn't even mention it, or doesn't seem to miss it. Along with his father."

"Isn't he always quiet? Does he seem angry?"

"No. I wish he seemed angry, but he doesn't. When he told me Crystal was pregnant, it was very deadpan. I was very upset, asking him all sorts of questions, but he just sat there quietly. Kaipo is the only one he talks to. And not in my presence. The only reason why I know this is because Kaipo told me he does when I told him that Brandon never talks. Kaipo just said, 'He talks.' I'm really worried."

Soong sighed. "We will fix it. Where was it that Crystal used to work?"

"Club Mirage."

"And no one has found her there?"

"No one has looked. Who is going to go? Her brother? Donny? He doesn't even want to see her."

"She's keeping the baby?"

"Brandon thinks so. And I understand that."

Won Ju paid for the box of wine with cash. She gave the short, chubby girl her Club Card. After ringing it out, the checkout girl, handing Won Ju the receipt, said, "Thank you, Mrs. Akana." The change slid out of the change machine. Yes, she understood it, too. As they walked out of the store with a box of white zinfandel, walking towards Kaipo's truck, which had absurdly big tires, Soong understood that as mother, grandmother, now great-grandmother, responsibility grew with age. Kaipo's enormous silhouette hunched over the steering wheel. She felt like one of those back-bent women in Korea. Time just kept adding responsibility after responsibility. But Soong wondered whether it was really time that aged people, or was it people that aged people. Either way, walking to the truck, Soong felt older than she'd ever felt before. She swore she heard her body making a creaking sound with each step, and there was no way she would be able to carry that frighteningly big figure in the truck, too. "Crystal's brother is here to pick you up?"

"Yes."

"The truck matches him."

"Yes, it's a big truck. Come, we will take you back to town."

She'd been on the bus for over an hour to come to Waianae and have an unpleasant half-an-hour conversation with her daughter. The thought angered her. "No, I will catch the bus."

"Are you sure?"

"Yes."

"OK."

The fact that her daughter didn't argue more with her concerning a ride back to Honolulu angered her more. She quickly waved to Won Ju and began walking to the bus stop. She would have to fix this. Everyone else was just too lazy to do it. She took her bus schedule out of her purse and looked at how she was going to get from Waianae to Kailua. It looked as if she was going to have to go all the way back to Honolulu and transfer there. She was looking at about three hours of travel. The combination of the sun beating down on her and her thoughts of travel reminded her of the long walk she'd taken when she was fourteen. There was hope then. What was there now? She did not know. There was the prospect of death. There were accounts to be closed. Her dream was much different now than it had been then. As a child, she dreamed of imaginary things, a palace, a prince, and a paradise. But now, knowing that the world was not ideal, but very real, she simply dreamed of eternal sleep with a clear conscience. She dreamed of dying, knowing that her family was OK. She did not think of it as a very ambitious dream, which was why she was so puzzled at the fact that it was so difficult to achieve. She sat down at the brown-painted, shoddy gazebo bus stop next to a mother trying to control her three screaming children. She tried to enjoy the shade. Cars whizzed past in the two lanes, traveling in opposite directions. The speed of the cars scared her. All one had to do was turn a steering wheel forty-five degrees, and disaster. Life was so precarious. A simple gesture, a split-second decision could end it all. The slight jerk of a wheel, and it could be over. A silver knife, no matter how sharp, could not protect one from that. How did she manage to survive for so long?

An old Nissan sedan pulled up to the bus stop. It was Darian. "C'mon, Mother, let's go to Kailua. I'll take you."

Soong raised her voice over the yelling children playing tag, running in circles around the bus stop. "I'll catch the bus."

Darian shook her head. "Stop trying to be a martyr, Mother, and get in this car."

"I need to call Chung Yun."

"I have a cellular phone. We can call him."

Soong stood up and entered the car. As Darian pulled away and dialed the number of the restaurant, Soong sat quietly thinking about what her daughter had just said. Was she trying to be a martyr? Darian sped toward the freeway. "Guess what, Mother, I'm happy."

Soong smiled for the sake of her daughter. It will not last, she thought. Everything human is temporary.

-2-

DONNY DIDN'T SEE any light. There was no moment of redemption for him, no enlightenment; he didn't see God, there was no epiphany. He didn't look at his life, constructively reflect upon the error of his ways, or decide to put his foot down and make a change for the better. He didn't accidentally stumble upon an eight-fold path, nor did he run into a twelve-step program. He didn't let bygones be bygones. He wasn't trying to right wrongs. He wasn't turning the other cheek. He wasn't trying to start over again. He wasn't settling old debts, nor was he preparing for Judgment Day, whether that entailed a possibility of eternity in hell, returning to earth as a cockroach or the fungus that causes ringworm, or simply decomposing six feet under. Donny was simply doing what he knew hundreds of millions of other people did every day. He was working. Even though his sisters looked at him as if he were turning staffs into snakes, he was just working. It was just work. He didn't seem to have anything better to do.

He was forty years old, single, and childless. He'd received the divorce papers a week before in the mail. He didn't feel horrible about it, but he sensed an acute melancholy, a sort of emptiness that befuddled him because he didn't really feel like he'd lost anything. It was a curious pain, a nagging muscle ache, like one that originates in the state of slumber. He'd slept wrong, but work seemed to help. Work for him was like stretching a sore muscle.

There were a couple of things that he did realize, though. When he'd found out what really happened to his sister years ago in Las Vegas from Kenny, it had made him sad. He didn't want to talk about it with her or his mother, which surprised him. He also found it funny that, after the years of halfheartedly searching for the green light at the end of Daisy Buchanan's dock, the idea of becoming wealthy didn't even really appeal to him anymore. So Donny didn't see any light; instead it seemed to him that he gave up. He submitted, like he supposed most people did when they reached adulthood. He laughed at this. He just became legal at forty. But this resignation, this dying of vague dreams wasn't a sad thing to him. It comforted him. He didn't feel like he had to chase anymore, even if his twenty-year chase had been done in a low-impact jog, or sometimes in a wheelchair pushed by his mother, where what he was chasing was never in sight.

So when his mother had called him that afternoon, from Waianae of all places, saying that she and Darian were going to cover the evening shift, and that she had something important to tell him, he wasn't anxious or irritated. In fact, when Soong and Darian walked through the door while he was re-stocking napkins and straws behind the counter, he was surprised to see them. He'd momentarily forgotten that they were even coming.

Soong slouched into one of the chairs and hunched over the table. It was the first time Donny remembered seeing his mother hunched over. It looked especially awkward because she wasn't tall enough to lean completely over the table. It was like a seventy-degree lean. Darian walked behind the counter and whispered to Donny that their mother wanted to talk to him. The clicking of her black platform shoes faded as she walked to the kitchen. Donny shrugged and went to sit across from his mother. He wanted to make it quick, just in case a customer came in soon.

"Mother."

Soong sighed. "I don't know how to tell you this."

"Quickly would be good. A customer could come in any minute."

Soong rubbed her eyes. "Crystal is pregnant."

"And?" The fact that he was neither shocked nor really interested surprised him.

Soong sat up. "You don't care?"

"I don't think I do." Not caring felt liberating, but he supposed he should act like he cared a little for his mother's sake, so he added, "How do you know this, anyway?"

"Brandon."

Donny smiled. "Wow." Then he began to laugh loudly. He found it very funny. Did ludicrous things like this happen outside of the imagination? Donny supposed that anything was possible.

Soong stood up and yelled. From her training as a stage actress, her voice could reach ear-piercing volumes. "This is not funny! This is not funny!"

Donny began laughing even harder. It developed into an uncontrollable laughter, and tears soon followed. Every time he tried to respond, he was cut off by a burst of howling laughter. "Your sister is crushed!"

He stopped, wiped his eyes, and frowned. "Yes, this must be hard on her."

Soong sat back down. Her weariness disappeared. She sat straight up. "Do you suppose she will keep the baby? Won Ju said that Brandon thinks she will."

"Yes, she will probably keep it. Crystal didn't think she could have children."

Soong sighed. "Do you know where I can find her?"

"What are you planning to do? What are you going to do, try to buy the baby from her or something? What could you possibly do? Let it go, Mother. Just let go. It's Crystal's baby."

"It's family. It's my great-grandson."

"The embryo is family? What could you possibly want with this child? You could just forget about it." Donny was listening to himself, and for the first time, he felt like the sane one in the family.

A man walked in with two children. The children were at that touch-everything, motor-mouth age, where it seemed like they had to have the metabolism of hummingbirds to keep up that sort of energy.

Darian immediately emerged from the back. She smiled as she took the family's order. As Donny turned back to his mother, it just occurred to him that she hadn't stopped talking since the threesome walked in. He understood that. When you speak a foreign language, a conversation is private by default. "I'm sorry, Mother, what were you saying?"

"You never listen."

"Customers just walked in." He paused to check his voice, resisting the urge to yell. "So why can't you just let it go?"

"I don't think Brandon can."

"He's a child. What, is he going to raise this child? Is he going to marry Crystal? Drop out of school to support his new family? Crystal wouldn't even marry him."

Soong bit her lip. "She married you."

"Yes, she did. And look how that turned out. You are insane. Look at yourself. Crisis management. You are always trying to solve problems instead of trying to prevent them. And you are always trying to solve problems, not where they lay, but just everything around them. You're…you're…like a bad doctor or something. The heart is bad, so you check for cancers in the arms, legs, and head. And you amputate anything suspect."

"I try!"

The two children in the restaurant immediately became quiet. They stared at Soong. Donny shook his head. "Just because you blame me, you hate me, I try," Soong said.

"This is the first time we're having a conversation about this."

"I try."

"Why is it the first time? What are you going to do? Try to find Crystal, try to fix this? Is it not Brandon that's broken, not Crystal? What about Won Ju?"

"Won Ju needs help. Will you not help your sister?"

The customers hurried outside with their food. "Why didn't either of you tell me about what happened in Las Vegas?"

Soong seemed unsurprised by the question. She shrugged. "How could you not know? A mugging. You must be stupid. You saw her at the hospital."

"I was a teenager, of course I was stupid. And nobody talked to me."

"You were a child."

"Yes, I was. So was Won Ju. And you were a mother who left her children. And I am not saying this now because I want to hurt you. But Brandon is a child, too. So I guess you will not talk to him either."

"Are you going to tell me where she is?"

Donny stood up. "She's working at the club again."

He walked to the kitchen to grab a cigarette. He also felt the sudden need to chop cabbage.

Darian was smiling and handed Donny a cigarette. He lit it, sat down on a stool, and leaned against the enormous stainless-steel refrigerator. The coolness of the door felt good. "Aren't we a scandalous family," Darian said in English.

His younger sister had been in an unbearably perpetual good mood ever since she'd started up with Kaipo. They were such a strange couple to Donny, more so physically than anything else. It looked disturbingly like pedophilia when they went off together. "When are you going back to California?" Donny asked as he took a long drag from his cigarette.

"Don't take this out on me. Besides, I think I'll stay here, get married, have a couple of kids. I'll get nuclear."

"Won't that be 'problematic' with Kaipo?"

"See, you're stereotyping him. Racist. Won Ju sees the light. He's been great to her and Brandon, the little spoiled shit. Jeez, do you see how Won Ju, Kenny, and Mom give him everything, and he acts all sullen and unhappy? You ever notice that before?"

Spoiled. She was one to talk. "Maybe certain stereotypes have some validity to them, like the ex-con one. Don't most of them go back to jail?"

"He's a changed man."

"Are you taking credit?"

"I sure am. He's even reading *Moby Dick* now."

Donny put out his cigarette and began packing his things. Wallet, house keys and car keys to his just-purchased, used nineteen-eighty-three Honda Civic, cigarettes, lighter, accounting book for the restaurant. The BMW days were over for him. He looked once more at Darian. Soong walked to the back. They looked amazingly alike. Donny walked away in wonderment that he was the only sane one in the family. He felt prophetic. Bad things were going to happen, and no one could see it but him. Donny saw no light, instead he saw that darkness was coming.

-3-

IN CHINA, THEY mutilated feet. In the West, they made corsets. In Africa, they made lip plates and neck rings. In the Middle East, they covered it all in black robes in hundred-degree heat. And in America, they made saline and razor blades. All to accentuate the feminine features that men found attractive. Feet, waist, lips, neck, breasts, hair, or the lack thereof, everything. Most of it also seemed to make women immobile. These thoughts immediately popped into Soong's mind at her arrival to Club Mirage.

The dancers did not dance. Most simply changed imaginary sexual positions. The ones with the saline-charged chests seemed to be drawing the most attention. The others leaned on fluorescent-lit plexiglass poles filled with water bubbles. They either smoked cigarettes or tried to get the attention of men sitting in booths, men who stared at their beer-bottle labels. All were in various stages of undress. About a third of them were completely naked, and this embarrassed Soong. She didn't know who she was embarrassed for, the young girls or herself. Loud rock-and-roll music blared. One of the girls leaning against one of the poles put out her cigarette, and halfheartedly moved her feet to the percussions.

It occurred to Soong that perhaps every woman should come to a place like this before they get married. The men were of all sorts;

old, young, of all ethnicities. The ones at the stages ogled round breasts and shaved crotches. Some of them looked like hunched-over stamp collectors. Others slapped each other on the back, musing about what a good time they were having. There were a few who were trying to look into a naked girl's eyes, Soong supposed to try to show them they had decency and consideration, which, of course, they didn't. She again focused on the bubble-filled poles. The owners probably spent a huge amount of money installing them, probably because they thought it was classy. Soong demanded that someone had to be embarrassed. Whether a naked girl, a male pervert, or proprietor, someone should shout, "I can't believe this place exists, and I no longer want to be a part of it!" She was tempted to yell it herself.

The bouncer, a Samoan man as wide as Crystal's brother, but not as tall, demanded a seven-dollar cover charge at the register. Soong reached into her purse, just as, as far as Soong knew, the most gaudy Korean woman approached her. The plump woman with thinning, burnt hair, who looked like she was dressed by Armani and accessorized by a pawn-shop dealer, was about Soong's age. She put her hands on Soong's shoulders. "Mul Ui Yau Wang?" The Queen of Tears?

Soong twisted the earring in her right lobe, and nodded. The woman laughed. She looked at the bouncer angrily. "No charge. What's wrong, you. This great actress."

This amused Soong. Of course the bouncer would not recognize her. Only middle-aged Koreans who were hardcore movie fans would recognize her. The woman took Soong's arm. "Come with me."

They walked towards the bar, then the woman stopped. "What are you doing here?"

"I am looking for one of your employees. Crystal?"

"Crystal? Why?"

Soong was embarrassed for having any ties to this place. "She used to be married to my son."

"Donny? That's your son? Wow, he used to be a very good customer. How is he doing?"

"Fine. But I really need to see Crystal."

"How is your daughter? I saw a picture of your family, years ago, when I was in Korea. I remember thinking how great it must have been to be you. So rich, so beautiful. What are you doing now?"

Soong was growing impatient. She looked around the club without really looking. "Is she working tonight?"

"I made tons of money when I got here. Just think, I was a poor Korean girl selling myself to American soldiers in Seoul for close to nothing, now I have over a million dollars."

Soong frowned. Why was this stranger telling all of this to her? She was bragging, but why and about what? A million dollars made on doing this? Just as Soong was about to insult this woman, the woman said, "Crystal is in the dressing room. I'll show you."

Soong was relieved that she wouldn't have to sit at the stage and talk to the girl from between her legs.

Just as Soong and the woman, who mentioned that her name was Kilcha, were about to walk into the dressing room, Crystal came walking out in a black teddy with no underwear. Her thick hair was piled up on the top of her head, deftly held together by a well-placed lacquer chopstick. "Jesus," she said. "What the hell are you doing here?"

Kilcha laughed. "I thought same ting when I first see her. She look for you."

Soong could barely hear them because of the loud music, which progressed to rap. The bass shook the walls. A waiter called Kilcha, so she ran off. Soong looked up at Crystal. She towered above her on her huge platform shoes. "I need talk," she said, as loudly as she could.

Crystal shrugged. She grabbed Soong by the arm and led her towards the front door. Soong stopped. "Outside? But you naked. No panty!"

Crystal laughed. "So I'll give a free show. C'mon."

Soong shook her head as she followed Crystal, looking at her bare ass.

They walked through a red velvet curtain at the back door. The parking lot was filled with a variety of cars: sedans, SUVs, pick-ups, and luxury vehicles. The asphalt was littered with cigarette butts, most with rings of red lipstick. A big, blue plastic barrel was filled with empty beer bottles, both brown and green, emanating the smell of rotten barley. The moon was a perfect half, and light clouds slowly floated in front of it. The light from the moon made Soong's discomfort over Crystal's lack of dress increased. She wanted desperately to find a robe and put it on Crystal. Crystal stopped and simply stood there as if things were natural. She smiled. "So Soong Nan, what can I do for you?"

The headlights of a car blinded Soong momentarily. "I… I … I worried. You pregnant?"

"Not that it's your business, and I'm not trying to be rude, but yes, I am."

Soong sighed. "You, you, how you take care?"

"Are you kidding? Like half of the girls that work here are single mothers. They manage."

Crystal's curtness surprised Soong. When she'd first met the girl, she was certainly lewd and boisterous, in fact very silly. Crystal seemed very serious now. "By yourself?"

Crystal shook her head. "This isn't like the Middle Ages. I don't need a man or a mother-in-law. God, lady, you make me want to smoke a cigarette. Which I don't do, by the way. Big surprise, the slut Crystal believes in prenatal care. Listen, I have to go on. What do you want?"

Soong felt completely powerless. She could not talk to this woman like this. Besides, Crystal was the one with power. She had the unborn child, and like Chung Yun said, it was hers. As much as she wanted to reach her hands into this woman's womb and tear the child away to rescue it, she knew she couldn't. She needed to approach this differently.

"How's Brandon?" Crystal asked. The question was posed in a way that showed genuine interest. Soong wanted to give a genuine answer, but it occurred to her that she didn't really know how Brandon was. According to Won Ju, he was despondent, and if this were true, then the woman standing in front of her was at fault.

"Why you do what you do?"

"You mean, dance?"

"No, you not dance, but why you...Brandon?"

Crystal sighed. "I liked him. I don't know, he seemed so pure. I guess I felt like I needed some purity in my life."

"Brandon not good. Why you do?"

Crystal wrung her hands and shook her head. A couple of men across the street whistled at her. She glanced across the street, then held up her middle finger. The catcalls persisted. What did she expect? Soong thought. "Men," Crystal said. "I didn't want to hurt Brandon. I didn't think I could hurt him. He's a guy. I thought he'd look back on what we did, how he lost his cherry, and be happy about it. I mean, and I don't want to sound conceited, but what fifteen-year-old wouldn't love to have me for their first time and tell their friends about it?"

She was talking a bit too quickly for Soong now. "I don't understand you."

"I don't understand you either."

"What I do?" She meant the question. She had no real idea what she was trying to accomplish here, and at the same time she knew that she wasn't accomplishing it.

"You go home. I have to work now."

"I don't know what to do. Why I here?"

"I don't know. But let's be real. We're not family. We're too different. I'm keeping the baby, and, hey, maybe you guys can visit. Tell Brandon, once the kid is born, he can stop by anytime."

Soong was distracted by a scar on Crystal's abdomen. She could barely see it at night, but through the teddy, she saw a distinct scar. Crystal suddenly yelled to the men across the street. "Get a fuckin' life!"

They began to walk away. Soong pointed at the scar. "What happen?"

Crystal looked down and rubbed the scar. "I got hit by a car when I was fourteen."

Soong clasped her hands together. "Me too! What happen?"

"I guess what happens to everybody who gets hit by a car. I went to the hospital. Surgery. Actually, I almost couldn't get it because I didn't have insurance. It kind of fucked up my life."

"Oh."

"But I moved here to town. My big move after the accident. You know, Waianae is only like fifty miles away, but it's farther than that. Anyway, I had to get the hell out of there. Do you know what that's like? You just gotta go? Listen, I have to get back. Tell Brandon I said, 'What's up.' Bye."

Crystal walked back through the red curtain. Left standing in the parking lot, Soong turned her head back and forth. She was surrounded by one- and two-story buildings. There was a back street in front of her off the city bus route. She could not tell in what direction the mountains or ocean were. She knew she was in Honolulu, on the south side of the island, but could not tell if she was facing north, south, east, or west. She looked up to try to locate the North Star, but could not find it. Only the seemingly geometrically perfect half moon illuminated the sky behind a transparent mist of clouds being pushed slowly by the weak wind. Even if she'd been able to locate the star, she wasn't sure that it would have been much help to her. She looked down at the blacktop at the cigarette butts and shards of brown and green glass. Old gum, now hardened black disks, overwhelmed some of the small valleys in between the rugged peaks of asphalt. Several bubbly globs of male spit also sat in stillness. This is where I am, she thought. Why did I come here? Where do I go from here? I still have twenty thousand dollars, she thought. She felt a sudden, deep desire to spend it.

-4-

THE TRUCK WAS in line at a stoplight on the corner of Kapiolani and Kalakaua. As the light changed, the traffic slowly rolled eastward. It was nine at night, and there was still traffic. Won Ju had spent the ride from Waianae to Honolulu looking at town and street names. Many of them were Hawaiian. On the freeway, there were exit signs indicating towns: Waipahu, Aiea, Honolulu, Likelike, Pali, Kinau. But as they got into town and on Kapiolani Boulevard, six lanes of traffic lights, bars, business buildings, a shopping center, and a convention center, the names varied: Cooke, Ward, Pensacola, Piikoi, Keeaumoku, Kalakaua. But she didn't let the Hawaiian names fool her. A convention center? A shopping center with a gigantic Sears and Neiman Marcus? This was an American city. "Why do you drive me around?" she asked.

"You need help," Kaipo said.

"But you don't owe me anything. You take care of me and Brandon, sure, you're dating my sister, but you don't complain, and I feel so bad; you're not my driver."

Kaipo shook his head. His huge forearms extended toward the steering wheel. Curly red hair sprouted from hand to elbow. "You no get it? Listen, you tink, jus' like most odda people, 'Oh, I goin' owe him,' or 'Oh, he must want something from me.' I just helping out. I mean, I not one saint or anyting, but what's da big deal. Someone need help, you can help, help um."

The light turned green. They were headed toward the apartment. Won Ju had set up a meeting with Kenny to discuss Brandon. She'd already told him what had happened on the phone, and he wanted to get together.

They passed McCully Street. After spending so much time in Waianae, she looked up at her former home and realized how pretentious it was. The surface was more tinted glass than cement.

The condominium was sealed from the outside by a parking gate, computerized coded entry, and a handful of blue-shirted security guards. It was called Iolani Towers, named after King Kamehameha II.

Not that she thought of Waianae as any sort of paradise. The small town on the west side of the island scared her. She found the size of the people and poverty very intimidating. The pit bulls secured to houses with rusted, iron chains. The barefoot boys, some of them not even teenagers but bigger than her, strutting around like roosters. Cars that looked more expensive than some of the houses they were parked in front of. But the thing that intimidated her the most was the look on most of their faces. They looked so mad. Not just the men, but the women, too. It was as if the people were waiting for someone to punch them in the face. But it wasn't a doomed look; it was one of defiance. "Just try it," most of their faces said. She envied the look.

Kaipo's entire body had the look. And from what Darian had told her about him, he had cause. He had, in fact, learned to brace himself for sudden, unexpected punches in the face since childhood. His father, schoolmates, juvenile detention, prison; and the fact that he was a red-headed, light-skinned Hawaiian didn't help. Apparently, he was also short and skinny as a child. But he'd said something funny to Darian. Darian had told Won Ju that he'd told her, "Was funny, though. I swear every time I got whacked, I think I grew half one inch wider and taller."

As Kaipo pulled up to the entrance of the condominium, Won Ju asked, "How tall are you and how much do you weigh?"

"Six-five, three-thirty," he said. "I guess I go pick you up in about one hour."

"Thank you."

"No prob."

As she entered the building, and waited for the elevator, Won Ju thought about Darian's attraction to Kaipo and understood it. The alpha-male thing was of course a factor. In caveman days, Kaipo probably would have been tribal chief. Kaipo's lack of education was probably security for Darian, too. You are obviously the strong one, so I get to be the smart one. He also had eccentricities that made him, according to Darian, a round character. He was a neat freak. He was also incredibly punctual. Won Ju knew these traits by now. He'd said he'd be back in an hour, which meant that he'd be back in anywhere from fifty-six to fifty-eight minutes. Darian thought of him as a character in a book, which made Won Ju feel uneasy. Real people just didn't cut it for Darian.

His most attractive quality, Won Ju guessed, for Darian was that he made her feel guilty. His life had been much harder than hers, and she knew it. Won Ju believed that guilt was one of the most powerful emotions a person could feel because it was almost impossible to put down. Maybe whenever Darian felt self-pitying, another strong emotion, having Kaipo around made her feel bad so she felt better.

The elevator doors opened, and Won Ju was relieved to find that no one was there. She hated standing in elevators with people. The person could be on the other side of the car, but to Won Ju it always felt like she was rubbing shoulders with a complete stranger. She would become conscious of her breathing, and stare at the upward or downward countdown of lighted numbers above the door.

She wasn't anxious about seeing Kenny. But as she thought about him as the elevator ascended, she felt nostalgic about when they had first started dating. He'd come to the place where she was bartending, Club New Office, a name that to this day baffled her, a hostess bar. Pretty Korean women with four-inch heels, layers of makeup, and false eyelashes served drinks and rubbed slack-covered legs; it was during the pre-karaoke days, so most of the music was imported contemporary Korean stuff that made her miss home. Kenny had come in with his friends. He was a lot skinnier back then, and seemingly shy. She'd also found his name charming. It reminded her of her brother's boy-like name.

When they'd first started going out, it was like he was trying to balance a tray full of cocktails, being careful not to spill one drop. In turn, she'd peel his oranges and shrimp, and when they finally started to sleep together, she'd tickle his back to help him fall asleep. It took years before he started to throw beer bottles against the wall. She wondered if all men were like this. She wondered if her son was going to grow up and be like this.

When she got off the elevator and entered the apartment, she was surprised to see how little it had changed. The fish tank was gone, of course, but the glass dining table, the television, the leather sofa, all of these things were in the same spot. Even Kenny seemed like an unmoved piece of furniture. He was sitting at the table, reading the sports section and drinking a bottle of water. He looked up. "Hey."

"Hey."

She sat down. "So about what I told you on the phone."

Kenny put down the paper and shook his head. "Dumb kid. I told him about condoms."

"Maybe you should have had the same talk with Crystal."

"You seem to be taking this well."

"Don't comedians always say humor masks pain?"

Kenny took a gigantic swig from his plastic bottle, finishing off the water. "Listen, drop the kid off tomorrow. Let him spend the weekend with me. Maybe I'll take him to the Club to have lunch or something. I'll try to talk with him."

"I'll ask Kaipo if he can drop him off."

"I would pick him up, but I have business stuff to do, and Waianae is so far away."

"That's O.K."

"So she's keeping it?"

"That's what Brandon says."

"What did your mother say?"

"Not much. But Donny said she stopped by the restaurant today, asking where Crystal was."

"Your mother is nuts. Gotta love her. So are you guys ever going to come home?"

"I don't know."

"You're welcome anytime."

"Thanks."

"The kid will be O.K. Jeez, I wish I had that my first time."

Kenny winced. Won Ju stared at him. "Don't start," he said. "It's not a me thing, it's a gender thing."

"I think he's sad."

"I'd be sad, too. Stop! Stop! Don't leave; I'm just joking."

Won Ju sat back down. "Why do you take everything so seriously?" Kenny asked.

"There's a baby involved, Grandpa." She hoped the word would hurt his vanity.

Kenny's face turned serious. "Are you willing to work with me on this?"

"What?"

"I have connections. What Crystal did was illegal. Statutory rape. I think I can get custody."

"And Crystal?"

Kenny slapped his palm on the table. "Fuck Crystal."

"But she's Kaipo's sister, and Kaipo has been so good to us."

Kenny slapped his palm on the table, this time even louder. "Fuck Kaipo. Listen, this is the way the world works. You want something, you take it with the law on your side. This is the real world, not the boondocks. Do you really want a stripper raising our grandchild? Do you want the kid? I know your mother must be going nuts. I know she'd agree with me. We can get custody, and we can adopt. I already talked to John, you remember, John from the Club? He's a big time lawyer, and he thinks we have a good chance if we stay married."

"And Brandon's role?"

"C'mon, Won Ju. He's still a kid with his whole life ahead of him. Finish high school, college. We take care of the kid; he doesn't have to worry about it."

"What if he wants to?"

"Sure, he'll be like an affectionate older brother. Then off to the mainland for college."

Won Ju sat quietly. Kenny was on a roll, and she felt herself being persuaded. "A couple of things, though, Won Ju."

"What?"

"We wait until Crystal has the kid, then we move legally. I don't want anything to upset the pregnancy. And we don't tell Brandon. I mean, we may not get our hands on the kid for another year or two. Let him grow out of it. A year or two more in high school, girlfriends, driver's license, he'll forget about the baby."

Won Ju nodded. She still had one more question. Who were they doing this for? But she kept the question to herself. Maybe she knew that Kenny had an answer ready to fire back. Maybe she was afraid that the real answer would somehow emerge if she asked.

-5-

KAIPO HAD NO idea what he was doing with these people. When he'd first seen them at the Club, at the get-together after his sister's wedding, he'd decided that he didn't want anything to do with them. Private haole clubs, old Korean women with earrings that were worth more than his truck, Hawaiian guys who were trying to be haole, unemployed Korean guys who were momma's boys, spoiled college girls, and sulky mothers and sons, none of it appealed to him. He'd gone to the dinner because his sister asked him to, but he figured that'd be it. He didn't know why his sister was getting mixed up with these people, but he didn't say anything. It was her life.

He had a bad attitude about people with money, and he knew it. He figured most people thought that his bad attitude sprouted from jealousy, but they were wrong. He didn't have any desire to have a lot of money. He just took what he needed. He figured in the old days, it was probably similar, Hawaiians living off the land. But there was no land left, so he picked rich people's stuff like he was picking taro. And most of the time it wasn't like it was stuff they needed anyway. Jewelry, car stereos, golf clubs, and laptop computers. He could understand punishing people who took what people needed, but punishing for taking things like these? It didn't make much sense to him.

So he didn't dislike people with money because he envied the fact that they had money, he didn't like money because of what it turned these people into. It made them think that they had power, protection, and freedom. The shackles of cash were invisible to them, and to Kaipo, there was nothing worse than talking to somebody who thought that they had more or were more than they really were. He wanted to punch people like that in the face. And sometimes he did. Just to show them that he had no money, but he had the power and the freedom to hurt them, maybe even kill them, if he wanted to. He couldn't believe how people with money were fooling themselves.

So when he'd seen those Koreans, that one token Hawaiian with all the plastic-looking muscles at the Club who had the nerve to call him "brother," and the haoles all around him, he saw a bunch of fools. The funniest thing was that they looked down on him, but they also feared him. What could they do, make spears, helmets, and shields out of green paper? They knew what was up, but none of them had the guts to admit it to themselves.

When he'd arrived and sat down that night, facing the beach and the docked outrigger canoes, which were modeled after what his ancestors had made centuries before, he knew this Korean family was talking about money. He didn't have to understand the language to know that that was what they were talking about. Controlled anger in words was the language of money.

He'd stared out at the canoes, thinking how even though he was half-Hawaiian, he'd never paddled one before, while the family spat back and forth in sharp and loud dialogue. There was a song-like quality to it; the words all seemed to vary in volume, and some words had even more than one tone to them. While listening to them sing about money, he thought back to when he'd entered the club just five minutes before, when he saw the trophies from the Hawaiian Canoe Club canoe racing victories, and the pictures of the winning crews—mostly white. So with the Koreans going at it in their language about money, and thinking about Hawaiian canoe paddling, Kaipo felt like a foreigner there, on the beach, in Hawaii.

He thought about that first night as he and Brandon coasted on the freeway, heading for the Pali. Brandon stuck his head out of the window like a dog and smiled as the wind tossed his hair. It was a strong wind that shimmied his cheeks. He hadn't said anything since they'd left. But Brandon's quietness never bothered Kaipo; in fact, he liked it.

Brandon had been the only quiet one that night at the Hawaiian Canoe Club. He'd barely even noticed Kaipo, it seemed, and immediately Kaipo knew why he was so quiet. Brandon didn't have anything to say to these people. He was a foreigner, too. So Kaipo liked him, and decided to sit there quietly, too, until Darian started to talk to him.

Darian. She was a sweet kid. Full of ideas and long, not necessarily big, words. Always reading books, talking about how there was so much reality and truth in ink and paper. At least her fake world wasn't made out of green paper. At first, after he'd gotten the phone call from his sister offering part-time work, which he'd known would make his PO happy, he thought that he'd just be in and out of there on weekends. Then Darian came on to him, and he figured, why not? She was good-looking. He wasn't stupid.

But something funny happened. He didn't fall in love or anything like that; he thought of it more along the lines of flea infestation. You bring a dog into your house; you're not only bringing in the dog, you're bringing in all of the fleas attached to the dog, too. But he liked them. He liked Darian, Won Ju, and the kid; besides, they weren't messy. They didn't mess with his ghost mother, who had been a transparent spectre in that house as long as he could remember, either, so he saw no reason to put a flea collar on Darian. Besides, the entire family amused him, and it seemed like he had his own little flea circus.

"So what? Rough day, yestaday?" he asked.

Brandon pulled his head away from the window. "Nah. Where was everybody, anyway?"

"I took your madda fo' meet your grandmadda. Den I took your madda fo' meet your fadda. I tink Darian and your grandmadda went work wit' your uncle."

"You're like a taxi. They don't piss you off?"

"Nah. Whatevas."

"Yeah."

They took the Pali Highway cutoff. The ascent up the Koʻolau Mountains sloped up gradually, unlike the decent, which would consist of steep drops and a notorious hairpin turn. To both the left and right there was foliage so thick that the ground seemed to consist of tops of trees. Far to the right, the mountains were veined with the faint white lines of waterfalls from the heavy morning showers. Though the news had said nothing about a hurricane or tropical storm, Kaipo sensed something coming. The sun seemed to be fighting with the clouds over whether there would be rain or shine. A vortex of air blew through the open window, into the cab of the truck, twirling old receipts, empty cigarette packs, crumpled gum foils, and loose clothing. "Roll up da window. I tink going storm."

Brandon obeyed. As they traveled further up, a sunny drizzle started. "Only in Hawaii, can be sunny and rainy at da same time."

Brandon didn't say anything. He was staring out the window. Just then, it seemed as if someone dumped a bucket of water on the windshield. It poured heavily for just a few seconds, then the rain completely stopped, and the sun shone strongly. The wind was getting more and more powerful. Leaves were being ripped from their branches.

As they neared the top, the tunnels, Brandon cleared his throat, then looked at Kaipo excitedly. "Hey, Kaipo, let's check out the Lookout."

"What if we late?"

"Just for a few minutes. Look how strong the wind is."

The windshield wipers were vibrating. A weak drizzle started again. "Nah, raining."

"It's only drizzling."

"O.K., O.K. We go."

Kaipo took the Pali Lookout cut-off. There were tour buses and rental cars in the parking lot. Both Japanese and haole tourists were walking toward the Lookout point, toting cameras and children. Charges of wind rippled through their clothes and hair as they leaned forward against the wind. The tourists with children began turning back. "Must be one good day," Kaipo said.

They got out of the truck. Kaipo looked up. He could see that it was raining, but raindrops were not hitting them. The wind was blowing the water back up, creating a cloud mist suspended a couple of stories above their heads. It was the first time Kaipo saw anything like this. The wind at the Pali Lookout was almost always strong, because it was a small gap at the top of the mountain range, much like a gap between two front teeth constantly causing whistling, but he never saw the wind stop rain before.

They walked past the defeated tourists. As they neared the cement railing, Kaipo had to lean more and more forward to move through the whistling wind. Brandon walked beside him, smiling as he squinted. A faint trail of tears was streaming toward his temples. They walked down the old cement stairs. More and more tourists passed them, complaining about the strength of the wind. Some children were crying. Some had scraped knees. Kaipo was amazed at how much effort he had to put into the last several paces to the edge of the cliff.

By the time Kaipo and Brandon reached the cement railing, and held on to the top of three horizontal safety bars above it, they were the only ones left. The sun was winning its fight with the clouds, but Kaipo could not tell if it was hot or cold. The sun rays warmed him, while the wind chilled his skin.

Over the railing, right below the cliff, was a thick canopy about a hundred feet below. Beyond the canopy, further out and down, was a golf course. Beyond that, Kaipo could see an ant line of cars on Kamehameha Highway, all of the suburbs of Kaneohe town, and Kaneohe Bay. The Bay was a mixture of warm, shallow, coral-reef greens and deep, cold-channel blues. Coconut Island was there. Kaipo pointed to it. "That's Gilligan's Island," he said.

The wind made his voice practically inaudible. Brandon seemed not to hear him. He tapped Brandon on the shoulder. "We betta go," he said.

Brandon smiled. "How many leaves to you think are down there on all those trees?"

Kaipo looked down. From that angle, the trees looked as if they were made entirely of leaves. "Billions," he said.

More tears streamed toward Brandon's temples. They looked like transparent crow's feet. "They all look the same, don't they?"

Kaipo looked down again. He supposed Brandon was right. "We so high, dat's why."

"My science teacher told me, you know, about all that genetic research and stuff. He told me all human beings were ninety-nine-point-nine percent like each other."

After he finished talking, Brandon quickly climbed up on the railing. He straddled the top bar, holding on to it with one hand, like he was riding a bull. Kaipo grabbed his leg. "What da fuck you doing?"

Brandon smiled. "I'm tired. Flying or sinking."

Kaipo wasn't sure if he'd let go. He never would remember if he did or not. He didn't think the boy was strong enough to break his grip, but who knew? Brandon was determined. Maybe he wanted to see it; maybe he'd figured that it was Brandon's life, but he couldn't remember letting go. What he would never forget, though, was the image of Brandon being levitated by the wind. For a moment, it was as if God was under Brandon, and He pursed his giant God lips and gently blew. Brandon looked like a mullet jumping out of a glassy pool of brackish water in slow motion. He wore the sun as a halo for a second, smiling ten feet above Kaipo. He was a stained-glass window. Kaipo remembered that smile, that glorious smile that was brighter than the sun itself for that split second, right before he crashed toward the canopy like an ill-constructed paper airplane. God inhaled, but Kaipo would never forget that victorious, angel-for-a-second smile that outshone the sun. Just like the moment before a wave rolls and consumes itself on a stormy day, the moment of death can be so beautiful, and like the mullet jumping from the pool, or the marbled, misty breaker, it often goes unnoticed.

-6-

THE NAMELESS, EGG-shaped man. Soong remembered Henry had mentioned him at least thirty times. The nameless, egg-shaped man had gone through basic training with Henry. Actually, it wasn't that he'd completed or somehow graduated from basic training, but it was World War II, and like in all wars, the armies need bodies, so corners were cut. Henry'd said, "We all knew. We all knew from the start that this guy wasn't going to make it. He couldn't do a pull-up, much less a push-up, and his running was even worse. I'd look at him most often in disgust, but sometimes with pity. Because when I looked at him, I think he knew he wasn't going to make it, too."

Soong had often wondered why Henry would always talk about the weak and unlucky men he'd served with. He seemed never to talk about the ones who won medals or saved lives. But now, she thought that maybe he was trying to pass on some wisdom to her. Maybe he was saying that it's a fact that the weak perish and so do the strong sometimes, because of bad luck. Maybe he was saying that this is so, and there's nothing anybody can do about it. The nameless, egg-shaped man indeed perished on that first day, and as Henry said, probably within the first few steps he took on the Old World. "What happens when you roll an egg down a hill with rough terrain?"

Had Brandon been an egg or unlucky? Soong asked herself as she sat alone in her aisle, onboard the still Korean Airlines DC-10 in front of Gate 42. It could be considered that bad luck, that one moment where Crystal had been allowed to stay at Won Ju's home, a simple decision, doomed them. But even then, it wasn't luck, was it? Crystal wasn't a mortar that made heads disappear, was she? No, even though she'd considered Chung Yun as the egg all these years, it was indeed Brandon. She supposed all people were eggs; the raw ones were the weak ones, and the boiled ones were strong. Brandon had been a raw egg, an egg carefully coddled by layers and layers of tissue. Tissue. What has tissue ever protected? Tissue does not protect; it cleans.

The legacy of her family that started with an orphan girl named Kwang Ja, the matriarch, was ending. Won Ju and Chung Yun would not bear children. Whatever Darian would give birth to would be the start of a new, American line. And Crystal had vanished. Despite the desperate searches conducted by Kenny to find her, or more specifically, his grandson, she was gone. Soong knew well the advantages of letting go of your name. There could be new beginnings, and since Crystal had changed it once before, why not again, and someplace else? Soong had been overboiled. As she thought of the end of the family she started cracking without moisture.

Chung Yun would go on. Won Ju had become like that ghost woman who lived in Kaipo's house after Brandon died, except she haunted canned-vegetable aisles. Kenny continued on his search for Crystal, at the same time doing everything in his power to convince himself and anyone else that Kaipo had murdered his son, tossed him off the cliff at the Pali Lookout, even though Kaipo was the one who'd contacted the police before he'd even contacted family. But Kenny had the ears of powerful people, so nevertheless, Kaipo sat in jail awaiting trial. Darian had flown back to California where, Soong figured, she belonged. And here she was, on her way to Korea, to sell her artifacts to a museum, including the silver knife. What was hers belonged in a museum. She did not understand this world, and her artifacts proved useless. She would die in Korea.

The plane began taxiing down the runway. Soong thought about reincarnation and wished it were so. She wanted another chance. She still wasn't quite sure what she'd done wrong, but she hoped with no delusion that she could have another opportunity. But she knew that hope without delusion was not hope at all. Suddenly, she remembered that fortuneteller years ago, the one who had renamed her. She thought she had been properly skeptical. But perhaps she was not. Perhaps a part of her believed that her new name was a lucky one, because she had hope. She had hopes for her family. She felt like she had been duped, which, she supposed, hope often does.

The plane stopped on the runway. The engines wound loudly. The wings of the plane shook. The flight attendants appeared, going over the safety tips and instructions on what to do if the plane were to drop out of the sky thirty thousand feet high. Had she been crying? Her body convulsed. She wiped her face with her fingers. There were no tears. Suddenly, she felt sick. She grabbed for the bag in front of her and vomited into it.

The plane raced down the runway, then slowly lifted. Soong vomited again. As the plane ascended, Soong experienced a series of dry heaves that sent tears rolling down the sides of her face. She could not stop.

Other novels
from Mutual Publishing

Luzon

by Malcolm Champlin and Steven Goldsberry

This smashing novel of love and combat in the war-torn Philippines is based on a true story. Authors Malcolm Champlin (who fought in many of these battles) and Steven Goldsberry bring a rare mix of authenticity and glorious writing to this nearly forgotten and utterly harrowing chapter of World War II.

> "Malcolm Champlin's unique battle experiences
> and novelist Steven Goldsberry's expert storytelling combine in a
> powerful and moving account of the desperate struggle by Americans
> and Filipinos against the imperial Japanese. *LUZON* is an epic tale of
> courage, endurance, love, and glory."
> —W.E.B. Griffin, author of the series
> *Brotherhood of War, The Corps,* and *Honor Bound*

casebound: ISBN 1-56647-185-0, $22.95
softcover: ISBN 1-56647-190-7, $15.95

The Red Wind

by Ian MacMillan

Set in Hawai'i making its way into the post-statehood era, this is the story of half a century in the life of an Island family experiencing its share of joy and tragedy. Centered around its patriarch—a canoe builder—who thinks of the Hawaiian canoe as a living being of majestic artistic beauty, *The Red Wind* is a story of one man's devotion to the preservation of tradition in an era of rapid change.

> In *The Red Wind,* Ian MacMillan writes vividly
> of Hawaiian family life on windward Oahu in postwar
> Hawaii…MacMillan takes us into the rich physical and emotional life
> of his characters in this remarkable novel which transcends four
> generations and takes us from Hawaii just after
> World War II to the nineties.
> —Marjorie Sinclair, author of *Kona, The Wild Wind*
> and *Nahi'ena'ena: Sacred Daughter of Hawai'i*

casebound: ISBN 1-56647-205-9, $22.95
softcover: ISBN 1-56647-203-2, $15.95